THE LAST DOGS

THE LONG ROAD

THE
LAST DOGS
THE LONG ROAD

by
CHRISTOPHER HOLT

illustrated by Allen Douglas

LITTLE, BROWN AND COMPANY
NEW YORK   BOSTON

Text copyright © 2013 by The Inkhouse

Illustrations copyright © 2013 by Allen Douglas

Little, Brown and Company

Hachette Book Group
237 Park Avenue, New York, NY 10017
Visit our website at www.lb-kids.com

Little, Brown and Company is a division of Hachette Book Group, Inc.
The Little, Brown name and logo are trademarks of Hachette Book Group, Inc.

The publisher is not responsible for websites (or their content) that are not owned by the publisher.

First Edition: November 2013

Library of Congress Cataloging-in-Publication Data
Holt, Christopher, 1980–
The long road / by Christopher Holt ; illustrated by Allen Douglas.—First edition.
pages cm.—(The last dogs ; [3])
Summary: "Dogs Max, Rocky, and Gizmo continue on their quest to find their families and uncover the mysteries behind the Praxis virus as they travel through the swamplands toward Baton Rouge, making new friends and facing old enemies along the way"—Provided by publisher.
ISBN 978-0-316-20013-4 (hc)—ISBN 978-0-316-25193-8 (e-book)
[1. Dogs—Fiction. 2. Adventure and adventurers—Fiction. 3. Science fiction.] I. Douglas, Allen, 1972– illustrator. II. Title.
PZ7.H7388Lon 2013   [Fic]—dc23   2013001040

10 9 8 7 6 5 4 3 2 1

RRD-C

Printed in the United States of America

For Donnie, M Flo, and Josh,
who let me make characters of their cats

BEACONS

———◆———

Max was resting by a river.

He lay in the thick, coiled roots of a great tree. Bright daylight filtered through its leaves. The mud beneath Max's belly was damp and warm in the heat, and the air that brushed his golden fur was thick with moisture.

Nearby, the river roared and gurgled. Max had followed it along forests and fields, past cities and towns and farms. According to maps, his destination lay past the opposite shore, in the direction of the setting sun. Once he'd reached the river's end, he'd have to find some way across.

Croaking bullfrogs and buzzing insects joined the river's din. From the other side of the tree came doggy snores—Max's friends Rocky and Gizmo. Typical afternoon sounds, except for one. There were no bird-calls. No chirping sparrows, no warbling ducks. All the birds were gone.

Just like the humans.

Max curled into the roots, pretending he was being held by loving, human arms. But the roots smelled of dirt and dead leaves, and it wasn't the same as being hugged by his family, not even close. He and his friends had traveled so far, and still he hadn't found his pack leaders, the children named Charlie and Emma, nor had he led Rocky and Gizmo to theirs. He'd made promises to other lost friends to find their missing loved ones, too.

But he was so tired, and so hungry. . . .

Max's floppy ears twitched. Amid the noise of the river and its animals he thought he heard laughter. Human laughter! He leaped to his feet.

There it was again: the giggles of a little girl. The gleeful shriek of a little boy. Max bounded over the tree roots and burst through the tall grass until his paws met smooth, wet rocks.

"Charlie!" Max barked. "Emma! I'm here!"

Max! he thought he heard Emma squeal in delight.

Max stopped circling, his tail wagging madly. And finally he saw his young pack leaders.

They ran atop the rushing river as if it were a solid thing. The water sparkled silver and gold beneath their feet, and the children themselves were merely silhouettes.

The shadow that was Charlie stopped splashing his sister to wave at Max. *Hi, Max!* Charlie's voice rang out. *Come play with us, boy!*

"I've been trying," Max barked. "Please don't run away again!"

The grass rustled behind him, and Max looked back to see a large, old Australian Shepherd padding out of the underbrush. The dog nodded, then sat beside him on the pebbly shore.

"Hi, Boss," Max said.

Well, hello there, son, Boss said. His jaws did not open as he spoke, but Max heard the words in his head anyway.

Boss watched the children with sad, weary eyes. *You miss them, just like I miss my friend Belle,* Boss said. *Remember, son? Before I died, you promised to find her for me.*

Max lowered his tail, then dropped to his belly next to Boss. Together they looked out over the glistening, rushing waves. Now Max saw a new figure, a full-grown Collie, prancing atop the water, her chest puffed out proudly.

Ain't she the loveliest, kindest dog you ever seen, son?

Max nodded, then rested his head on his paws.

The figure that was Belle lowered her snout to the river. She nosed the surface one, two, three times. And as Max watched in amazement, three white rings, connected at the edges, rose above the water.

The rings emitted their own light, like a trio of small

suns. They were a symbol that represented Praxis—the virus that had started everything. People had once painted the rings in places where animals were infected with the Praxis virus, but now those animals were everywhere.

Raising his head, Max saw another dog walking along the shore. It was his long-gone friend, Madame Curie. *You're tired, but you can't give up yet, my sweet Maxie. You're far closer than you know.*

Madame Curie was old, and her big brown eyes spoke of many events she'd witnessed in her long lifetime. She was a Labrador like Max, though her fur was black and speckled with white, like a night sky filled with stars. Around her neck was a collar that shimmered with the same three-ringed symbol that floated above the waves.

Max climbed to his feet and nuzzled Madame, inhaling her familiar scent. "I miss you so much," Max whispered. "I'm afraid of losing more friends, the way I lost you and Boss."

I know, Maxie, Madame said. *But your friends will be fine. You can protect them.*

Max looked back at the giant tree where his two small companions slept.

Look to the river, Max, Madame's voice echoed.

Max did as he was told. The silent children played with the figure of Belle, while the glowing three-ringed symbol bobbed above the waves. The rings represented hope for Max, even though the humans viewed them with fear.

Someone new walked atop the river: an older woman with a kind, wrinkled face. She wore a lab coat like the one worn by Max's veterinarian.

As Max watched, the woman—Madame's owner—approached the hovering rings. She grabbed them and crushed them together, forming a glowing orange disk with an *X* in its middle. Satisfied, she let go and smiled.

The glowing disk was a beacon, a signal for Max to follow.

Now the river grew louder. Still laughing, the figures of Charlie and Emma danced in the waves, followed by the old woman and Belle.

Max heard Boss's voice. *Don't forget your promise, my friend. Please find Belle.*

Your pack leaders are close, but you can't see them yet, Madame's voice echoed. *Find my pack leader. She can help you. There is peril ahead, but you are smart and can handle it. Keep your friends safe. Find Belle. Never give up on seeing your own pack leaders.*

"Thank you," Max whispered.

And in a burst of light, she and Boss were gone.

The orange beacon grew, giving off an irritating buzz that made his nose tingle.

Max awoke.

CHAPTER 1
RIVER'S END

The first thing Max realized when he awoke was that the buzzing and tingling on his nose were not part of his dream at all.

Crossing his eyes, he could just make out the blurry outline of a bug with flapping wings and spiky legs. The thing was big, black, and bloated with blood. He felt a jab of pain as it stuck its needlelike nose into his tender skin.

A mosquito!

Before Max could react, something wet and heavy slapped his nose. The buzzing stopped, and Max saw a fleshy pink tongue snap back into its owner's mouth.

Max recoiled, only to find himself trapped in the spongy, snakelike tree roots where he'd lain down to rest. He must have fallen asleep without realizing it and had one of his dreams—dreams that had become all the more vivid over the past few weeks.

Shaking his head, Max peered up at the mosquito eater. It was a squat, bulbous bullfrog with slick, bumpy skin. Slowly it blinked its big yellow eyes.

"Uh, thanks," Max said.

The bullfrog merely blinked once more.

Clearing his throat, Max said, "It seems there are a lot more mosquitoes and other bugs around since all the birds went away. But I guess that's good for you, huh?"

Max was met with a stare. "Since you eat bugs, I mean?" he continued. "No more competition."

The frog's pale throat bulged. With a croak it leaped over Max's head in a flash of long limbs and webbed feet.

"All right," Max muttered. "Nice to meet you, too."

Max rose to all fours. He felt stiff, and his fur stank of rancid mud. He couldn't be sure how much time he'd spent asleep.

Not that it mattered. He'd lost track of how long this journey had lasted. It must have been a few months, maybe longer. All he knew was that he was farther from his old home on the farm than ever before.

The farm. That was where he'd lived with Charlie and Emma and their parents before all the people disappeared, leaving the animals to fend for themselves. Max had been trapped in a kennel, but luckily Rocky was around to help him escape. Soon they'd met Gizmo, and it wasn't long before the three new friends decided that living under Gizmo's tyrannical pack leader wasn't what they wanted.

Max's dream of Charlie and Emma had felt so vivid and real, but his family and friends often came to him this way, bringing warnings of upcoming danger, as well as messages of hope.

"Big guy! You're finally awake!"

Craning his neck, Max looked up to see his two companions.

The one who'd spoken was Rocky, a Dachshund with a pointed snout, a spiky tail, and a long black body held up by short legs. The floppy-eared dog was notorious for his love of kibble.

Beside Rocky was Gizmo, a chipper, fearless little Yorkshire Terrier. She had tan-and-black fur; bright, friendly eyes; and tufted, pointed ears that were always alert. Brave and charming, she'd lost her people even before the other humans left.

Max padded out from between the tangled tree roots. "How long was I asleep?" he asked.

"All afternoon and all night!" Gizmo said. "But we didn't want to bother you." Wagging her stubby tail, she flicked out her small pink tongue to lick Max's nose.

Rocky waddled toward the river's edge. "Yeah, we figured you needed your beauty rest. Hate to break it to you, buddy, but your coat ain't exactly got the sheen it used to."

9

Max looked down at the mud crusting his over-grown golden fur. Not that any of the dogs looked their best. Gizmo's once-fluffy fur was matted and knotted, and Rocky's coat was coarse and patchy. They were all thin, though they weren't starving. They'd been on the road long enough to tell where they might find something to eat.

"Come on, Max," Gizmo said as she trotted after Rocky through the underbrush. "The water is nice and cool."

"Thanks for looking out for me," Max said as he joined Rocky and Gizmo on the slick, pebbly shore.

"It's the least we can do," Rocky said as Max dunked himself into the river to clean the mud from his fur and lap up the cool water, which tasted of fish and drowned plants.

"You've been leading and protecting us ever since we saved the dogs on the riverboat," Gizmo added. "Lately you've forgotten important stuff, like eating and sleeping!"

Rocky shook his head. "I'll never understand how you can forget to eat, big guy! I mean ... kibble. I could—"

Rocky stopped speaking, his whole body gone rigid.

"You hear that?" he whispered.

Max waded out of the water and looked along the shore. For a moment, he almost expected to hear his pack leaders' laughter, just like in his dream.

Instead, he heard a distant croak.

"Aw, it's back!" Rocky turned to Max. "Say, big guy, you hungry for some frog legs? I hear they're a delicacy."

Max chuckled. "Now why would I eat a bullfrog? They seem so . . . slimy."

Rocky stared up at Max. "Because if you don't eat it, it's gonna eat *me*!" The Dachshund paced back and forth on the bank. "You should have seen it, just watching me. Licking its oversize lips. *Waiting.* I'm telling ya, big guy, it was hungry for dog!"

Gizmo darted to the water's edge, then splashed Rocky. She laughed as he sputtered and backed away.

"Snap out of it, Rocky," she said. "The bullfrog isn't *that* big. How could it eat you?"

Rocky dropped to his belly and rested his head on his paws. "I've heard stories. And everyone tells me I look like a sausage. It's not easy being mistaken for a tasty treat, okay?"

Shaking his head, Max padded back up onto the muddy, grassy bank.

"How about we start walking again," he said to his two companions. "That way we won't be here when the bullfrog comes back."

With a happy bark and a wag of his spiky tail, Rocky jumped up and waddled over to Max's side. Gizmo joined them.

"Do you think we're close?" Gizmo asked as they started walking south on the grass, following the river.

All Max could see in the distance was the glittering water and more trees. Still, his dreams gave him hope that they'd be reaching the next stage of their journey very soon.

"I'm not sure, Gizmo," Max said as he stepped carefully over a fallen log. "But I have a good feeling. Today might be the day we get to the end of the river."

The three friends spent most of the morning in silence. As the sun rose, the day grew hotter, but the shade of the large, twisting trees kept them comfortable.

Max peered into the branches as they walked, looking for the glowing orange beacon he'd seen in his dream. He'd seen the beacons first in real life.

Several weeks ago, Max, Rocky, and Gizmo had stumbled upon a riverboat full of dogs who had made their home inside. It was there that Max and his companions had met Boss, the Australian Shepherd who proved to be a good friend.

With Boss's help, the three dogs had found the laboratories where the old woman, Madame's pack leader, worked. There they discovered that pets and other animals had been infected with a virus called Praxis that was meant to make animals smarter. But the virus could spread to the humans and hurt them. That was why all the people had left. Something about the virus had made the birds fly away, too. A pig named Gertrude had told Max to seek out the glowing orange beacons that the old woman was leaving to mark her trail.

Then some bad humans and a pack of vicious wolves had attacked the riverboat, and Max, Rocky, and Gizmo had helped save the dogs who lived there. The riverboat had gone up in flames, and Boss was too badly hurt to live. Boss had asked Max to find his lost love, Belle, in a city called Baton Rouge, and Max had given his word that he would.

Max and his friends had left behind the riverboat dogs several weeks ago, but they hadn't seen any beacons yet.

Even earlier, in a city far to the north, Madame also had told Max to find the woman, who had been her pack leader. Just like Boss, Madame, who was old and very sick, had asked Max to continue the journey. Because of his two fallen friends, Max would never give up. He knew the beacons had to be somewhere, and Belle was waiting in Baton Rouge for word of Boss.

"Hey, is it just me, or is the river getting wider?" Rocky asked.

Max shook his head, ready to insist that it was just Rocky's imagination—but it wasn't. The little dog was right.

The river had been a wide, gushing, turbulent thing for as long as the dogs had followed it. But now it seemed to double in width, the opposite shore farther away than ever.

His heart pounding with excitement, Max broke into a run. "Come on!" he called.

Up ahead through a break in the trees was a small, muddy incline. Max dug his paws into the dirt and climbed up to find himself walking on asphalt.

A road!

As Rocky and Gizmo came to stand near him, panting, Max darted back and forth. To his left, the road stretched long and straight. There were great swaths of dried mud on the asphalt, and broken branches littered the path, as if some storm had come through.

To his right, the road turned into a long metal bridge that spanned the river. Vines dangled from the rusting metal, and dead weeds and other debris lay scattered everywhere.

Straight ahead, the river fanned out on a sandy beach into a body of water that seemed to stretch on forever. Max remembered old images from his pack leaders' television. "It's the ocean," he gasped.

Strong winds rose up off the waves and carried with them the pungent scent of brine and fish and water plants. It was unlike anything Max had ever smelled before.

He studied the beach. The ocean waves crashed against the shore in a burst of froth and foam before receding, leaving wet sand. He could see slick weeds with bulbs at the ends and branches strewn across the shore. There were animals, too, strange creatures that looked like hard-shelled, smooth spiders and one that looked like a star.

"Have we reached the end of the world, big guy?" Rocky whispered.

Max shook his head, the salty wind swirling through his golden fur. "I don't think so. But we've reached the end of the river."

"So where do we go now?" Rocky asked.

Before Max could answer, Gizmo barked in excitement. She leaped forward, her tail a blur.

"Look!" she said as she spun in a circle. "Do you see them? Boats!"

Narrowing his eyes, Max gazed past the beach and the crashing waves, far out into the ocean.

And he saw them.

Beneath puffy white clouds that floated lazily in the blue sky were three distant ships. Judging by how far they were from shore, Max guessed they were much larger than the riverboat.

"Good eyes, Gizmo!" Rocky said, nuzzling the terrier affectionately.

"Thanks," Gizmo said. She looked up at Max, her eyes wide. "Do you think there are people on those boats? Where do you think they're going?"

Max tilted his head. "Well, the last boat we found was full of dogs, but most pets couldn't sail out to sea on such big ships. So it must be humans, heading in the direction we need to go in, too."

"And where's that?" Rocky asked.

Max nodded toward the bridge. "West."

"Yay!" Gizmo said, bouncing up and down. "Let's not wait anymore, Max."

Together, the three dogs ran toward the bridge, where a green sign hung between the arches. It read FOOD AND ENTERTAINMENT—1 MILE.

Reading human words—not something a dog could usually do.

But as Max, Rocky, and Gizmo had learned, that was just one of the many perks of Praxis.

Gertrude, the pig, had explained that the Praxis virus was dangerous to humans but harmless to animals. In fact, it was the first step in a process that, when completed, would make an animal as smart as a human. Back at the lab, Gertrude had put Max, Gizmo, and Rocky through the second step of the process, and ever since then Max had understood more of the world around him. He could see the change in his friends, too, by the way they spoke and acted. It was frightening but exciting—especially since Gertrude claimed that finishing the second step meant they could no longer infect humans.

If only the rest of the animals could be made safe, too. Then the humans could come home and everything could go back to normal.

But first things first—Max needed to find Madame's pack leader.

The three dogs swiftly crossed the bridge. Far beneath their feet, the river splashed and roared into dangerous currents as it met the ocean.

Not exactly water they'd want to dive into.

It was late afternoon by the time they reached the town, and the setting sun cast long shadows. First they passed a small bait shop, its windows boarded up and a CLOSED sign dangling on a chain. A rusty truck sat on concrete blocks in its driveway.

But the farther they walked, the more modern the buildings became. On the right side of the road, opposite the beach, they passed shop after shop, all painted a pale summery blue with white scalloped shutters. One of the shops had jars of brightly colored candy in its window alongside rainbow-patterned kites and racks of postcards. Next to that was a restaurant. Its sign read JIM'S CRAB SHACK.

"Ohhh," Rocky moaned. He plopped belly-down on the road.

"Are you okay?" Gizmo asked, licking Rocky's fur.

"I'm fine," Rocky said, "but I'm really hungry. We've been walking for ages."

Max's own stomach growled, and his legs were tired, too. He scanned the storefronts, but he didn't see a grocery store.

But there was another building down the road on

the sand. Squinting, Max read its sign. SUNNYSIDE RESORT AND SPA. A smaller sign read, LUNCHES AND DINNERS PROVIDED BY OUR RESIDENT CHEF. PETS WELCOME.

Rocky perked up as he read the signs. " 'Lunches and dinners'? 'Pets welcome'? Sounds like my kind of place!"

"Let's check it out!" Gizmo yipped.

With Max in the lead, the three dogs ran forward with renewed energy. They bounded up the weathered, wooden steps of the resort onto a wide porch. Stepping forward, Max nudged the glass front door with his head. It didn't budge. Looking up, he read the word on the door: PUSH.

Which meant the door was locked.

"Come on," Max said. "Let's see if there's a way in around the back."

They followed the porch around the side of the building to where it stretched out into a wide-open area. Wooden beach chairs were arranged around an empty swimming pool that stank of chlorine and mildew. A few chairs were tilted on their sides, and one lay up against the railing. Umbrellas were lying torn and tattered on the ground.

At the back of the resort building, there were two sliding glass doors. One showed symbols Max equated with bathrooms. That door was wide open.

They had a way in!

Max was about to tell his friends the good news when he felt Rocky bump into his hind legs.

"I don't mean to alarm you," Rocky whispered. "But I don't think we're alone, big guy."

The musk of animal fur met Max's nose. He turned to see four small creatures on the opposite side of the pool. They huddled in the early evening shadows next to the porch railing: three cats and a tiny dog.

The largest of the cats—a fat orange tabby with a square of black fur beneath its nose—stepped forward into the light, its green eyes narrowed into slits.

"Hi!" Gizmo said with a wag of her tail. "Maybe you can help us. We're looking for food and thought this place might have some."

The orange cat didn't have a chance to answer.

They heard a distant *thwump thwump* from the north.

As the sound grew louder, great gusts of wind rose up, carrying fallen leaves and stinging sand.

Blazing, man-made lights flooded through the resort windows.

And the big cat, its fur standing on end, cried out, "Don't just stand there! Run!"

CHAPTER 2

LIGHTS IN THE SKY

For a moment, Max was frozen.

The thumping from the sky sent vibrations into his bones, until the entire world was quaking beneath him. The rushing wind spun into tornadoes of dirt and sand that blasted his fur and flew into his mouth and eyes. Searing lights flashed all around, blinding him.

The cats, the tiny dog, Rocky, and Gizmo shrieked and ran. They screamed warnings and cried in fear, but Max couldn't understand a single word over the noise.

THWUMP THWUMP THWUMP.

Spitting grit from his mouth, Max ran blindly toward the back of the porch. His front legs banged against a lounge chair, and he hissed through his teeth. But he couldn't let the sharp burst of pain stop him. He crouched against the porch railing with his belly to the sand-covered deck.

The source of the noise was right above him now, casting black shadows in the final rays of the setting sun. Max looked up just in time to see one of the tattered yellow umbrellas rise up toward the sky. It hung there for a moment, then flipped over and landed on the beach below.

Peering up with blurry eyes, Max saw two black man-made objects hovering above, so close they almost grazed the top of the resort building. Giant, spinning blades rose from their tops.

Helicopters.

The wind from the blades twisted and tangled Max's yellow fur and blasted sand into his face, but he didn't care anymore. Because if there were helicopters above— that meant there were humans, too. He could almost see their shadowy figures through the windows.

No longer frightened, Max jumped atop a lounge chair and barked as loudly as he could.

"Hey!" he shouted. "We're down here! Please take us with you!"

But his barks were lost in the din of the whirring blades, and in seconds the two helicopters were soaring over the beach.

Still on the lounge chair, Max watched with despair as the twin helicopters flew away. Their floodlights swirled across the beach, illuminating cats, dogs, and other animals who were running to hide in the dunes. There were many more pets here than just the four they'd seen, but the helicopters did not stop.

The people inside them had to have seen the animals. They just didn't care.

Whimpering, Max watched the helicopters grow smaller, soaring over the ocean. The big ships were out there, brighter than ever in the approaching darkness, and that was where the helicopters were headed.

To all the other people. People who wanted nothing to do with the pets they'd left behind.

No, Max scolded himself. The humans had no choice—if they hadn't left, they'd have gotten sick. His job was to find Madame Curie's pack leader, and both Madame and Gertrude had insisted the woman would be found on land.

One by one, everyone who had been on the deck emerged from their hiding spots.

"What was *that*?" Rocky asked. "Were they UFOs? I saw them on TV once." He gaped at Max. "Were you standing out in the open the whole time, big guy? Did you see the aliens?"

Shaking his head, Max stepped off the lounge chair. "It wasn't aliens, Rocky; it was people in helicopters."

"That's strange," Gizmo said. "I wonder what they were doing."

Appearing out of nowhere, the fat orange cat leaped atop the railing above Max's head.

"Does it matter what they're doing?" the cat grumbled. "As long as they leave us alone on the beach, no harm is done except some scary noises." It licked a paw and ran it over its face, cleaning it of sand. "The name is Grendel, by the way."

Max introduced himself and his friends, then asked, "Don't you miss the humans?"

Someone snorted behind him, and Max turned to see the other cats and the tiny dog—a Chihuahua—sitting at the edge of the empty pool. Both cats were slender with white bellies, though one had black fur and the other, gray.

The gray-and-white cat—who Max guessed had snorted—rolled its eyes and said, "The people abandoned us to our fates; why should we care about them? We have all we'll ever need here at the beach, thanks to that lady in the hat."

Something about the way the cat and its companions looked seemed immediately familiar. A whiff of its musky fur met Max's nostrils, and with it came a flash of memory.

It had been weeks, maybe even months, but he had met these animals before, way back at the start of their journey. They looked thinner now, but they were definitely them. All three had been residents of a house for cats—and one Chihuahua who *thought* he was a cat. Raoul, their leader, had let the dogs spend the night. These two cats—sisters—had been the kindest, sharing their food and water.

Just after Max and his friends had left the cat house, it was overrun by a pack of wolves—the same wolves who would later attack the riverboat. Their leader, Dolph, had been following Max and his friends on some irrational quest for vengeance. Raoul died protecting his charges, and the cats who had lived in the house had fled. Max never expected to see any of them again.

"Hey," Max, his tail wagging, said to the cat sisters and the Chihuahua. "We know you, don't we?"

"Oh!" Gizmo yipped. "Of course! It's Panda, right?" she asked the black-and-white cat. "And you're her sister, Possum?" she said, addressing the one with the gray fur.

The two cats glanced at each other. "Yes," Possum mewed. "That's who we are."

"And little Buddha!" Gizmo yipped at the Chihuahua. "You've turned into a dashing feline, I must say."

Buddha snapped his slender tail, catlike, but didn't respond.

"You're those dogs," Panda said in her soft voice. "The ones we helped."

"That's us," Rocky said.

Gizmo's ears drooped. "We thought those bad wolves might have hurt you. I'm glad you're safe."

Possum let out a sharp laugh. "Luckily, if there's anyone who knows how to scatter in every direction, it's cats."

"But how did you end up all the way down here?" Gizmo asked.

"Well..." Panda began.

Groaning, Rocky dramatically flopped onto his side and covered his snout with a paw. "It's nice everyone's safe and happy and all, but can we share stories later? I'm practically wasting away over here."

Licking his lips, Max took a step forward. "If it's okay with you, can we try to find some kibble?"

"Why are you asking us?" Buddha grunted.

"It's a free beach," Grendel drawled from the railing. "Do whatever you want."

Max could only stare. So far, every group of animals they'd met had been protective of their food and homes. The last thing he was expecting was to be told to do as he pleased.

"Hey, nice!" Rocky said, rolling back onto his belly. "Finally, some laid-back animals." Glancing up at Max, he added, "Must be the ocean air."

Max looked at the beach. The ocean had turned a deep gray as the sun started to set. The waves crashed heavily before exploding into foam against the shore.

"Must be," he agreed. To the cats, he said, "You're telling me no one here listens to anybody? You just play on the beach all day?"

"Sure," Grendel said. "We've got plenty of food—"

"Food," Rocky moaned.

"—and places to sleep and play on the beach. It's pretty nice." The fat cat grimaced. "Well, except for the fleas."

The other cats meowed in agreement.

Max looked between Grendel and Possum, confused. "It's been months since all the people disappeared," he said. "How is it you still have food? We didn't see any grocery stores nearby."

Grendel began to pace. "There's a town not too far north of here, with a shopping mall and a pet store. We don't bother going there much, though. The hat lady left us with enough food to last for ages."

"Hat lady?" Max asked.

Rocky sighed. "Max, buddy, big guy—seriously, can we just eat already?"

Clearing her throat, Panda took a few cautious steps forward. "You can share some of our food tonight, if you like. There's dog food out on the beach, but it's so dark you might not be able to find it."

"What?" Buddha yowled. He jumped in front of Panda. "That's *cat* food! You can't go giving it away to a bunch of dumb dogs!"

Panda swatted his backside with her paw. Startled, Buddha let out a distinctly doglike yip and hid behind Possum.

"Is that all right with you, Sister?" Panda asked, craning her head at her gray-and-white twin.

Possum slowly blinked her yellow eyes. "Why not?" she said.

"Ohhh, finally!" Rocky said with a wag of his spiky tail. "Kibble! Lead the way, ladies."

"It's not exactly the kibble you're used to," Possum said, a smirk playing at her feline lips.

Rocky tilted his head. "How's that?"

"We've only got kitty chow," she said. "Salmon-flavored."

"Kitty chow?" Rocky grimaced.

Panda licked her lips. "The *best* kitty chow."

Rocky said, "Well, I guess it can't hurt to try new things. Take us to this"—he swallowed nervously—"kitty chow."

Max had only ever eaten kibble meant for dogs. The kitty-chow bits were so *small* in comparison. But after going without food for a few days, he felt as if the kitty chow offered up by Panda, Possum, Buddha, and Grendel was the best thing he'd ever eaten.

The cats' hideout was in the shade beneath the pool deck. One of their bags of kitty chow had already been wrenched open by their surprisingly strong jaws. They all ate, silent save for the crunching of food and the satisfied moans from Rocky.

After they'd eaten their fill, the seven animals cuddled together atop the warm sand. The briny ocean breeze rose up in gusts, colder now that it was night, and Max stared at the horizon, at the bobbing lights that told him humans were out there. He half considered diving into the dark waves and swimming for the boats, but he knew they were too far.

"This place is nice," Rocky mumbled as he curled up against Max's belly, his eyes half closed. "Looks like there will be plenty of friends to play with, tons of food, and no one trying to boss everyone around. Maybe we should stay here for a while."

"A beach vacation," Gizmo said with a wistful sigh.

Rocky licked her nose, and she curled up against him.

"We can't stay long," Max said softly. Images from his dream by the river came to him. "Tomorrow we have to continue on. We need to find our families, and Belle, and Madame's pack leader, and the beacons."

"Mmm," Rocky said, his voice muffled in Gizmo's fur.

But Max knew his small friend hadn't really heard, and Gizmo was already asleep.

"You're still on that journey, huh?"

"What's that?" Max asked.

It was Possum who had spoken. "We met you not long after the people left," she reminded him, licking her paws. "You said you were going to find your family. Seems like you've come a long way without much to show for it."

Max tried not to bristle at her tone. "If that's the case, why did you bother coming this far? Why not let the wolves take you, too?"

With a sigh, Possum glanced over at Buddha and Panda. "My sister is a fool for love," she said. "All that gets her through this is thinking one day she'll have her human back again." The gray-and-white cat swatted at

29

the air and turned away from her sleeping twin. "Besides, we didn't actually walk all the way here. That woman in the hat found us and drove us here in her truck."

Max's brow furrowed. "The hat woman Grendel was mentioning," he said. Memories flashed in Max's mind of a photo he'd seen at the laboratory. "Did she wear a lab coat, like a vet? Did she have white hair and a friendly smile?"

Possum's whiskers twitched, her eyes glowing in the dim light.

"She wore pink and yellow and purple," the cat said. "Her shirts had flowers on them. And she had a big straw hat."

"Do you remember anything else?" Max asked. "Did she leave glowing orange beacons as she drove?"

"I can't say I noticed," Possum said. "All I know is that she brought my sister and Buddha and me here. She fed all the animals on the beach and the ones with numbers for names, who came from that pet store up the road, and then she left us." She let out a bitter laugh. "If you ask me, that's why everyone on this beach is so lazy. With all the food in the world here, why do anything but play and feast? I'm sure the food will run out eventually, but until then, let's enjoy our lives as best we can."

"Oh," Max said. "Well, it was nice of the hat lady to feed you."

Possum didn't respond, resuming her grooming session.

Max rested his chin in the sand and turned his gaze to the ships. "I was there with Raoul before he died, you know," he said.

Possum stopped swiping at her fur.

"He distracted those evil wolves so all the other cats could live," Max went on. "He did it because he hoped that even if he couldn't see his lady again, you still would have a chance to be with your families one day."

Max met Possum's eyes once more. "I am going to find the people. I've promised too many animals to give up now, and I won't rest until I do. There's a way to cure the virus that made all the humans leave. So don't let your sister lose hope, all right? The people will come back for you soon."

Silence. For a long moment, there was no sound but lapping waves and doggy snores and insects chirping in the trees.

"You think so?" Possum finally asked, her voice a whisper.

"I know so," Max said.

They didn't speak after that. But Max felt the cat's warm body against his side, cuddling with him as the world drifted into dreams.

CHAPTER 3

A RUMOR OF MONSTERS

Max awoke to the sound of barking laughter, the slosh of waves over sand, and the whoosh of wind past his ears. The air was still cool, the sun newly risen, but already the beach was alive with animals—dozens of dogs, cats, and other pets.

After a mouthful of kitty chow, Max padded slowly through the sand. He didn't see snout or tail of Rocky or Gizmo or any of the cats, but he assumed they were out there somewhere.

Music met Max's ears, carried to him by the ocean breeze. He followed the sound until he found several young dogs surrounding a large radio. The music was peppy with a fast drumbeat, and several of the dogs leaped up onto their hind legs to mimic human dancing.

They couldn't keep it up for long, though, and soon they fell into a furry heap.

Not far from the dancing dogs, a trio of puppies tossed a branch wildly over the sand. A herd of cats swatted playfully at ocean weeds as though they were cornered mice. Two Border Collie puppies chased a rainbow-striped beach ball.

And in big piles all over the beach were sacks upon sacks of dog and cat food. Some bags were open, their pellets spilling onto the sand, but most were stacked neatly. The cats had been right—the lady in the hat, whoever she was, had left more than enough food to last these animals for months.

Max spun in a circle, absorbing all that he could see and hear and smell. Everywhere he looked, there were animals enjoying themselves. No one was fighting. It seemed like one big, never-ending party.

Max knew he should find Rocky and Gizmo so they could continue their journey. But he couldn't stop staring at the ocean. Its vastness, its smells, and its beauty were unlike anything he'd ever seen.

Before he could stop himself, Max raced into the surf.

The sand beneath his paws went from dry, shifting, and warm to packed and wet as the waves rushed toward him in a burst of wind.

The cold water crashed into his body, almost toppling him. Closing his eyes tight, Max dug his paws in the sand—and the waves receded, leaving him soaked and dripping.

Max laughed, loud and long. What a teasing thing, these waves! Splashing him before running away! Well, two could play at that game. Darting forward, he met the waves head on as they rushed back in, sending a big splash right back at the ocean.

He opened his jaws—only to take in a big gulp of the seawater. It wasn't like the river water, which had a strange taste but was drinkable. No, the ocean water was foul and vile, like a cocktail of fish and plants and salt—so much *salt*.

Soggy and cold and with his mouth filled with that awful taste, Max padded back toward the dry sand. He saw other big dogs splashing in the waves, and he guessed they'd already figured out not to drink the water. It looked like fun to splash with dog friends. Too bad Rocky and Gizmo were much too little to face the ocean's full strength.

Barking echoed from above. Max looked up to see Rocky and Gizmo back by the resort, next to the two Border Collie puppies. The puppies were yipping loudly—apparently trying to get the attention of Grendel on the deck railing.

Max shook his whole body, sending water splashing off his fur in every direction. Then he ran through the sand to hear what the commotion was about.

"Come on, Grendel, tell them the story!" the boy puppy barked.

The girl puppy spun in a circle. "Grendel, you're not gonna let them go out there with the creatures, are you? They seem so nice!"

Grendel ignored the frantic puppies, carefully cleaning his orange face and little black mustache.

"What's happening?" Max asked Rocky and Gizmo as he padded through the warm sand to join them.

"Oh!" Gizmo said. "Hi, Max! Rocky and I met these cute puppies and told them about our journey. They insisted we talk to Grendel first before we leave again."

Rocky shuddered. "Supposedly there's something dangerous in the swamps. Not that I'm afraid of danger, of course." He ducked his head. "But, uh, I figured it couldn't hurt to know what we're up against."

Realizing that someone new had arrived, the two black-and-white puppies stopped barking. They swarmed Max, sniffing at his fur, their furry tails wagging.

Max laughed. "Nice to meet you, too! I'm Max."

The boy Border Collie jumped back. "I'm Seventeen!" he barked happily. "And my friend here is Twelve."

"Hello," Twelve said politely, though her yellow eyes were filled with worry. "We just met Gizmo and Rocky, and they said you were going west to Baton Rouge."

"That's right," Max said. "A friend of ours who used to live there asked us to look for a dog named Belle."

"Belle? Hey! We know her!" said Seventeen. "A Collie, right? Belle used to come play with us at the farm in Baton Rouge. She was so nice, wasn't she, Twelve?"

"Sure was," Twelve said, her voice still shaking with concern.

"Oh, you know Belle?" Gizmo asked. "How wonderful!"

"Everyone knows her!" Seventeen said. "Just ask around when you get near the city, and you're sure to find her."

"Oh, good," Rocky said. "At least one part of this journey won't be hard."

Max looked down and saw that Twelve was shivering now, glancing past the resort at the road that divided the beach and the woods.

Nudging the puppy's side, he asked her, "Is everything all right? When I ran up, I heard you barking about creatures in the swamp."

From the railing above, Grendel yawned. "The puppies just have an active imagination."

Twelve shook her head furiously. "That's not true, Grendel! You know they gotta be careful out there." To Max, Rocky, and Gizmo, she said, "There have been animals that started off to the mall and never came back. And some who went off and returned with stories of monsters in the woods. Dark things as big as houses, with skin made of iron scales and teeth like razors. And they like to eat us pets."

Max chuckled. "I'm sure that's just a story the bigger

animals told to scare you. If any animals disappeared, they probably just decided to move on. There's no such thing as monsters."

Seventeen shook his head. "I dunno, mister. We all heard the howling. Grendel knows; I know he does."

Three pairs of eyes glowed in the darkness beneath the deck, and then Possum, Panda, and Buddha crept out into the daylight. Possum's tail snapped back and forth.

"These dogs are our friends, Grendel," Possum meowed up at the fat cat. "They need to know what's out there and why we stay on the beach."

With a sigh, Grendel rose to all fours and stretched. "Fine," he said. "I suppose I can take a break from sunning to tell you what I've heard. But I'm telling it only once, so listen close.

"After the hat lady left," Grendel began, "most of us at the beach did our own thing, but there was one animal who kept us working. He was a great big beast of a canine who slobbered endlessly, so large he would tower over Max."

Grendel paced as he spoke. Above him, the morning sky darkened as gray clouds swirled in from the ocean.

"The dog's name was Georgie," he went on. "Before the people disappeared, he lived at the inn up the road. He taught everyone to share the food that the hat lady left behind, and he figured out how we could flip the levers in the bathrooms to drink, what with the ocean water being so salty. He led expeditions to the board-walk to find toys for everyone.

"After a time, though, Georgie got fed up with taking care of everyone else. He decided he'd follow the hat woman and try to make his way back to where he lived before his pack leaders moved to the inn. He walked right up to the swamp road that leads to the mall…and disappeared."

Grendel paused, and the dogs huddled close together, silent and listening.

"That night, we all heard it," Grendel continued. "A loud, anguished howl from the woods that echoed throughout the beach, lasting a minute or more." Grendel's whiskers twitched. "And then Georgie went silent, and we never heard from him again."

Max studied the trees on the other side of the road, past the resort. It couldn't be later than midmorning, and yet the shadows there were long and dark. Was it a trick of the leaves, or was there some animal in the depths of the forest, watching them?

Rocky chuckled nervously. "Okay, so a dog ran away. That doesn't mean anything bad happened to him." He shivered. "Does it?"

"Maybe not," Grendel went on. "But it wasn't long after Georgie disappeared that we lost the bunnies."

"Oh, no," Gizmo gasped. "There were bunnies here?"

"There still are," Grendel said. "But a couple of them were lost. Some of the cats and dogs goaded them into exploring the trees near the inn. But there was something in those woods, and the bunnies never came back.

All we remember is those cats and dogs running back to the beach, yowling and barking in terror."

"Wh-what did they see?" Rocky asked.

"It was dark, so they couldn't be sure. But they thought they saw giant beasts covered in dark, hard ridges. And their eyes were black hollow things. Blacker than the night and evil."

"One of the cats told me they had millions of teeth," Seventeen said. "Teeth like steel daggers."

"And I heard they move fast," Twelve said. "They can lunge from the trees and then sink into the waters."

"And you can't see them until it's too late," Seventeen added.

Gizmo shook her head. "That sounds incredible. I mean, superscary and all, but I've never heard of anything like that."

"Oh, and I wish I never had," Rocky said. "Snatching up bunnies is one thing, but taking a dog even bigger than Max here? They must be as big as trucks!"

Max suddenly felt small and insignificant beneath the swirling gray sky, a speck on the endless beach.

"Anyway," Grendel said as he lay down once more on the railing. "So far we've been safe in large groups. None of you will end up like Georgie as long as you stick together, so I don't see why these puppies are raising a fuss." His whiskers twitched again. "Though I have to say, that's only as long as you get through the forest and to the mall before it's night out."

"Then what are we waiting for?" Rocky yipped as he jumped to his feet. "Let's get on our way before night monsters come to eat us up!"

Max stood and shook the sand from his fur. "Thanks for the warning," he said to the puppies and the cats.

The two cat sisters and Buddha sauntered back to the safety of their home beneath the deck.

"It was nice seeing you again," Panda whispered over her shoulder. "Good luck."

"Thank you," Max said.

Briefly meeting Max's eyes, Possum said, "I won't forget what you said. I hope we'll see you again soon."

Then the gray-and-white cat was gone.

The puppies started back toward the beach to resume playing with the other dogs. As Twelve passed, she lowered her head. "Please be careful, all right?"

"I promise I'll be safe," Max told her. "Nothing is going to stop me from finding Belle and my family. Not even a monster."

Max watched the puppies bound through the shifting sand, then looked once more at the swampy woods, now darker than ever under the suddenly overcast sky. Surely all that lurked out there were more animals. And Max could handle most animals.

Unless they had iron scales and teeth as sharp as razors.

CHAPTER 4

THROUGH THE FOREST

After pestering Grendel for directions, Max, Rocky, and Gizmo left behind the beach and its laughing, playful animals. The music from the dancing dogs' radio grew faint as they walked west to the road that would take them to the mall.

They padded over the concrete parking lot next to the resort, careful to avoid broken glass, and soon they were back on the main road. Its surface was coated with swirls of dried mud and littered with driftwood. They passed more shops and a wooden boardwalk before reaching a side street that veered north, into the trees.

"This must be the way," Max said. He padded toward the shadowed street, then stopped, an uneasy feeling coming over him.

"Is everything all right?" Gizmo asked.

Max peered back over his shoulder to find his friends also hesitating.

Max nodded and said, "Yes, it's fine. The shopping center can't be too far. Let's go."

As he stepped onto the street, Max felt as if he were entering a new world. Coiled, thick-trunked trees towered over the asphalt, shrouding it in shadow. There was more debris here—decaying leaves and fallen twigs and plastic bags. He even caught sight of a rusted motorcycle leaning against a tree, overgrown with fluffy moss.

The farther they walked, the heavier the air became, until Max found himself panting. Sounds echoed all around him. Some were familiar, like the buzzing of insects and croaks of frogs, but there were other noises, too—strange ones. He heard groans and creaks, as if the trees were settling all around him. An occasional distant, unearthly shriek pierced the sky.

Max swallowed, nervously eyeing the darkness between the trees. Neither of the others spoke. Aside from the noises of the forest, the only sounds were their panting breaths and the pads of their feet on the overgrown road.

Even though the beach was not that far behind them, Max thought it seemed a thousand miles away. This place was some new, untamed land, where wild, unusual things could lurk around any corner.

Suddenly, the idea of monsters in the woods didn't seem so silly.

Rocky cleared his throat. "I'm not sure I'm feeling brave right now."

"It's just noises," Max said. "Probably just more frogs or birds—"

"But the birds all left," Rocky muttered.

"—or...or...bats or something. We'll be fine. Right, Gizmo?"

"Definitely!" she said. "Um, though maybe we should hurry a little."

Silent again, the animals trotted steadily and quickly down the overgrown road. Max kept his eyes aimed forward, refusing to look into the trees and scare himself even more.

It was Gizmo who saw it first.

"Hey, what's that?" she asked.

"What's what?" Rocky said, following her gaze. Immediately the Dachshund yelped in fear. He darted between Max's front legs and huddled underneath his belly.

"Rocky, what's wrong?" Max asked.

Trembling, Rocky tried to answer, but he couldn't get out the words. Instead, Gizmo pointed with her snout toward the trees on the side of the road.

There, in the dark, were two glimmering amber circles. They glowed and flashed in the shadows, like the eyes of some great, terrifying beast.

"It's those creatures!" Rocky howled. "They've come to eat us all up!"

Max froze, unable to look away from the two glowing circles. His instincts told him to run, while his brain told him to stay still to avoid capturing the creature's attention.

He and his companions huddled together, staring at the amber eyes. Max expected the beast to stomp out of the trees at any moment, the ground trembling beneath its feet. He expected a steel-plated body the size of a bus and a mouth filled with jagged razors.

Instead, the eyes stayed still, flashing at a steady rhythm.

Wait, Max thought. *Didn't the puppies say the monster's eyes were black, like the night?*

And wasn't the blinking too steady, too mechanical, to belong to an animal?

Max let out a long, shaky breath, then chuckled.

"Why are you laughing, big guy?" Rocky whispered. "We're about to become a monster's lunch!"

"Actually, it's kind of funny," Max said as he carefully stepped over Rocky. "All those stories are getting us scared over nothing."

Max padded purposefully across the road to the blinking lights. As he drew near, he laughed again, louder this time.

The glowing circles weren't the eyes of some terrifying creature. They were two round, plastic yellow-orange beacons with *X*s on their fronts. They were on top of a small traffic barricade painted with orange and white stripes, though the paint was scratched and faded.

And spray-painted on the tree behind the barricade was a neon-orange circle with a black *X* in its center.

These weren't just any beacons. These were *the* beacons, the ones that Madame Curie's owner was leaving to mark her trail. The three of them were on the right track!

Facing his companions, Max called out, "Hey, it's safe! In fact, this is exactly what we were looking for!"

With a relieved bark, Rocky waddled after Max, with Gizmo close behind him.

"Is that what I think it is?" Gizmo asked as she approached.

"It sure is!" Max said.

"See?" Gizmo said to Rocky. "Nothing to be afraid of."

"Not this time," Rocky muttered. "But one of these days my tendency to be overly cautious is gonna keep us from getting eaten."

Gizmo licked his side, giggling.

Rocky sniffed at the barricade, and his eyes went wide. "Hey, you know what this means, right? The only human the beach animals saw come this way was the hat lady—which means she and our scientist lady are one and the same!"

"Oh!" Gizmo said. "Yay! And since she left here only a few weeks ago, we can still catch up with her."

"Gertrude the pig was right, back at the laboratory," Max said. "Madame's owner is trying to fix us animals so that the Praxis virus we have inside us won't be harmful to people. I'm sure of it."

Max sniffed at the painted wood barricade and the glowing beacons and the tree behind them. The old woman's scent was faint and distant, washed away by weather and time. But there was just enough left that Max could recognize the peculiar musk of human mixed with the perfume of lilacs and something sharp and antiseptic.

He took in deep, gulping breaths of the faded scent, letting it swirl through his nostrils and into his brain. The old woman might have shed her lab coat for brightly colored, flowery shirts and a big straw hat, but he'd know her by her scent.

Finding some of the orange beacons he'd been searching for since leaving the riverboat filled Max with happiness. The forest no longer seemed quite so dark and ominous.

Not that he planned to stay on the overgrown road any longer than he had to.

Turning away from the beacons, Max met his friends' eyes. "We're safe from monsters for now. Let's get out of these trees before it's dark!"

Soon, the trees thinned out and sunshine beat down once more on their fur, the stormy clouds having drifted away. A breeze washed over them, carrying the musty smells of the forest.

Rocky darted ahead. "Oh, sweet freedom!" he yipped. "I thought we'd never get out of those woods."

They had reached a big concrete parking lot. To Max's right, a small billboard read INLAND SHOPPING CENTER—NEXT LEFT. Across the vast, open lot was the biggest shopping mall Max had ever seen, several stories tall with wide windows that glittered in the sunlight.

Taking up most of the enormous building's side was a movie theater. Next to the theater was the mall entrance, and next to that was a storefront with cartoon fish and puppies and cats painted on the windows.

"That place is huge," Gizmo said. "I bet it's filled with all sorts of neat stuff!"

"Grendel said we should find a way to spend the night inside," Max said. "We still don't know what's lurking out here."

"Uh, yeah," Rocky said, peering up at Max. "I like that plan."

"I wonder if there ever really was anything in the woods," Gizmo said as they walked through the lot toward the mall. "It would be nice if, for once, we didn't have any dangerous beasts after us."

Rocky nudged her side. "I thought you loved everybody, Giz."

She sniffed. "Well, I do," she said. "Except when they're trying to eat us."

Max chuckled. He was about to say something when a stray scent met his nose.

He stopped walking, one paw raised midstep. All day, he'd been surrounded by the murk of the swampy woods and the briny smells of the ocean. Now this new, fleeting smell set off an immediate alarm in his head.

It was the musk of wolves.

At least, he thought it was. The scent was so briefly in and out of his nostrils that he couldn't be sure.

Sniffing at the air, Max turned in a tight circle. Nothing. He didn't think he'd imagined it, but he had to be careful. The last time he'd thought he smelled wolves, he'd been right.

There was still a chance Dolph could be following Max and his friends, wanting revenge. He had already tracked them from Max's hometown all the way to the riverboat. The animal was relentless.

And in the dark of night, hidden by trees, could wolves hunting for a rabbit meal be mistaken for giant, iron-clad monsters?

"What is it, Max?" Gizmo asked. "Do you smell something?"

Rocky gasped. "Is it the monster? Is it here?"

Max didn't want to worry his friends, so he said, "No, it's nothing. Let's just get to the mall, okay?"

Darting ahead, Rocky called out, "Don't have to ask me twice. Let's hurry!"

As they neared the mall, Max looked toward the massive pet store. Twin orange lights caught his eye.

"Hey," he said to his friends. "Over here."

Another of the small white-and-orange barricades was set up at the edge of the pet store. Just like the barrier in the woods, the beacons on top blinked with a steady rhythm, and the old woman's faint scent swirled in the air. Painted on the wall behind the barricade was another crude orange circle with a black X through its middle.

"The old woman was here, too," Rocky said. "But why leave a beacon here?"

"It's a pet store," Gizmo said. "Maybe it's just to let people know that she already came through."

Max angled his head back and studied the pet store. It was dark inside, though far in the back he could see faint blue lights refracted by murky water. Fish tanks.

But more importantly, the three-ringed symbol that had been on Madame's collar was spray-painted crudely all over the store's facade. The circles were black and misshapen. Drips of paint fell from their bottoms, leaving goopy trails.

The symbol was for the laboratory that had made the Praxis virus. But, as Max had discovered, many humans had chosen to paint the three rings as a warning on any building containing animals that might have been infected.

He could only be thankful to the kind humans who must have freed Twelve, Seventeen, and the other pets inside this store. Memories of the time he'd spent in the kennel immediately after the humans disappeared came back to Max. His loneliness. The combination of aching hunger and his worry that he might never see his family again.

Max shook his head. He didn't want to think about what could have happened if he hadn't escaped. "It doesn't matter why she left the beacon," Max said. "All it means is that we're still on the right path to finding her. Let's get inside."

As they neared the entrance to the pet store, they saw a plain white door next to the dark display windows. On it was a sign that read EMPLOYEES ONLY.

The door was slightly open. The hallway beyond was narrow and plain—white floor, white walls, white ceiling. Quietly, the three dogs padded down the dark hallway to another door. It opened with a squeak of hinges, revealing a room flooded with light. They were in a storeroom filled with doggy beds, toys, and—most importantly—kibble.

With flashes of black-and-tan fur, Rocky and Gizmo darted inside.

"This is heaven!" Rocky said as he sniffed the bags of kibble lining the shelves.

Gizmo lunged into a stack of plush, plaid pet beds, and they collapsed around her in a heap. She laughed. "This is fantastic," she said. "What a great place to spend the night!"

Max wrenched open a bag of beef-flavored kibble, spilling the pellets all over the dusty floor. He, Rocky, and Gizmo ate until their bellies were full. An upsidedown jug of water on a white, square base stood beside the door. It was easy enough to figure out how to press down the lever on the front, and one by one the dogs drank the water that streamed out.

They spent some time exploring the storeroom, discovering jars of tiny turquoise rocks for the bottom of aquariums, plastic tubes for small rodents to crawl through, and toys—so many toys. But soon exhaustion caught up with them, and Max decided they were ready for an early bedtime.

They all agreed to keep the bright fluorescent lights on in the storeroom. Just in case they helped keep monsters away.

Climbing atop the mound of doggy beds, Max, Rocky, and Gizmo spun in tight circles and then lay down to get comfortable. Rocky was the first to fall asleep, clutching a nubby red rubber ball between his teeth.

Max didn't fall asleep right away. He kept thinking about all sorts of things—his family, promises he'd made, the dangers that might lie ahead. In his mind's eye, he saw enormous, metal-plated monsters breathing fire and tossing aside trees.

It was one of the downsides of being smarter, Max supposed. His brain always wanted to work now, when in the past he could just close his eyes and drift off.

A small, wet nose nudged Max's neck.

"Are you awake?" Gizmo asked.

Max lifted his head off his paws. "Sure," he said softly, so as not to disturb Rocky. "Is everything all right?"

"I'm not sure," Gizmo said. "Do you ever have trouble falling asleep?"

"It depends," Max said. "If we've been walking from morning to night, sometimes I'm so tired I doze right off. But other times, my thoughts keep me from sleeping. It's been that way ever since—"

"Praxis," they said at the same time.

Gizmo giggled. "Oh, good, it's not just me."

Max licked Gizmo's side. "Are you having scary thoughts because of all the monster talk?"

"Not really," she said. "I keep remembering the day I last saw my pack leaders. I saw that squirrel outside their RV, and I jumped out the window to chase it. Even though I knew better!" She sighed. "There are squirrels everywhere. But there's only one Ann, who loved me so much, and I loved her, and now I might never see her again." Gizmo dug herself into the crevice between two upturned doggy beds until Max could only see the tufts of her tan fur.

"I was such a dumb, silly dog," she whispered, her voice muffled.

Max climbed onto all fours, stretching his legs. As Rocky continued to gnaw on his rubber ball in his sleep, Max climbed over the mounded pet beds to where Gizmo hid.

"Hey," he said. "You were never a dumb or silly dog."

She peered up at him, a shimmer of tears in her dark eyes. "I sure acted like one."

"Maybe," Max said. "But there's nothing we can do about it now, right? We can't go back and change it."

"No, it's probably not possible to go backward in time," Gizmo said, nodding in agreement.

Max lay down next to Gizmo. "I think these thoughts are called regret. I remember all the friends we lost, like Madame and Boss, because I didn't know how to save them."

"What are we supposed to do?" Gizmo whispered.

"Well," Max said, "we can learn from our mistakes. And we can imagine different things."

Gizmo's tail wagged slowly. "Like what will happen once we find Madame's pack leader and her big hat! I wonder if she'll let me wear it."

Max chuckled. "Exactly! But that hat is so big, it would wear *you*."

Max imagined a big straw hat with a wide brim and a pink bow plopping down on Gizmo. And Gizmo running around, making it look as if the hat had sprouted legs.

Gizmo must have imagined the same thing, because both dogs burst into loud, snorting laughter.

Nearby, Rocky grumbled in his sleep. Max and Gizmo put their paws over their snouts to quiet themselves.

"Thanks, Max," Gizmo said. "You really cheered me up."

"I'm glad," Max said. "I'm still learning, too. Being smart is new for all of us."

Gizmo's small mouth opened wide in a yawn. "Good night, Max," she whispered as she curled into the plush beds.

"Good night," Max whispered back. And though worry and regret still threatened to keep Max awake, he made himself imagine a future where he and Gizmo and Rocky were surrounded by their families, and soon he drifted off to sleep.

CHAPTER 5

BRAND-NEW DAY

Max was back on the dark, overgrown road between the peaceful beach and the empty mall.

The leaves above him shuddered, and he could hear the fluttering of hundreds upon hundreds of wings.

Birds? Had the birds returned?

He looked up at the canopy, hope rising in his chest. What he wouldn't give to see feathers of white, brown, red, and yellow as robins and cardinals, sparrows and warblers flitted above him.

Instead he saw a blanket of bats dangling from the branches, their leathery black wings unfurled.

From deep within the shadowy woods came a piercing, frightened howl.

The bats screeched and dropped from their perches,

taking wing and swarming out of the woods, a living black cloud.

Max trembled at the lonesome sound—until two dogs appeared at his side.

It's all right, Maxie, Madame said. *His howl is nothing to fear.*

We're right here with you, son, said Boss.

And though the howl grew louder and louder, Max's fear faded away. The warmth of his friends leaning against his side comforted him.

"Who is he?" Max asked.

He has many names, Boss said.

Madame added, *But you will come to know him as "friend."*

The howling faded to an echo. As Max watched, the largest dog he'd ever seen slunk out of the trees. His shape and breed were unclear to Max—in fact, it seemed to shift by the second—but he could see the beastly dog's sad, watery eyes and the lines of drool trailing from his snout.

Tail held low and head drooping, the large dog walked down the road away from Max. Far beyond him was the figure of a woman, a silhouette in the dim light. Madame's pack leader. Next to her shadowy figure, an orange circle glowed.

Keep going, Max, Boss said. *Take it one step at a time.*

We believe in you, Maxie, Madame said.

Holding his head high, Max stepped away from Madame and Boss, following the large dog deeper into the overgrown woods. With each step forward, he felt his friends' presence fade and recede until they were gone altogether.

And with each step, he felt the old woman grow even closer.

Max opened his jaws to bark at the sad dog ahead of him, to ask him to wait.

And Max awoke.

Max raised his head and yawned. Even though the room they were in had no windows, something told him it was dawn.

He roused Rocky and Gizmo and dragged the partially eaten bag of kibble over for a quick morning meal. After eating their fill and drinking from the water jug, the three dogs left the bright storeroom and padded down the dim, plain hallway they'd come through yesterday.

As they neared the EMPLOYEES ONLY door, a steady patter of rain met Max's ears, and he looked out to see that the sky was a roiling, swirling gray.

"Oh, great," Rocky grumbled. "It's storming! I say we go back to sleep and wait till it's over."

Max nosed Rocky's side playfully. "You should be used to it," he said. "We've dove into more rivers than I can remember by now."

"Used to it, sure. But that doesn't mean I like it."

The three dogs left the building, making their way under a wide awning around the side of the shopping mall. Suddenly, Max realized the little terrier was no longer trailing behind him.

Panic seized Max's chest. Had she gotten lost? Or worse—did one of those slithering monsters find her?

Max scanned the parking lot—and there, near an entrance to the mall, was the tiny tan-and-black fuzzball that was Gizmo. She sniffed loudly at a wide rubber mat.

Max trotted swiftly to her side. "What do you smell?" he asked.

"Hi!" Gizmo said. "Sorry, I didn't mean to run off. It's just that I got a whiff of a doggy smell, and I followed it here. It makes me think of a big, big dog." She wagged her tail. "There's dried slobber here, too," she added. "Grendel said in his story that a big dog named Georgie was following the old woman to find his way back home, so that gives us one more trail to follow."

Max's dream from the night before came back to him in bits and pieces. He understood completely now: He was meant to follow Georgie, who would lead him to Madame's pack leader. His tail wagged, and he licked Gizmo's forehead. "Good work picking up his scent. I have a feeling finding Georgie will help us out a lot."

"What's good work?" Rocky asked as he waddled up. "What's happening?"

"We found Georgie!" Gizmo squealed with a triumphant jump.

Rocky spun in a circle. "Where? Here?"

"No, silly," Gizmo said as she nuzzled Rocky's neck.

"Just his scent. But Max thinks if we follow him, he'll lead us to the hat lady. Between Georgie and the beacons, we won't ever get lost."

"Oh, good," Rocky said. "Losing our way out there wouldn't be fun."

Max looked up at the awning. The patter of rain had lessened, but it was still gray outside, and a mist hung in the air.

"Ready to face the elements?" Max asked.

"No," Rocky muttered.

"Sure!" Gizmo said at the same time.

"Let's go," Max said.

The rain was no longer a torrent but a gentle sprinkle as the storm came to an end. The air was heavy and thick, however, and it coated their fur with moisture.

The parking lot on the north side of the mall was smaller than the one they'd walked through the day before. Keeping their heads low, the three dogs splashed across the empty lot as quickly as they could.

Before long, they reached the main street and then veered left, just as Grendel had told them to. The road west was covered with branches. Soon, Max realized that it was raised above the land like a bridge.

At the top of the incline, the three dogs stopped to catch their breath. Something about the humid air made every step feel harder, every breath more laborious. Max looked ahead and saw that, much like the road from the beach, nature had overtaken their path.

The trees on either side of the elevated roadway were

thick and tall. They grew from the water far below, water that was covered with slimy lily pads and green algae.

The road itself was overgrown with tall, untamed grass. Leafy vines sprouted from the surface and climbed up the nearby trees or dangled from metal railings. Blankets of lush, gray-green moss hung in sheets from the branches and railings, floating ghostlike in the breeze.

Though it wasn't quite as dark here as in the woods, there was an eerie, verdant hue to everything that made the path ahead seem dreamlike. More of the strange animal shrieks echoed through the trees, and down below there was a splash as something—or some*one*—plopped into the water.

Max was about to ask Rocky and Gizmo if they were ready to continue when a rustling came from the tree closest to them.

Rocky darted behind Max. "Get back, Gizmo," he whispered. "Did you hear that?"

The branches rustled, and there was the briefest flash of gray fur. Not taking her eyes off the tree, Gizmo slowly backed around Max's hind legs to join Rocky.

"What is it, Max?" she asked.

"I don't know," Max whispered back.

With a shudder of leaves and a scrabble of claws, the branches and moss parted. A dozen glowing yellow eyes glared down at the dogs.

Rocky screamed, "The monster is back! And this time it's in the trees!"

CHAPTER 6

THE TREE DWELLERS

The creature—or whatever it was—hissed and growled, and Max took a step back.

"It's going to eat us!" Rocky yowled.

Panicked, the Dachshund sprinted to the opposite side of the cracked road, running in a wild zigzag. Meeting the concrete ledge on the far side, he spun around in a desperate circle.

Max's instincts told him to flee as well, but he remembered the last few times he'd thought a monster or some other beast was out to get them.

Instead of running away, Max took a purposeful step forward. Though the sprinkling, misty rain made him blink, he was able to see that the dozen yellow eyes belonged to six different small faces. It wasn't the dark, deadly gaze of the monsters described by the beach pets. And it certainly wasn't the icy glare of Dolph or his wolves, who wouldn't be up in a tree, anyway.

"Don't get close!" Rocky howled. "We gotta run away!"

Max moved closer so that the tree canopy blocked some of the rainfall, and he finally got a good view.

The creatures looked like giant rats with messy gray fur. One was bigger even than Gizmo or Rocky, but the other five were younger and smaller. They dangled upside down from the mossy branch, holding on with their thick, hairless pink tails. The strange things stared at Max with beady eyes, their rounded ears perked up.

For a long moment, Max and the six creatures watched each other silently. Then, from behind Max, came a loud thud. He spun around to see that Rocky had run headfirst into a guardrail. The Dachshund sat upon a patch of weeds, looking confused.

"Rocky!" Gizmo barked, and she ran to his side to sniff and lick his forehead.

From the trees, the tiniest rat-creature giggled. She raised her tiny front claws to cover her snout, but she couldn't stop laughing. Soon, she was joined by the other four small ones.

"Did ya see that, Papa?" one of the creatures squealed. He pointed at Rocky. "That dog there done hit his head! Isn't that silly?"

"It was funny, it was!" the smallest one squeaked.

"He went 'round and 'round and 'round, and then he smacked his head like this!" She bounced her fist square in the center of her forehead.

All the small rat-creatures burst into another bout of laughter. Only the largest one remained unamused.

"Hey, it's not funny!" Rocky barked from across the road. "You can't go around scaring people and then laughing at them. It's not right."

Next to him, Gizmo giggled, then ducked her head when Rocky glared at her. "It was a little funny," she said. "But only because you're not hurt!"

The big creature growled again, and Max turned his attention to him. The younger things seemed harmless enough, but if the big one decided to attack Rocky or Gizmo, they could be in a lot of trouble. He was fat-bellied, with long whiskers that twisted off his snout like metal wire. Part of his left ear was missing, and there were scars all over his face. The creature's jaws were clamped shut, but Max had seen the tiny, sharp teeth that filled the snouts of the babies. He could imagine how much bigger those teeth would be in an animal who'd clearly been in more than a few fights.

"Sorry about my friend," Max said, gesturing to Rocky. "We've heard lots of stories about monsters in these woods, so he gets scared easily. I'm Max. Who are you?"

"He's *Papa*," said one of the tiny creatures, rolling his eyes.

"In actuality," the big thing said, "the name is Hank. These be my children."

"Nice to meet you," Max said warily.

Hank looked Max up and down. "Uh-huh," he said.

Rocky tilted his head at the creatures. "What are you supposed to be, anyway?" he asked.

"We're possums!" the youngest girl squealed.

Gizmo furrowed her brow. "We know a Possum," she said. "But she's a cat."

Hank grunted. "She musta been named after us real possums, then. Or she's trying to be mistook for one of us. Lots of animals wish they was as nimble as us."

Rocky nodded. "I've heard of animals like you. But why don't you have any hair on your tails? Don't you get cold?"

"Nah," a boy possum said, his voice deeper than his sister's. "Don't need no hair. That would make it hard to dangle from branches."

"And why do you hang upside down?"

The smallest one sniffed and crossed her arms. "Why *don't* you?"

"Let's not insult our new friends, Rocky," Max said. To Hank, he nodded once more. "We'd best be on our way. It was nice to meet you."

"Oh, yeah," Hank said. "It was real pleasurable-like. Enjoy the swamp, ya hear? It plans to enjoy you back."

"Uh, all right," Max said. Something about what the possum had just said felt very strange to him.

The possums watched silently as Max, Rocky, and Gizmo started down the road again. Once more, Max was astounded by the sudden shift in the world around them. A hazy green fog hung in the air, a mixture of the moisture rising off the swamp and mist from the earlier storm. Grass, weeds, and moss squelched between their toes, and mosquitoes buzzed around the puddles.

The tall trees and the dangling moss waved gently in the breeze, and Max heard distant splashes and shrieks. He ignored the noises until he heard creaks and cracks from the branches immediately to his left.

"What was that?" Rocky wheezed.

Max looked up and saw, once more, twelve eyes looking down at them. It was the possum family, only this time they sat atop the branch in a neat row, with Hank nearest to the road.

"Uh, hello again," Max said.

"Hi!" Gizmo said.

Hank's messy whiskers twitched. "Where you all headed?" he asked. As the possum spoke, Max caught flashes of his teeth, sharp and yellowed with age.

The possum children stared at them with unreadable expressions.

Something in the back of Max's brain tingled, saying, *Don't trust this possum.*

But that was silly, wasn't it? Walking forward, Max answered, "We're just passing through on our way to Baton Rouge."

"Hmm," Hank said.

The branch swayed as the possums leaped to another tree, keeping pace with the dogs. They watched silently.

Max led Rocky and Gizmo around an abandoned car. Its wheels were flat, and vines and moss dangled from its open doors.

Again the trees creaked, and the possums jumped to a branch up ahead. Rocky shivered, but Gizmo trotted in front of the others.

"Hi!" she called. "It's Gizmo. I have a question."

"What question?" Hank said from his new perch.

"I was wondering if a great big slobbery dog came through here not too long ago," she said. "I smelled him back at the mall, but the rain's washed away his scent."

Leaves rustled as the five small possums dropped down to dangle from the branch by their naked tails. They whispered to one another, but Max couldn't make out what they were saying.

Hank, meanwhile, stayed perched above them. His notched ear twitched as he listened to his children's whispers, and slowly he nodded.

The largest of the five smaller possums peered up at his father. "Papa?" he asked.

"I done heard," Hank said. To Gizmo, he said, "Yeah, a few weeks back some dog came through. He was awful confused and whiny, but no one ever did say big things is always smart."

"He slobbered all over!" one of the young possums squealed.

Coming up to Gizmo's side, Rocky called out, "Okay, thanks for the help! You can shoo now. We'll be fine traveling on our own."

Hank's whiskers twitched. "If you say so."

Despite Rocky's clear irritation, the possums did not shoo. They stood where they were, still watching.

Rocky whispered to Max, "How about we pick up the pace and lose these guys? I don't like how they're watching us."

Max nodded.

"Aw," Gizmo said. "Their dad sure is a grump, but the little ones are cute in their own way."

"Yeah, yeah, they're cute," Rocky said. "Now can we get out of this swamp before we make any new creepy friends? Like those giant monsters everyone went on about?"

With one last glance at the dangling possums, Max led the way back up the overgrown road, this time at a full trot, and soon the three dogs found themselves cresting the top of the hill.

As far as Max could see, they were surrounded by the swamp, and the road, though it leveled off, was still overgrown. A little ways ahead was a big green sign, elevated high above them by steel posts. More of the gray-green moss dangled from the sign, and it was splattered with mud. There was a location printed on the sign in bold white type, but half of it was obscured by a spray-painted version of the three-ring symbol.

The paint was dark red, all the more garish amid the green of the swamp. Drips of paint made long trails down the sign, leaving spots of red on the road below. Max managed to make out the words NATIONAL WETLANDS PRESERVE, the white letters barely showing through the red paint. SOUTHERN ENTRANCE—ONE MILE.

"What do you think that means?" Gizmo asked.

Rocky stuck his head through the guardrail. "The land down there sure is *wet*. I'm not sure why they'd want to preserve this place, though. It's stuffy, and it smells awful."

"If we're already in the wetlands, why is there an entrance in a mile?" Gizmo asked. "Unless it's a special type of swamp. Maybe it's nicer than this one!"

Max stretched his legs. "The sign says it's only a mile away, so I guess we'll find out."

Gizmo's stubby tail wagged. "That's not far at all! Maybe Georgie will be there, or the old woman. Let's go see!"

A branch next to the sign rustled and bounced, and a flash of gray fur burst from between the leaves. The fat possum, Hank, landed with a thud on a slender ledge at the base of the sign, sending the moss and vines waving.

"What you dumb dogs playing at?" the possum hissed. "Acting like you learned how to read people symbols? Animals can't read."

"You're still following us?" Rocky yipped. "Don't you have anything better to do?"

Gripping the metal ledge, Hank regarded Rocky with narrowed, beady eyes.

"Maybe I do, and maybe I don't. It ain't none of your business."

Rocky growled. "Then I don't see how it's your business if—"

"It's fine, Rocky," Max said. He looked up at the fat possum. "Hank, it's a long story, but we actually can read. That's why we're on this journey. We're looking for an old woman with a big hat who might have come through here. She's involved with why all the people left and why some animals are smarter now."

Hank waved a dismissive paw. "You go on and pretend you understand what these symbols mean. I'll have you mutts know that we ain't following you, we're just going the same direction."

"We are?" Gizmo asked. "You're going to Baton Rouge, too?"

"Naw!" Hank spat. "Who wants to go all the way there? No, that old lady with the hat is having a party down the road. I'm taking my children. I'd invite you, but—"

Max's ears perked up. "The hat lady? She's here?"

"And she's having a party?" Rocky asked. He spun in an excited circle. "With food?"

"Why didn't you tell us before?" Gizmo asked.

The leaves above the sign rustled, and three of the small possums' heads popped out. "Yeah, Papa," one squealed. "We didn't know about no party!"

Hank shook his head. "It was supposed to be a surprise. But now it's all ruined."

Gizmo sniffed at the cracked asphalt. "I don't smell the lady's scent," she said.

Hank glared down at the dogs. "Well, you wouldn't, would ya? Not with all the rain. You said that yourself."

Gizmo sighed. "That's true."

Hank stroked the underside of his scarred snout with his paw. "I suppose it wouldn't hurt if you dogs went to the party. That dog you asked about is probably there, too."

"Where is this party?" Max asked.

Stringing his thick, naked tail through a gap in the ledge, Hank dropped to dangle beneath the sign. He pointed down the road with his front paws.

"It's thataway. You'll see another sign and a dirt road on the right. Just keep going straight and you'll find it in no time."

"What about us, Papa?" one of the children squeaked.

"You hush," Hank called. "You ain't near clean enough to go to a party yet. You best start grooming yourselves afore all the possum food is ate up by these dogs."

The smallest children let out a disappointed "Aww!" but they were quickly herded away by their elder siblings to get ready. Hank watched them go with a stern glare.

"Thank you for letting us know," Max called up to Hank. "We appreciate it."

"Yeah, yeah," the fat possum said. "Have fun."

Max, Rocky, and Gizmo quickly trotted toward the sign and the branch that held the large possum. Just as they passed beneath, Max dared a glance up at him.

There was a strange look in the possum's eyes. Once more the little voice in his head told him to be wary, but he didn't know how to read possum expressions. And he so wanted to meet Madame's owner. If she was truly just down the road, it meant this part of their desperate journey was finally over.

Once the sign was far behind and the possums out of earshot, Gizmo stopped to shake herself free of water from the mist and damp foliage. Max did the same, even though he knew it wouldn't help much.

"You know, I usually like *everybody*," Gizmo said. "But I'm not sure about Hank. Did you guys think he might be making all this up?"

Max nodded. "I can't shake the feeling there's something strange going on with him."

"I hope he's not lying," Rocky moaned. "I've had enough of this dampness. Someplace festive and filled with food sounds amazing."

"It does," Max said. "I guess we'll find out."

As the three dogs walked on in silence, Max sensed the elevated road slanting down. He caught glimpses of mud and dirt through the guardrails, islands of dry land peeking up through the slimy green swamp water.

The sky above was still gray, and the air was much too warm. Max felt as though someone had thrown a hot, wet blanket on top of him. The idea that Madame's owner would throw a party for animals out here in a swamp seemed strange, but he also never would have expected a scientist to end up helping a colony of animals at an abandoned beach resort.

So maybe Hank's odd tale did have some truth to it.

"Hey!" shouted Gizmo.

Following the small terrier's gaze, Max looked into the clustered trees on the right side of the road. There, partially hidden by overgrown branches, was another green sign. This one was smaller than the sign a ways back, but Max read the same words on it: NATIONAL WETLANDS PRESERVE. There was an arrow pointing to the right.

And just like on the bigger sign, someone had spray-painted a three-ringed symbol on this sign as a warning that Praxis-infected animals were nearby.

Max licked Gizmo's forehead. "Good eye! Let's go check it out."

The three dogs darted to the side of the road. Now that it was level with the land once more, the guardrails had disappeared, replaced by a narrow ditch between the road and the swampy woods.

Max sniffed the ground as they passed the sign. He

74

couldn't hear any party sounds, and there weren't any human or dog smells, but that didn't necessarily mean anything. The storm would have cleansed the air of many scents, and maybe the party wasn't a loud one.

Not far past the sign, they saw a hard-packed dirt road that disappeared into the trees. Without asphalt to keep the plants at bay, it was more grass and weeds than road, though there were still evenly spaced ruts where cars and trucks would have driven through.

Were they fresh? Max sniffed and pawed at the dirt, but he couldn't tell.

"It sure is dark down there," Rocky whispered.

"Yeah," Max said. "Maybe this is the wrong road?"

"I don't think so," Gizmo said. "Hank's directions said it would be this one. But I think he must have been lying to us, don't you? I don't see any sign of a party."

"What's gotten into you? You're superwary today," Rocky said to the small terrier. "Usually you'd be the first one to dart into a dark forest." He wagged his tail. "It's one of the things I like about you."

Ducking her head, Gizmo said, "Thanks, Rocky. It's just, sometimes running ahead without thinking can get us into trouble, so I thought I'd try to be more like you."

Rocky's spiky tail wagged even faster. "You want to be like me? That's the nicest thing anyone has ever said to me!"

While the others talked, Max took a few cautious steps down the grassy dirt road. All around him the trees swayed, the strands of moss floating on the breeze like ghostly beings. It was strangely silent in the woods. There wasn't even the sound of bugs or frogs or other swamp creatures.

Despite the day's heat, Max shivered.

Then, something caught his eye, and he went rigid. It wasn't movement, but a flash of unnatural color that shouldn't have been in the swamp. Up ahead, partially hidden by the tall grass, were a half-dozen barriers set in a line across the road. Orange-and-white-striped barriers.

His tail a blur, Max spun to face his friends. "Hey, guys! I see the old woman's beacons! Hank wasn't lying: She's here!"

"Forget everything bad I ever said about that possum," Rocky said as he ran to Max's side. "Let's party!"

"Wait, Max, are you sure it's—" Gizmo started to say, but Max and Rocky were already bounding through the tall grass, and Gizmo was forced to run to keep up.

Images of being petted and fed by a human—a *nice* person!—flooded Max's brain. He no longer cared about the stench or the humidity or the threat of monsters. The nagging voice from before kept trying to ruin his day, but he ignored it, because Gertrude the pig had said to follow the beacons. Now the beacons were here, and so was the old woman! He just knew it!

"Max!" Gizmo barked, panting. "Max, stop and look!"

They were almost up to the barriers. A hazy green

darkness enveloped them, but there were still no festive noises and no human smells. Even so, Max wouldn't stop running until he found the old woman's party.

"Max, *stop!*" Gizmo bellowed. "Look at the barriers. There aren't any beacons!"

Max skidded to a stop in the slick grass. Panting, Rocky stopped next to him, and Gizmo finally caught up. Together the three dogs looked up at the barriers.

And Max realized that Gizmo was right: There were no beacons atop the barriers, no flashing amber lights. No spray-painted orange circles on nearby tree trunks.

In fact, the barriers looked *old*, as if they had been on this road for a very long time. They were orange and white, sure, but months or years of being in the woods had coated them with a thick layer of grime. Vines sprouted from the dirt and twined up the metal supports, weaving leafy patterns.

Max had only seen what he *wanted* to see. Tail drooping, he sat down. "These aren't hers," he said softly.

"Are you sure?" Rocky asked. "Maybe the beacons fell off."

Gizmo nuzzled Rocky's side. "Look at how old these are compared with the other barriers we saw," she said. "Plus, these have words on them. The old lady's barriers didn't."

She was right again—Max saw there had once been something printed on each barrier, but the words were so faded that he couldn't read them.

Looking into the trees, Max saw another sign. It was

brown instead of green, with a cartoon boat beneath the words TWO MILES TO SWAMP BOTTOM/BOAT LAUNCH.

"There's another sign," Max said.

Rocky let out a whine. "Swamp bottom? That doesn't sound very dry. And boats! I'm tired of boats."

"I don't think there's a party down there," Gizmo said. "I'm sorry, guys."

"It's not your fault," Max said. "It was silly of me to get so excited. It's just... I wanted to finally meet Madame's owner."

"Me, too," Gizmo said.

Rocky offered Gizmo a comforting nuzzle. "We should have listened to you," he said. "You're getting good at this caution stuff."

Gizmo giggled. "I learned from the best!"

Their spirits dampened, the three dogs shook themselves off and turned to walk back up the dirt path to the main road. It seemed much farther away than when they were running in the other direction.

"Why do you think Hank lied to us?" Gizmo asked. "We didn't do anything to him."

"I don't know," Max said. "Maybe he—"

Before he could finish his sentence, a loud crack sounded to their left.

The three dogs froze. There was another crack, from the right this time. And then a squelching, sucking sound.

"Nice doggies," a voice whispered.

The sound was low, a hiss almost, but it echoed all around them.

"Come play, doggies," the voice said. Or maybe it was another voice. Max couldn't tell.

"I-is that Hank?" Rocky asked.

"I don't think so," Gizmo said.

Heavy footsteps filled the air, and the grass on the side of the road rustled. Max stared wide-eyed as a head appeared—a head as long as Max.

It was a narrow, bumpy head, a green so dark it was almost black. Sharp teeth lined its long mouth, and inky eyes blinked slowly on either side.

The creature was massive and ancient, and there was no mistaking what it was.

"The monster," Max gasped.

CHAPTER 7

SCALES AND FANGS

The creature's long snout opened ever so slightly, and it chuckled, a sound like mud and gravel churning together. "I'm no monster, doggies," it hissed as its breath whooshed between sharp yellow teeth. It was rancid and sour, as if the giant beast exhaled the stench of death.

With another squelch, the monster stepped closer to the three cowering dogs. Max could just barely make out the creature's body, still hidden in the trees. It seemed impossibly long, and its skin was tough and shiny, as though it had been carved from rock.

Or, as the beach pets had said, pure metal.

The monster blinked its round black eyes. "Nice doggies," it said. "Sit and stay. No need to be afraid."

Next to Max, Rocky and Gizmo trembled and shook. Max's own hind legs quaked, and he felt as if his limbs might collapse beneath him. His golden fur stood on end, and his heart thumped so fast he thought it might burst. He knew there was only one thing they could do to save themselves.

"Run," Max said, but the word caught in his throat. Panicked, he tried again. "Run," he barked. "Run!"

Max, Rocky, and Gizmo barreled forward.

Just as they did, the monster attacked.

Max dared a glance back over his shoulder to see the creature leap out from between two trees. Its long, flat jaw was opened wide, its teeth glimmering with saliva. In a flash the jaws snapped shut—right where the dogs had been standing, frozen with fear.

A rustle in the undergrowth came from the opposite side of the dirt road as another of the beasts crawled forward from the shadows, almost as if it had formed from the darkness itself.

"You missed," the second monster hissed. "After them!"

Max turned away, galloping down the dirt path, the asphalt highway terribly far ahead.

"Keep running!" he barked between heaving, panting breaths. "And don't look back!"

Heavy, thudding footsteps echoed through the trees, growing closer. A shadow loomed on Max's left, and he glanced to the side to see one of the horrific, giant heads thumping toward Gizmo.

The small terrier's legs were a blur as she matched Max's stride, but the terrifying creature was right there beside her, looking for a meal. Its mouth was open, and its razor-sharp teeth looked like daggers, but Max wasn't about to let them bite into his friend.

Max gripped Gizmo in his mouth by the extra skin at the nape of her neck and, jerking his head, tossed her forward. Startled, the terrier flew through the air to land awkwardly in the waving grass, a car's length ahead.

A second later, the monster's jaws clamped together with a fleshy, slicing sound.

"You missed, too!" the other monster hissed.

While Rocky and Gizmo raced ahead, Max skidded to a stop. Growling, he rounded on the beast that had just tried to make a snack out of Gizmo. He raised a paw and smacked the creature on the end of its snout.

"No!" Max shouted. "We are not food!"

To his surprise, the second monster also stopped. It snorted in and out and blinked its black eyes in confusion.

"Did you just *hit* me?" the creature asked, bewildered.

Max didn't stick around to answer. His hind legs flinging up dirt, he propelled himself after his friends. The beasts huffed and hissed as they thumped after him, but at least Rocky and Gizmo were now far enough away that they wouldn't get caught.

Just run, Max told himself. *Run and don't look back.*

The world turned into a blur of green as Max

focused on the dark gray asphalt up ahead. His friends had already reached the highway.

He didn't think his heart could pound any faster. It ached in his chest, and his lungs hurt for air. His legs quivered with exhaustion, but all Max could imagine were those monsters right behind him, their mouths opened wide to grab his tail and pull him into their swamp, where they would delight in making him their dinner.

Finally, Max felt the rough road beneath his paws. He veered right, skidding on a patch of slick moss. But he quickly regained his footing, splashing through stagnant puddles and around fallen branches. He was vaguely aware of meeting up with the tiny blurs that were Rocky and Gizmo, but he couldn't feel relief, not yet.

The monsters were real, and he didn't know if he could keep his friends safe.

Max ran until his legs could no longer handle it. They turned to jelly beneath him, and he slipped, dropping to the ground and scraping his furry stomach on the rough asphalt. His chest rose and fell as he heaved for air, his tongue lolling free.

Rocky and Gizmo collapsed beside him, and for a moment they all stared up at the blanket of swirling gray clouds.

There were no thumping footsteps coming up behind them, no hissing voices, no stench of swampy death. Now that they were so far away, the sounds of the wetlands had returned—throaty animal calls and gentle splashes and an incessant buzzing. Max felt the nip of a mosquito on his flank, and he slapped his tail to scare it off.

"I think we lost 'em," Rocky said.

"I think so, too," Gizmo said, looking back. "They sure were monsters after all. I thought the other animals might have been exaggerating."

Gulping in another large breath of air, Max sat up. His heart had calmed down, but his fur still stood on end. "I don't know if they're monsters, exactly," he said. "They looked like giant lizards. They're just animals."

"Yeah, lizards the size of cars!" Rocky said. "Animals or not, they sure seemed like monsters to me."

"I'm just glad you two are safe," Max said. "That was a close call."

"Oh!" Gizmo said, her ears perked up. "You tossed me out of the way right in time. That was superbrave of you. Thank you!"

"Hey, I made you guys a promise, remember?" Max said. "I'll never let anything hurt you."

Rocky growled, and Max and Gizmo saw him staring back the way they'd come with angry, narrowed eyes.

"What is it?" Gizmo asked. "Do you smell something?"

Rocky shook his head. "No, I'm just angry that we got set up."

"What do you mean?" Max asked.

Rocky started to pace. "Think about it. That possum lied to us. It's like he wanted us to run into those monsters!"

"But why?" Gizmo asked. "We never did anything

bad to him. Maybe it was just a coincidence he sent us where there were monsters."

"I don't think so," Rocky said. "I knew we shouldn't have trusted that guy."

"I don't know what Hank was trying to do," Max said. "But I do know that there's no shelter here. We need to get out of this swamp before it's night again."

"Lead the way!" Gizmo yipped as she ran to Max's side.

Groaning, Max climbed to all fours. His muscles throbbed with a dull ache, but he felt rested enough to continue. "Follow me," he said, padding forward over the broken road. "And if we see any barriers, let's make sure they have beacons, too!"

Afternoon came quickly, with occasional glimpses of sunlight through the clouds. A rainbow glowed in the mist on the western horizon, but Max couldn't enjoy it. He was too busy going tense at every unusual sound, certain that he and his friends were being followed.

None of the dogs could walk very fast after their terrified run. Max was almost limping, each step sending a jolt of pain through his legs.

Before long, a bridge came into view. A sign on its metal archways showed there would be restaurants and gas stations and other human buildings up ahead.

"Hey, look," Max said as he picked up his pace.

"Yeah, I saw, buddy," Rocky said. "Gizmo pointed out that rainbow ages ago."

"It's pretty!" Gizmo protested.

Max chuckled. "No, look ahead. I think we might be getting somewhere."

Both of the small dogs looked up, and immediately their tails started wagging. Together, the three friends trotted quickly down the cracked highway.

The land on either side of the entrance to the bridge sloped away from them, down to a valley filled with stagnant green water and lily pads. The bridge was much shorter than the one they'd crossed on their way to the beach town. Sheets of moss and tangled vines enveloped the metal railings, turning the man-made crossing into a thing that almost lived and breathed.

At the center of the bridge, a thick, coiled *something* hung from a rusted metal beam. It was much too large to be a vine, so Max guessed it was a tree branch that had twisted to fit through the bridge's trusses. It was slick and shiny and pale green, with spots of blackened bark along its sides.

Max stopped and sat down in front of the bridge. Peering up, he tried to read the sign.

"Can you see what it says?" Gizmo asked. "I can see the symbols for rest areas, and some words about a town, but there are also the words *right* and *left*."

Max shook his head—this sign was too overgrown to read clearly.

Ahead of him, Rocky let out a groan. The Dachshund had stepped onto the bridge, his eyes on the road at the opposite side of the valley.

"There's a fork in the road," he said. "That's why the sign says *right* and *left*. It's giving directions." Turning to face his friends, he let his tail droop. "But if we can't read the sign, how are we supposed to know which way to go?"

Max climbed back to his feet. "We'll figure something out. Maybe we'll see a beacon."

He began walking down the center of the bridge. The metal beneath his paws wasn't terribly comfortable, but they would be back on the regular road soon. He listened to the gentle splashes of the swamp water beneath their feet and studied the strange coiled branch. The branch seemed different now, as though the coils had rearranged, but perhaps it was just a trick of the light.

As they neared the center of the bridge, Max saw the branch move.

It wasn't a branch or a vine at all. It was an animal.

And with a rustle of leaves and moss, half of the creature uncoiled from the high beam and dropped in front of them, a few feet above the bridge's metal floor.

"Snake!" Rocky yipped.

"Watch out!" Gizmo barked.

Max stopped a yard from the dangling, giant snake. Its thick body seemed to stretch forever. Rocky and Gizmo backed away, their fur on end.

It was a boa constrictor, Max realized as the snake

slowly raised its head. A small, forked tongue slipped in and out of its mouth.

"None shall pass," the boa constrictor hissed.

"Oh, yeah?" Gizmo barked. "Says who?"

The boa constrictor focused its beady eyes on Gizmo. It flicked out its tongue once more.

"Says me," it hissed again. "And a dog your size is in no position to argue."

Growling and baring his teeth, Max took a step forward. "She's not alone, snake."

The boa raised its head to meet Max's angry gaze. "I noticed," the snake said. "But don't you worry. I could give a big dog like you a nice, long squeeze. You would take more effort to eat than the little ones." Its tongue slipped in and out. "But I would relish the challenge."

Max stood his ground, but he did stop growling. "We could always outrun you."

"Perhaps," the snake hissed.

Slowly uncoiling, the boa let its tail release the high beam, and it fell to the ground with a heavy plop. The metal bridge vibrated from the force of the landing.

The boa constrictor reared its head while the rest of its impossibly long body slithered and coiled beneath it.

"But," the snake continued, "are you willing to risk that the little ones are as fast as you?"

"We are!" Gizmo barked.

"Shh, Gizmo!" Rocky whispered.

The snake ignored them. "I heard you talking.

You have no idea where to go. One of the roads ahead leads to shelter. The other will take you deeper into the swamp, to the lair of the Mudlurker."

"The what?" Max asked.

The snake slithered back and forth across the center of the bridge. "Oh, you haven't heard tales of the Mud-lurker? He's a terrible, giant creature with jaws like *this*."

The snake's jaws opened wide, and it snapped its mouth closed a foot away from Max's snout. Instinctively, Max scrambled backward.

Hissing, the snake pulled its head up, away from the dogs. "So you might get past me only to head in the wrong direction. Sadly for you, only I know the correct path."

Gizmo growled. "We're not afraid," she barked. "Not of you and not of this Mudlurker. We actually just fought off some swamp monsters a little while ago. It was easy!"

The snake tilted its head. "I'm not sure I believe that. But the Mudlurker? He's the monster that the *monsters* are afraid of."

To Max's surprise, Rocky waddled forward. "Okay, we get it. We deal with you or we get eaten. I'm tired and hungry, so why don't you tell us what you want?"

Lowering itself so that its head was only half a foot off the ground, the boa constrictor slithered forward to meet Rocky nose-to-nose. Rocky trembled, but he did not back away.

"Right to the point," the snake hissed. "I can

appreciate that. Here's my offer: I will tell you the way to go for a price."

"And what price is that?" Max asked, already knowing he wouldn't like the answer.

The boa constrictor's tongue circled its mouth. "I want one of you," the snake said. "Just one." Its eyes darted past Max to Gizmo. "I'm hungry, too, and I need to eat."

"No way!" Gizmo barked.

"Don't be so hasty with an answer," the snake called. "I trust you'll make the right decision." Lifting its head, it slithered back to the center of the bridge.

Rocky shook his head. "This thing thinks he's so smart, but he's never met a *real* smart animal before. Let me talk to him."

"But Rocky—" Max said.

A gust of wind rose up, and the blankets of moss rippled above them. But that wasn't why Max stopped speaking.

With the wind came a familiar scent: the musky stench of wolves somewhere behind them in the swamp.

Gizmo went rigid. "Do you smell that?"

"Yes," Max said, peering into the trees.

"Wolves," Rocky whispered. "You've got to be kidding me. Lying possums, horrible monsters, hungry snakes, and now *wolves*? This swamp is just the worst."

Max raised his snout, facing their earlier path.

Behind him, the snake called out, "I'm still waiting!"

Max ignored the creature, focusing on the wolf

scent. He couldn't tell if it was just any pack of wolves . . . or if it was their old enemy, Dolph.

Gizmo asked, "Do you think it's Dolph? After he got burned in the riverboat fire, would he really come all this way just to get us?"

"Dolph is deranged," Rocky grumbled. "I'm surprised he's able to find other wolves to follow him."

"Dolph or not," Max said, "we need to get out of this swamp." He licked Rocky's forehead. "You sure you're up for talking to the snake?"

Rocky gulped. "Not at all. But I've managed to talk us out of danger before!"

Gizmo nuzzled Rocky's neck. "Be careful, Rocky. I don't know what I'd do if I lost you."

Rocky's spiky tail wagged. "Sure you do. You'd get vengeance on my behalf. That's why you're so great."

Gizmo sighed. "If he starts snapping at you, run. Okay?"

A loud, metallic clang echoed through the air, and all three dogs turned to see the boa constrictor, its fat tail raised. "Time's up!" the snake hissed. "What's your choice?"

Holding his head high, Rocky moved to stand in front of the boa constrictor. Gizmo curled into Max's side, her body trembling.

"They're not happy, as you can see," Rocky said. His voice was strong and confident, with no trace of fear. "But," the Dachshund went on, "I've decided to offer myself up to you in exchange for letting them pass."

The boa constrictor sat still, staring at Rocky. "How very...noble."

With a wave of his front paw, Rocky said, "It's nothing, really. You see, you might think the big dog back there is the leader, but he's just the muscle. I've always been the one in charge, and I vowed to protect these two simple, silly mutts. Even if I must make this most devastating of sacrifices."

The snake looked between Rocky and the other two dogs. Sensing the creature's suspicion, Max sobbed loudly. "I sure will miss our fearless leader," he cried.

Catching on, Gizmo let out a wail. "We'll always remember you, Rocky!"

Rocky shook his head. "Now, now, mutts. You know this is how it has to be. Just promise to live...for me."

The snake said, "Hmm. Usually my meals put up more of a fight. Well, a deal is a deal." And the boa opened its jaws wide, revealing pink gums.

"Wait!" Rocky bellowed.

Startled, the boa constrictor snapped its mouth shut. "What?"

"How am I supposed to know you'll live up to your end of the deal?" Rocky said. "Tell my friends which way to go, and let them free! I mean, this is a big deal for me. If I'm going to spend my evening being slowly digested, I need to know you're not lying."

The snake slapped the end of its tail against the bridge, and once more, the grating rattled beneath Max's feet.

"I'm not lying." The snake hissed. "How do I know *you're* not lying? If I point your friends toward the right path and let them go, how do I know you aren't going to play some trick on me?"

Rocky raised a paw. "Hey, I'm the one standing in front of your big, gummy mouth. Would I do that if I was trying to trick you?"

The snake flicked its tongue. "Well—"

"So really," Rocky interrupted, "it's just you who has to prove you're trustworthy. If you won't let my friends pass before you eat me, then show us some other proof that you're not lying."

"But I—"

Rocky jumped up on his hind legs. "Okay, I'm going to ask you a true or false question. Based on your answer, I'll know if we can trust you."

With a sigh, the boa constrictor pulled itself into a tight, tense coil. The creature was not pleased

"Fine!" the snake spat. "If it'll get you in my belly without any more yapping, ask away."

Rocky leaned in close to the snake. "Is it true," he asked, "that boa constrictors are too fat to swim?"

The snake laughed. "That's your question? That's false, of course! We're not too fat to swim. I am all muscle."

Rocky's tail drooped. "Oh, I hoped you would keep your word," he said sadly, turning to rejoin Max and Gizmo.

"Where are you going?" The snake hissed. "I told you the truth!"

"No, you didn't!" Rocky called over his shoulder. "Obviously nothing as big as you could swim without sinking to the bottom and drowning, especially since you don't have any legs to paddle with. If you'd lie about swimming, how can we trust anything you say?" Rocky shook his head. "No, we'll just have to find some other way across."

The snake thrashed back and forth in a rage, making the vines and moss tremble.

"Fine!" the boa constrictor bellowed. "I'll prove it to you! But just remember, you still need me to know which path to take. Go to the fork in the road. I'll *swim* there and meet you."

And as the dogs watched with barely contained glee, the giant boa constrictor slithered to the edge of the bridge, dangled over, and let itself drop to the swampy valley below. The three friends scrambled to the guardrail just in time to see the snake's body land in the murky water with a giant splash.

"You did it!" Gizmo said, leaping in the air. "You got it out of our way!"

Max laughed and licked Rocky. "You're one smooth talker!"

"Yeah, yeah," Rocky said, wagging his tail. "But we can't celebrate too long. Let's get across this stupid bridge and figure out which path to take before that snake actually swims to shore!"

CHAPTER 8

SWAMP ROADS

The dogs raced across the bridge and soon found themselves running on rough asphalt.

Behind them, Max could hear the slapping of waves as the boa constrictor slithered through the stagnant water. He had no idea how fast snakes could swim, but he didn't want to stick around and find out.

Reaching the fork in the road, the three dogs stopped and immediately spun in circles.

"Do you see any beacons?" Max asked. "Do any of the weeds look like they've been trampled by tires recently, the way they would have if the old lady had driven her car through?"

Rocky bounded back and forth. "I don't see anything," he said. "Both roads look exactly the same!"

Max had to agree. A forest of towering trees surrounded the two roads, and clinging vines and moss had overtaken everything in sight. Neither path looked particularly inviting. Both seemed as if they could easily lead to more of the giant lizard monsters.

Splashes echoed from the swamp valley, and the snake's voice sputtered out, "See! I made it to shore just fine! Now let me get up this hill, and we'll finish our deal."

Another gust of wind rustled through the trees, and mingling with the musty stench of the swamp was the sharp, distinct smell of nearby wolves.

Panicking, Rocky spun in a figure eight. "We gotta hurry, guys. I don't think I can trick the snake again."

Max was about to pick a road at random when he noticed Gizmo had run ahead, her snout to the ground.

"I smell Georgie!" she cried. "This way! We need to go right!"

"How do you know?" Max asked as he and Rocky trotted to her side.

"Because I picked up his scent," Gizmo said happily. "Georgie came this way, and since he's following the old lady, this is where we need to go."

Trembling, Rocky looked back over his shoulder. "Are you absolutely sure it's the right smell? I don't know if that snake was just making up stories, but I really don't want to go the wrong way and end up meeting that Mudlurker guy."

Gizmo opened her mouth to answer, just as they heard a rustling near the bridge. All three dogs could make out the slick, mottled green scales of the boa constrictor as it reached the top of the muddy incline.

"Never mind!" Rocky yipped. "I trust you! Let's go!"

The three dogs galloped down the darkened road. As they reached a bend, they heard the snake hiss in rage.

"I'll get you!" it screamed. "You lying mutts, I'll get all of you!"

But Max was sure there was no way the snake could catch up to the three dogs. For the first time in hours, he felt himself flooded with relief.

The winding stretch of road veered once more to the west—Max could tell by the hazy glow of the sun behind the clouds. Knowing directions by the position of the sun was a handy ability brought on by the Praxis virus. Confident that they were safe for the moment, he slowed down to a fast walk.

"Do you still smell Georgie?" Rocky asked Gizmo after he'd caught his breath.

Gizmo raised her head high and sniffed at the humid air. "I do," she confirmed. "But just barely. His scent was strong back there, though."

Max raised his own nose to smell. He did catch the faintest strains of another dog, but he'd have to take Gizmo's word that it was Georgie's, since he hadn't memorized the scent himself. Mostly, though, he was relieved not to smell any wolves.

He was about to lower his snout when his nose picked up another odor. Something instantly familiar.

99

Possum.

A tree branch to his left moved slightly, and through the leaves he caught a glimpse of a fat, gray body marked with scars.

Max marched toward the line of trees. Leaping over a puddle, he bared his teeth and growled up at the branch, hackles raised.

The branch ceased its rustle.

"Hey!" Max said. "I already saw you, Hank. I know you're up there."

"That possum is here?" Rocky asked.

Max didn't answer. Instead, he stomped to the base of the tree, then leaped up with his front paws pressed against the smooth bark. Rearing back his head, he barked as loudly and angrily as he could.

Terrified squeals rose up, and five small figures appeared from behind the leaves.

"What you scaring my kids for?" His beady eyes narrowed, Hank glared down at the three dogs.

"It *is* you!" Gizmo cried. "I've decided I don't like you much, Hank. And I usually like most animals."

The possum's whiskers twitched. "You think I care?" Gizmo growled.

Max dropped down to all fours and paced back and forth beneath the branch.

"So why'd you do it, Hank?" he asked.

"Do what?" the possum asked.

Rocky rolled his eyes. "You know what you did. You

lied! That old lady wasn't down that road, and there wasn't any food at all. Instead, *we* almost got eaten!"

"Maybe you went down the wrong road," said Hank. "That's what you dogs get for thinking you can read human words."

"I don't think so," Max growled. "I think you knew exactly where you were sending us." He glared up at the fat creature. "I'll ask again: Why'd you do it?"

"I—" Hank started to say.

"And don't you lie anymore," Max barked. "We almost got eaten by giant lizards and a snake today, so I'm not very happy with you swamp animals. You might think you're safe up in the trees, but I bet I could shake you loose."

"Wow, Max," Rocky whispered. "You ain't really gonna harm them, are you, buddy?"

"Hey!" a high-pitched voice called out.

The smallest possum dropped from the branch, dangling upside down. "You leave my papa alone," she squeaked. "He don't want to hurt nobody."

"Could have fooled us!" Gizmo said.

Sighing, Hank shook his head.

"Naw, she's right," he said. "I don't want to see no one get ate. But those monsters got mean after all the humans done left. They say, if I don't send other animals to them, they'll eat up my kids." The fat possum looked at the branch above him, where his children huddled together.

"They said that?" Gizmo asked softly.

"He's awful sorry, ain't you, Papa?" the small girl possum said.

Hank nodded.

Max couldn't be mad anymore. The dogs were passing through the swamp, but the possums had to live there. Max knew he'd do anything to keep his friends and family safe. Could he be mad that Hank would do the same?

"We're sorry, too," Max said. "You shouldn't have to be afraid. But we're on a journey to bring the humans back. Maybe then the monsters will go back where they came from."

Hank raised his snout. "You are?"

"Yes," Gizmo said. "We know where a human is, and she can fix everything. These monsters only started taking over the swamp once the people left, right? If they come back, the monsters are bound to run and hide and leave you alone!"

"You might well be right," Hank said. "In that case, I'm glad none of you got ate!"

"Me, too," Rocky grumbled.

Dropping down next to his daughter, Hank clapped his front hands together. "You northern dogs are on your way to Baton Rouge, from what I remember. Just keep heading this way and you'll reach there. Stick to the road and don't go veering off none, and you'll be safe."

"Thanks," Max said as he turned back to the road. "At least we know we took the right path back at the bridge."

"Just so you know, you ain't the only newcomers in the swamp today," Hank called. "There's been talk of wolves, and they ain't that far."

"Thanks for the warning!" said Gizmo. "I hope things get better for you and your family."

Hank hugged his small daughter close. "Me, too," he said.

The other four young possums dropped down next to their father. As the family watched, Max took the lead once more, and he and his friends continued down the long road.

Night was coming. Wolves and monsters, snakes and the Mudlurker...They needed shelter. And soon.

The three dogs walked on, mostly in silence, for the next several hours. The gray sky began to darken much sooner than Max had hoped. Gizmo assured them she could still smell Georgie's trail, but they hadn't seen any of the old lady's beacons since way back at the mall.

As the sun set, the trees cast long, twisting shadows that writhed like ghostly beasts. Deep in the woods, the swamp gurgled and splashed, and unseen animals called out. Max could almost imagine that the shadows and the sounds were the boa constrictor or the giant lizard monsters, their razor-filled jaws wide open.

Deep in the overgrown foliage, pinpoints of light darted back and forth—fireflies, Max realized. Occasionally he would hear the croak of a bullfrog, then a snap, and one of the lights would blink out. It seemed almost every swamp animal cared only about finding some smaller creature to sneak up on and devour.

As Max helped Rocky and Gizmo over the slick, decaying bark of a fallen tree, a click sounded from overhead. Tall streetlamps that were mostly hidden by the overgrowth began to blink on one by one all along the sides of the broken road. They were far apart, and the lights were a dim, flickering orange, but it was better than the utter darkness that otherwise would have surrounded them once the sun had fully set.

Even if those lights did bring new, frightening shadows that set Max's fur on edge.

After his friends were over the log, Max bunched up his hind legs and leaped over, too. But they walked only a few more feet before Max noticed that the road in front of them had disappeared.

"Stop!" he barked.

Rocky and Gizmo both halted midstep.

"What is it?" Rocky asked, trembling. "Is it monsters? Is it the Mudlurker?"

"No," Max said. "Just stand still. Something is wrong."

Max took a small step forward, his eyes trained on a circle of blackness. He didn't want to think what would have happened if the lights hadn't blinked on, if he hadn't called for his friends to stop.

The blackness was a giant hole in the ground that

had formed a deep, muddy pit. On either side, the road ended abruptly, its edges jagged. Broken slabs of asphalt littered the bottom of the pit. A streetlamp lay toppled, having tumbled down from above.

The pit was more of an oval than a circle, and a good chunk of the land that had once been to the right of the road had collapsed to the bottom as well. Max scanned that side of the pit, expecting to see upturned trees and dangling roots.

Instead, he saw a white concrete building. Its glass sign was fractured and broken, and wires dangled through the cracked glass. It appeared to be some sort of small convenience store, a rest stop for travelers.

"Whoa," Rocky whispered, taking in the mess. "What happened here?"

"I think it's a sinkhole," Max said. "I saw one on TV once. It's when the ground beneath a road washes away and everything up above falls in."

"Well, I'm glad we weren't around when that happened!" Rocky yipped.

"Look how far across the road is," Gizmo said, her gaze on the opposite side of the sinkhole. "How are we supposed to get over there?"

She was right. The sinkhole extended so far ahead that Max could just barely make out the crumbling edge where the road picked up again.

Max looked to his left and right. Towering trees surrounded them, darker than ever now that the sun had set. They'd been told many times never to stray too far from the road, what with all the beasts about. And certainly never to do so at night.

A gust of wind rose up, and several drops of rain plopped against Max's fur. One of the raindrops splashed Rocky, and the Dachshund jumped.

"Maybe we can go around?" Gizmo said. "We'll have to be careful not to fall into the hole, but maybe we can do it."

Rocky dropped to his belly. "No way, Gizmo. Who knows what's waiting for us in those trees?"

"Oh," Gizmo said, her ears drooping. "You're right."

Max paced back and forth. They hadn't seen any of the old lady's beacons in a long, long time, and with this hole in the ground, how could she have possibly gone this way? Unless it happened after she'd driven through?

"What do we do, big guy?" Rocky asked.

Max shook his head. "I don't know. Maybe we took the wrong path after all. Maybe we should go back and try the other way."

"But it's so dark!" Rocky yipped.

"And I can still smell Georgie," Gizmo added.

Max sighed. "For all we know Georgie went the wrong way, too."

Another burst of wind whooshed through the trees, so strong that it sent them stumbling sideways. High above, the clouds twisted and boiled into a deep, inky black, and then the rain came in slicing, warm sheets that soaked the dogs in seconds.

Rocky and Gizmo darted underneath Max's belly, hugging the ground and sheltering themselves as best they could. Max closed his eyes until they were merely slits—the sudden downpour was so dense he could barely see.

"How about we find us some shelter?" Rocky shouted over the rain.

"All right," Max shouted back. "We'll have to take our chances in the trees."

"What about that building that's partway in the pit?" Gizmo said.

"I don't know if that's safe," Max called. "Especially with all this rain turning the dirt to mud!"

"Can't we look anyway?" Gizmo asked. "It's an actual shelter, after all. It'd be much safer in there than anywhere we can find in the swamp."

Max had to admit that a building would give better protection than the trees. So, despite his better judgment, he nodded.

The way down to the half-collapsed building was a gradual slope, with plenty of rocks and exposed roots to grab on to, even though the dirt had turned to slick, goopy muck.

"It doesn't look so bad," Rocky said.

"Stay here," Max called over the rain. "I'll see how stable it is, then you two can follow me."

The two small dogs nodded. Gizmo's usually fluffy fur was matted and drooping, and streams of water fell from the ends of Rocky's floppy ears.

Taking a breath, Max stepped one paw off the road and onto the hill, then another. Mud squelched up between his toes.

He took another careful step forward, then another.

And then, his front paw met a wet rock, which tumbled down the incline. Max lurched and almost fell, but he caught himself, then quickly scrabbled backward up to the hard surface of the road.

Max was about to tell his friends that they'd need to find some other path when a voice echoed over the pounding rain.

"Yoo-hoo!"

The voice was slick and dangerous, sending a shiver of fear all along Max's spine.

"Oh, no," Gizmo gasped.

"Yoo-hoo!" the voice called again, closer. "Doggies! We're so happy to see you."

Slowly, Max turned away from the sinkhole and back toward the road. At the same time, a searing flash of white lit up the sky. It was followed seconds later by an explosion of thunder that made Rocky yelp in terror.

And in that brief moment of light, Max saw polished, ridged skin and glittering black eyes and the edges of daggerlike teeth.

The monsters had found them.

CHAPTER 9

A DESPERATE ESCAPE

The fear and tension that had been building up inside Max all day exploded into pure instinct. *Run away!* his brain screamed. *Protect your friends!*

But as the lightning and thunder faded, all Max could see was the blackness and small points of light, remnants of the bright flash that had blinded him. The only sound was a tinny whine inside his ear, an echo of the thunder. As he backed away from the approaching monsters, his hind foot met the edge of the broken road. Another step would send him tumbling deep into the muddy sinkhole.

Max blinked again and again, willing his eyes to regain their night vision. Rocky and Gizmo huddled beside him, quivering and silent.

The whine in Max's ears faded, and he heard the thud of loud, heavy footsteps. Water dripped into Max's eyes, but his night vision came back to him. They were trapped between the sinkhole and the approaching monsters. The three dogs had nowhere to hide.

"Stay calm," he whispered to the others.

"I'm trying," Gizmo whispered back, as three dark shapes moved toward the dogs. Two of them slithered in front of the fallen tree as their apparent leader stepped into the pale glow beneath the nearby streetlight.

The creature was the length of a car, its body flat and wide and low, with four strong, short legs that ended in claws. Its snout was also long and flat, open in a devious grin filled with overhanging sharp teeth.

Its skin was a murky mixture of brown and green and black that shimmered in the stormy night. Water streamed between the ridges that ran down the creature's body, all the way to the tip of its fat tail.

It was a giant lizard, like some mutant version of the tiny creatures that darted through Max's barn back home. One time Max had chased one of the small lizards and bit its tail, only to be surprised when the tail popped off, letting the animal run free and grow a new tail in safety.

Somehow Max guessed the same thing wouldn't happen with that creature's enormous cousin.

As the leader took another step forward, Max tried to reassure himself that this was just an animal. A swamp beast

who hadn't received the final Praxis procedure. A creature who, no matter how big and scary, could be outsmarted by Max, Rocky, and Gizmo. At least, Max hoped so.

"Ah, nice doggies."

The monster's voice was low and muddy, but with a strange warmth underneath. It reminded Max of Madame Curie, as if the swamp monster somehow shared the older dog's wisdom.

The creature slowly closed and opened its dark eyes. "What are you doing out here in the rain?" it asked. "We were hoping you were coming to our party. Our friend Hank was supposed to tell you all about it."

"He did!" Gizmo yipped, taking a defiant step forward. "He tricked us into going into the swamp to get eaten, just like you wanted. But we got away from the other monsters, and we're going to get away again."

The lead monster's eyes narrowed into slits. Lashing its tail, it glanced back at its followers.

"Did you try to eat the nice doggies?" it asked.

"Of course not," one of the other monsters said.

"We just wanted to carry them to the party," the other added. "Then they ran away."

Two creatures chuckled in the darkness, barely audible over the torrential rain. Max thought he heard more laughter in the trees, but he couldn't tell if it was just echoes or more of the beasts, lying in wait.

The lead monster turned back to Max and his friends. "You see, doggies?" It raised its clawed front foot, then stepped forward. "We're not so bad. You should give us a chance. It's the least you can do, considering you have nowhere to run."

Max clamped his jaw shut. He wouldn't give the beasts the satisfaction of seeing his fear—but they really were backed into a corner.

The monster parted its jaws once more in a mockery of a smile. "It will be all right, doggies," the creature said, its voice soothing and friendly. "I know it has been a long, frightening day."

The beast's tones were strangely comforting. For a moment, Max felt as though he were warm and dry inside his farm home, while his pack leaders told him what a good boy he was.

Max's heartbeat began to slow. Though he could still feel the pounding of rain against his fur, it no longer much concerned him.

"This swamp is such a dangerous place," the monster said as it took another step closer. "It is an endless place, one that dogs like you could never escape. You feel it, don't you?"

Rocky took a few steps forward as he whispered in response. "Yeah, I feel it. You're right."

"Rocky!" Gizmo shouted. "Don't listen to them! They're trying to trick you! Focus on anything but their words!"

She darted beneath Max's belly to nip at Rocky's hindquarters. The Dachshund shook his head and went still.

Stomping in front of Rocky, Gizmo glared once more at the lead monster. "We know all you want to do is eat us. It's not going to happen, so you should just go away, already!"

Laughter rose once more from the darkness, and this time the leader joined in. Its long tail whipped up and down, sending up a splash of water.

"Where do you think you can go, little doggy?" one of the unseen creatures called.

"The bayou is endless," another shouted. "If we don't catch you, one of our cousins will. We have spies everywhere."

"Like the possums."

"And that snake on the bridge that you made very, very angry."

More vicious cackling.

This time, Max was certain there were more monsters lying in wait and other swamp animals watching them.

But before he could react, the lead monster spoke, and its lulling, ancient tones hypnotized Max once more.

"Oh, my friends tease you, doggies," it said as it slithered forward, moving even closer to the dogs. "But they speak a certain truth, don't they? If there is no chance of escape, why try? Come. Be the most special guests at our party."

"No!" Gizmo barked. Rearing on her hind legs, she

swatted Max's face with a paw. "Right, Max? We won't give up!"

Max's own brain screamed, *Never give up*. But he could not look away from the creature's shimmering black eyes.

"Other dogs like you have searched for their people." The beast took another step closer. "Others have realized there is no hope." Another thudding step. "The humans don't want you." A rise and fall of dark, scaly flesh. "Even if you found your humans, they no longer love you. You have nothing."

And with those words, the monster's mesmerizing spell was lifted.

The creature had spoken Max's deepest fear: that Charlie and Emma never wanted to see him again.

But Max *knew* that his pack leaders never would have left him if they'd had a choice. He'd promised to find them and his friends' families, too.

And Max always kept his promises.

There *was* love out there, Max reminded himself. Max saw that love when animals rose up to protect one another and fight back against those beasts who chose darker paths. He saw it when Madame Curie and Raoul and Boss all sacrificed themselves to help keep others alive, to preserve the hope that one day the world would return to normal. He saw it every single day when his two small friends acted with bravery and compassion ten times their physical size.

And he'd *felt* it in every moment he had ever spent with his pack leaders. Charlie and Emma still loved him. They just had to.

The rain fell and the wind whipped past Max and his friends, and the night was filled with the sounds of deadly creatures, but Max no longer cared. Growling and baring his teeth, he took a defiant step forward.

"You're wrong," he said. "You will always be wrong. Even if I do fail, I will never stop hoping I can find my family, and I will never stop loving my friends until the moment I draw my last breath."

Gizmo jumped into the air and shouted, "That's right!"

"Yeah," Rocky said. "You tell 'em, big guy!"

The lead monster sighed a hissing, wheezing sound of exasperation as it glared at the three dogs.

"Fine," the monster grumbled. "I'd hoped you'd not make this difficult. But since you have…"

The beast's massive mouth snapped open, its top jaw slicing up into the air to reveal rows of sharp, jagged teeth. Its strong legs propelled it forward, slithering over the slick asphalt road.

"Come on!" Max shouted.

He leaped to his left, Rocky and Gizmo behind him. Seconds later, there was a clap of two strong jaws as the monster bit into empty air.

"Get them!" the lead monster shrieked as the dogs raced wildly through the rain. "Save the big one for me!"

Thudding, slapping footsteps came from the road as branches cracked and goopy splashes echoed from among the trees. The dark, deadly beasts were on the move—and so were their companions in the woods.

"Where do we go?" Rocky yelped. "That monster was right about one thing: There's nowhere to run!"

"Not true," Max called back. "There's one place!"

They'd reached the northern edge of the highway, and Max veered left once more—to the edge of the sinkhole. The downward slope into the pit was now an oozing slurry of mud and pebbles.

"In there?" Rocky said with a gulp.

"In there," Max confirmed, nodding toward the half-collapsed building. He glanced over his shoulder. The shadowy shapes of the three monsters were only a few yards away. And in that moment, another bolt of lightning snaked through the sky, illuminating the beasts as though it were the middle of the day.

The lead monster's black eyes no longer seemed ancient and wise. They were narrowed in pure hatred.

The electric bolt faded, replaced with a thunderous boom that pierced Max's ears. "Go!" he shouted, though he could barely even hear himself, let alone know if his friends had heard him.

He had to trust that even if they hadn't heard his shout, his friends knew to follow him. Running forward, he felt his paws sink deep into the muck. With squelching pops, they came free, and he ran forward blindly.

"They're going to the Mudlurker!" one of the monsters cried.

Another one repeated, "The Mudlurker? They are mad!"

"The Mudlurker!" still another voice screamed, muffled by trees and rain.

Max could hear other creatures screeching the name, and to his surprise, they seemed *scared*.

But he didn't get a chance to think about it for long. He stumbled on a sturdy root, knocking his front legs out from underneath him. His hind legs scrabbled to keep him upright, but the slick mud and the heaviness of his body and the pounding rain sent Max sprawling, sliding down into the depths of the pit.

"Max!" Gizmo called from above.

Max couldn't respond. A river of mud and water enveloped him as the incline became a steep, unclimbable thing, and he tumbled over and over into the bottom of the sinkhole. Rocks beat against his ribs as he fell, and mud gushed into his mouth, his nostrils, his eyes, and his ears. Then the thunder took away his hearing once more.

The world was black and silent as Max tumbled through the muck. Then, with a gulping splash, he fell into a deep puddle of water.

Dazed, it took Max a moment to realize he was no longer falling. He'd plummeted all the way to the bottom of the pit, into a murky pond.

Max flailed and twisted. His hind legs found purchase on the muddy ground and, shoving off, he swam the few feet up to the pond's surface.

His head burst free from the water only to be met with more water, as the falling rain sent up thousands of small splashes. Max spat out mud. The rain washed away the muck from his head and eyes, and, finally, he could see again.

As Max paddled, he tried to get his bearings. Right next to him was the hood of a car, its windows barely visible above the waterline. It was empty, swallowed up by the earth.

Beyond the car was a hill of debris. There had once been a parking lot there, he guessed, because slabs of concrete jutted out of the muddy incline.

The mud-and-concrete hill led to the doors of the convenience store, which lay at a slight angle above him.

Max squinted and could just barely make out the muddy forms of two small animals in front of the building's darkened, glass entrance. Max had no idea how his friends managed to make it unscathed. All that mattered was that the monsters were nowhere near them.

For now.

"Max!" Gizmo barked as she caught sight of him. "Max, are you okay?"

"Yes!" Max barked back. "Stay there! I'm coming!"

Max half swam and half walked toward the hill that

had once been a parking lot. Above and behind him, he heard snorts and angry hisses.

The monsters.

He glanced up at the craggy, broken edge of the road, where dark shapes stood lashing their tails, misty shadows in the torrential rain.

As Max swam, he noticed that more monsters had appeared up above. None made any move toward the building where Rocky and Gizmo waited for Max. And though surely these beasts could swim with ease, none leaped into the sinkhole.

Where, moments before, the creatures had been focused solely on capturing Max and his friends, now all they did was watch and whisper the same word.

Mudlurker.

Max didn't know what this Mudlurker was. He didn't want to know. All he cared about now was that he was no longer being chased, and he intended to take advantage of the situation.

At the edge of the water, Max tried to climb onto the muddy hill. Each time, he slipped on the muck and splashed back into the pond.

"Are you all right, buddy?" Rocky called down. "Can you make it?"

Growling, Max swam to one of the broken slabs of concrete. He leaped up, gripping the top edge of the slab with his front paws. The edge was rough and jagged and wet, but he refused to let go. Scrabbling at the mud with his back legs, he managed to shove his whole body out of the water, crouching precariously on the slab.

Max sat there, panting. A murmur of voices rumbled from above.

"Keep going, Max!" Gizmo cried over the rainfall.

"You can do it!" Rocky cheered.

"I'm coming, guys," he called back. "I'll be there before you know it."

Rivers of rainwater tumbled down the slope, cascading into waterfalls. Fat, heavy droplets of rain pelted his fur. The way up was slick, dangerous, and impossibly hard.

But Max drew on all his strength and leaped up to the next bit of broken concrete. Unlike the slope he'd fallen down, this hill was at an angle that he could climb. He rested another moment, then leaped again.

As he made his way slowly but surely up the incline, the leader of the monsters shouted from the road, unable—or unwilling—to climb down the sides of the pit to the building.

"Yoo-hoo!"

Max ignored it, focused on keeping his legs from trembling.

"Oh, doggy! Max, my dear boy!"

From the door of the convenience store, Rocky growled. "Leave him alone!"

But the monster continued on. "Poor doggy. You

think you've escaped us. But you'll meet the Mudlurker soon enough. And then you'll know I was right all along, and you should have come with me." It laughed, and the other monsters joined in.

Just above Max was a patch of concrete connected to the front of the convenience store. It jutted straight out, forming a makeshift cliff over Max's head. Rocky and Gizmo sat above Max at its broken edge, their tails wagging.

"No," Max said as he leaped up to the concrete edge.

"I," he added as his front legs gripped the ground.

"WON'T!" he bellowed as he propelled himself over the ledge.

Max landed on his side between Rocky and Gizmo, only a few feet from the entrance to the convenience store.

Climbing onto four unsteady legs, Max focused on the glass door. It said PUSH in bright red letters on its front. Gravity from the slight angle of the building kept it tightly shut.

"I tried to get the door open, big guy," Rocky said. "It's too heavy for me."

"You tried," Max said. "That's all that matters. Now let me give it a go."

Steeling himself, Max shoved his right side against the door. Though the rough ground was much sturdier than the mud in the sinkhole, Max didn't know if he could keep himself from slipping.

His body ached from the long day of running, from his tumble down into the pit, and from the climb up to the concrete slab.

But he had to get his friends inside and away from the monsters.

With a growl, Max shoved as hard as he could. He heard the tinkle of a small bell, and the glass door opened just wide enough for Rocky and Gizmo to slip through, darting out of the rain and into the dry store.

Above Max, the assembled monsters gasped.

"They're really going in there."

"The doggies are going to awaken the Mudlurker."

"Should we run?"

But to Max the monsters' words were just a jumble of noise. With another cry, he shoved the door open a few more inches and darted forward, his paws landing on smooth tile.

The door slammed shut, nearly closing on Max's tail, the glass rattling from the force.

It was dark in the slanted store, but dry and warm, the rain now a gentle rapping against the roof. Max took a few quivering steps forward and dropped to his belly.

As he lay there, his chest heaving, he heard Rocky and Gizmo just behind him. There came a metallic crash, and Max peered over his shoulder to see that the two had sent a metal rack falling onto its side to barricade the doorway.

"Good job," he said softly.

"Oh, Max, you look so exhausted," Gizmo said. She began to lick his forehead, her tongue lapping at a cut he hadn't even known was there.

"I'm so glad you're still with us, buddy," Rocky said as he curled against Max's belly. "We managed to stay on the slope until we made it to the door, but we saw you fall and thought you were done for."

"Never," Max said. "No matter how hard you try, I'll never leave you."

The three dogs just lay together, relieved, happy, and tired beyond belief.

"Why didn't the monsters chase us?" Gizmo said. "Were they afraid of falling in the pit?"

"Maybe," Rocky said. "Or maybe they were scared of something."

A noise echoed through the store.

Max jerked his head up, watching the darkness. It was hard to see—there was barely any light in the place—and many racks and shelves had fallen over. Cans and magazines and bags of chips lay scattered all over the floor near a smashed cash register.

As the dogs watched, silent, a small can of tuna fish rolled and bounced from the back of the store all the way to the front windows. It landed with a small thunk.

The force of the slammed door had set loose the can, Max reasoned. A can that had dangled there for days or weeks, just waiting for the right amount of vibration to fall.

But even as Max told himself this, he couldn't help but remember the monsters' fearful chants.

Mudlurker.

Max, Rocky, and Gizmo, wet and exhausted and trapped in the convenience store, were silent, watching and waiting.

And in the darkness at the back of the store, two large eyes, shot through with blood, blinked open, watching them back.

CHAPTER 10

THE MUDLURKER

Max wanted to run or shout or fight. He wanted to find someplace to hide his friends and keep them safe. More than anything, he wanted to collapse into sleep, into dreams where there weren't monstrous beasts hiding around every corner.

But he didn't dare succumb to sleep. Not with those unknown eyes peering at him. And no matter how much he tried, he couldn't roll over or get to his feet—his body was so exhausted and hurt that it wouldn't obey him. Not that there was anywhere to run anyway. Out there was only the pit and the forest and the many creatures who wanted to devour him and his friends.

So Max lay still, barely breathing, unable to look away from the bloodshot gaze before them.

A flash of white burst through the windows, revealing a bulbous, oozing body of brown muck. As the dogs watched, the swampy thing rose up and up, and a pair of jaws opened.

"That is what I am now," the creature said. Its voice was deep and rumbled like thunder. "I am the Mudlurker."

The creature closed its eyes and reared back its head, then let loose the loudest, longest howl Max had ever heard.

The Mudlurker's howl filled the space with a deep, reverberating din that spoke of despair and the end of days. Max, Rocky, and Gizmo all covered their ears with their paws, but nothing could shut out that sound. It penetrated the walls of the store. It echoed through the trees and the night sky, overwhelming even the din of the heavy rain. Max craned his neck to look out the windows and saw all the assembled monsters turn and scrabble away as fast as they could, slithering into the darkness to hide from the Mudlurker.

Finally, after several minutes, the Mudlurker lowered its snout and stopped howling. Gasping for air, the bulbous thing collapsed toward the floor as the last remnants of its bellowing sorrow faded away.

Once more the dogs sat silent, watching the creature in the back of the convenience store and waiting for it to make a move. Instead, the thing closed its eyes and let out strange, barely audible sounds, huffing and sniffing and whimpering.

And Max finally realized: It was *crying.*

"Uh, is that thing gonna attack us?" Rocky whispered nervously. "Should we run?"

"It doesn't look like it," Max whispered back. "I think it might be crying."

"Oh!" Gizmo said. "Poor thing. It must be so lonely with everyone too afraid to visit."

With her tail gently wagging, Gizmo took a few steps toward the sobbing, misshapen beast. As she did, the thing opened its yellow-tinged eyes once more.

"Hello," Gizmo said quietly. "I'm Gizmo. I'm not here to hurt you."

"You're a dog," the creature said. "What are you doing in here?"

"My friends and I were trying to escape those swamp monsters, and this seemed the safest place," she said.

"I had to escape those things, too," the Mudlurker said. "They almost got me before I ran in here a few weeks back."

Rocky narrowed his eyes. "Wait, I'm confused. Why were you running away from the monsters? They sure seem afraid of you."

"Why wouldn't they chase after me?" asked the Mudlurker. "I'm just a dog like you. Maybe a bit bigger, sure, but—"

"You're a dog?" Rocky yipped.

The Mudlurker whimpered. "Yes. You can't tell?"

"No offense meant," Max said, "but from here, you look like a big pile of mud with eyes."

The Mudlurker blinked. "Oh."

Groaning, the creature rose once more. As he did, he shook himself all over, sending clumps of earth flying every which way. Though he was still covered in muck, it was clear that he was indeed a dog, one that seemed almost as tall as a human, with a wide, stocky body; jowly cheeks; and big, floppy ears. He was ankle deep in a hill of dried mud that, Max saw, must have burst through the back wall of the store when the building collapsed.

And though he still looked more dirt-creature than dog, Max remembered his dream—this was the dog he was supposed to find.

Gizmo darted forward, sniffing wildly at the giant dog's lower limbs, her tail a blur.

"This isn't just any dog!" she barked. "It's Georgie!"

The dog—a Saint Bernard, Max could now tell—stepped off his pile of mud. "You know who I am?" he asked.

"We sure do," Gizmo said. "We've been following you, because you've been following the old lady in the hat! We're looking for her, too."

"Oh," Georgie said, his head drooping.

"Come meet my friends!" Gizmo yipped.

She darted back through the center of the store to where Max and Rocky lay. Georgie slowly followed her.

"I'd get up to greet you," Max said, "but I think my body won't let me."

"We've had a tough day," Gizmo told the Saint Bernard.

"It's fine," Georgie said as he sat in front of the three friends. "You still have better manners than most animals I've run across."

Rocky climbed out from between Max's legs. "So I gotta know, Georgie, how'd you get here, and how'd you make all the monsters afraid of you?"

"It wasn't really on purpose," Georgie said. "I got tired of how all the animals on the beach acted like nothing was wrong, so I set out on my own. My people ran the inn there before all the humans left. I figured the best way to find them was to follow the nice lady who had helped feed all of us. I followed her scent and signs until I ended up here in the swamp."

"You saw beacons here in the swamp?" Max asked. "We haven't seen any since the mall."

Georgie blinked his big, sad eyes at Max as a long line of slimy drool fell from his mouth.

"You didn't?" he asked. "I bet those gators knocked them over to hide them. That seems like something they'd do."

"Gators?" Gizmo asked.

"Gators," Georgie said. "Or alligators, if you want to talk fancy. That's what those monsters are called. And boy, they did hound me. Kept telling me I'd never escape and never find my people. And they were right."

"But that doesn't explain how you became the Mudlurker," Rocky said.

131

"Oh," Georgie said. "Well, one day the gators were chasing me right past this store and the car wash. I ran in here, and I howled and howled...and that's when it happened."

Rising back on all fours, the giant dog walked to the windows and looked down at the sinkhole.

"Just as I started to howl, the parking lot and the road rumbled and shook. All the gators went stock-still, and then the ground itself opened up and swallowed them whole."

Turning back to the three dogs, Georgie shook his head. "I thought I was a goner, too. The parking lot collapsed in a waterfall of mud, and the whole store started sliding down into the hole. But I got lucky. The store slid down a good ways, but it didn't tip over. The worst thing that happened was the wall gave way in the storeroom, which is where all that mud in the back came from."

Georgie sat down once more. "I've been here ever since. All the swamp animals thought I made the sinkhole, which is why they're afraid of me and why they started calling me the Mudlurker. So now they leave me alone. I got enough grub in here to last me awhile. And it's not like I have anywhere else to go."

"That can't be true," Max said. "You already said you were following the old woman in the big hat, just like us. We think she knows how to bring all the people back."

Georgie tilted his head as a glob of drool seeped between his lips and plopped to the floor.

"You *think*," the big dog asked, "or you *know*?"

"Well, we're *pretty* sure," Gizmo said. "Right, Max?"

"Yeah," Max said. "The old woman was the pack leader of a friend of mine. My friend told me that I should find her and she could help. And there were other animals, too."

"A great, big elephant!" Gizmo chimed in.

"And a super-rude pig," Rocky said.

Max nodded. "Those other animals knew the old woman, too. They said she was trying to fix the problem that made all the humans leave."

"Trying," Georgie repeated in a low grumble. "The gators were right when they said that this is all just a chase for wild geese." The Saint Bernard set his head on his muddy front paws. "I even thought about going back to Baton Rouge, where I grew up, to see if my old friends were there."

Gizmo trotted to Georgie's head and licked his nose. "Well, you're in luck, Georgie, 'cause we're also going to Baton Rouge. We're supposed to find a Collie named Belle."

Georgie's tail thumped against the floor. "Good ol' Belle," he mumbled. "She's a right treasure."

"You know her?" Rocky asked. "Yeesh, Belle is the most popular dog I've ever heard of."

"All the dogs in Baton Rouge know her," Georgie said. "A lot of us came from the farms or breeders near her home, and she always made the rounds to say hello.

But who knows if she's still there." The giant dog sighed and closed his big, sad eyes.

Max couldn't remember the last time he'd seen a dog in such low spirits. The disappearance of the humans and the taunts from the swamp animals—or gators, as Georgie called them—had done a number on the poor guy.

Not that Max could blame him. He wondered if he'd have continued his search without Rocky and Gizmo. Would Max just have given up and let the monstrous lizards have him? Would he have kept hoping to see his family if he'd been all alone?

Though his body still pounded with a dull ache, Max forced himself up on all fours. Legs wobbling, he padded to Georgie and lay down against the big dog's side. The Saint Bernard's fur was crusted with dried mud, but Max didn't move.

Gizmo lay down on Georgie's opposite side, joined a moment later by Rocky. Sensing their comforting warmth, Georgie opened his eyes.

"It sounds like you've had a tough time," Max said quietly. "And I understand why you might want to give up. What you really need, though, are some friends. You should come with us."

"Yes!" Gizmo said. "We'd love to have you along."

"Definitely," Rocky said. "No one will mess with us if we've got the Mudlurker on our side."

"The swamp is so big and dangerous," Georgie whimpered. "And there's no guarantee we'll find anyone."

"Maybe not," Max said. "But I can promise you that trying is better than doing nothing. At the very least we'll get you to Baton Rouge. You're bound to find some old friends, and then you won't have to be alone while you wait for your humans to come back."

"I suppose that's true," Georgie said. "It can get boring sitting in that mud pile all day."

"It's settled, then," Max said. "Tonight we'll sleep and regain our strength. Tomorrow, we'll set out."

On the cold, slanted tile floor, the four dogs settled themselves and closed their eyes, listening to the falling rain on the rooftop.

"You know, Georgie, I think you might need a bath," Max heard Gizmo say before he drifted off to sleep. "We're not in the best shape ourselves, but you're almost more mud than dog!"

"Hey," Rocky yipped sleepily. "Didn't you say something about a car wash?"

Too exhausted to wonder what he meant, Max closed his eyes and slept.

Max was on a road in the woods once more.

Nearby, the metal-skinned monsters cackled as they tore through the underbrush.

Serpents slipped through the branches, venom dripping from their fangs.

Giant wolves with glowing red eyes snarled as they paced, waiting to attack.

But Max didn't feel afraid. A giant dog plopped beside him. Watery drool fell from his lips.

Just ahead was a break in the darkness. The kind old woman, Madame's pack leader, sat in a lawn chair. She wore a wide-brim hat and sipping from a glass of lemonade that blinked with yellow light, beckoning like a beacon. She smiled and waved at Max and the other dog.

"Are we almost there?" Max asked.

The dog lifted his head back and howled as the lady took another sip of lemonade, still smiling.

Max awoke.

In the bright morning light, Max saw that every single one of the dogs was a mess. Max's, Rocky's, and Gizmo's bellies and legs were crusted with mud, and their fur was matted and tangled. They smelled awful.

But Georgie was dirtier than any dog Max had ever seen. Thick mud was slathered all over his body, as if he were a cake covered with chocolate frosting.

The dogs were definitely in need of a bath.

Once everyone was awake, Max announced that it was time to leave. Georgie carefully led Max, Rocky, and Gizmo up the sloped floor of the convenience store to his stock of kibble, near the dried mud pile that had been his bed. As they ate their fill, Max noticed the tiny flies that swarmed above the mud and the old human food. The insects came in through a vent on the ceiling. Max guessed it led outside and had amplified Georgie's howls. No wonder the Mudlurker's howls were so terrifying to the other swamp animals.

When their bellies were full, Georgie took the lead once more. They had to walk on top of the mounded mud to get into the storeroom. Most of the back wall had burst inward from the force of the mudslide, and mud and rocks had buried all the store's overstock.

Georgie had dug a small ditch beneath the broken wall and the mud. Without a word, Max dropped to his belly and scurried underneath and outside.

As he waited for his friends to follow, he studied the slope. His body still ached, reminding him of all they'd gone through the day before. He sniffed at the air and examined the trees, but he didn't find any sign of the monsters. A minute later, Rocky emerged, then Gizmo.

"Oof," Georgie grunted behind them.

Max turned to find the big, mud-coated dog struggling to pull his backside through the wall. The Saint Bernard gave one last tug and then barreled forward.

Rocky paced back and forth, nodding appreciatively.

"Not bad," he said. "You have a secret entrance, and those gators never knew."

"I guess," Georgie said. "I just didn't want to go to the bathroom inside. My pack leaders would have a fit if they knew I'd done that."

Gizmo scrunched her nose. "Oh, Georgie. How about you show us the car wash? It's time for a bath!"

Together, the four dogs bounded over the slabs of concrete into an asphalt lot with a Dumpster on one side. Behind the lot was a chain-link fence dividing the rear of the store from the swamp.

To their left was the car wash, completely intact.

At one point it had sat next to the convenience store. Now it stood alone atop its own concrete lot. The building had several big windows that revealed machinery and what looked like giant rolls of cloth. Near the back of the building was a smaller structure, an attendant's station.

The dogs trotted through the lot, jumping over hoses that snaked across the ground. There were two machines, one with letters stenciled on its side that spelled AIR. The other read VACUUM.

As they neared the attendant's station, Max saw a sign in the window.

"'Don't bring the swamp home with you,'" he read aloud. "'Basic wash only five dollars.'"

Georgie blinked at Max. "You know what those symbols mean?"

Max wagged his tail. "It's just a trick we learned."

"Huh," Georgie said. "That's neat, I guess."

"Yeah, reading is all right," Rocky said. "Unless what you read is bad news. This thing won't work without people money!"

"Oh, well," Georgie said, plopping to the ground. "Guess I'll have to stay all muddy, which means I can't leave the swamp."

Gizmo butted him with her head, but the big dog didn't budge.

"Oh, no, you don't," she said. "No more giving up!"

The Saint Bernard sniffed. "But I'm scared. If I'm not muddy, then I'm not the Mudlurker, and then what will keep the gators away?"

"He's got a point," Rocky said.

"We'll be fine," Max said. "We'll all feel more like ourselves once we're clean."

Max marched to the attendant's station, leaped up to press the door handle, and then shoved the door open with his snout.

He climbed onto the well-worn chair in front of the window. On the counter he saw a control panel with red buttons. The top button read SELF-WASH STATION ONE. Max pressed his paw against it, and a green light lit up.

"Oh, no, snakes!" Rocky yipped from outside.

Max leaped off the chair and burst through the door—and then laughed. Two of the hoses they'd passed were writhing and flipping over the concrete. One was squirting out soapy foam, and the other burst with clear water.

"It's just hoses, Rocky," Gizmo said.

"I turned them on!" Max said. "I guess people just paid some other human to press buttons for them inside this little building. You two should spray each other and get all that mud off you."

"What about Georgie?" Gizmo asked.

Max looked up at the machinery within the bigger building. He'd been in a car wash before, riding in his pack leaders' parents' car. With the windows rolled up, it was like driving through a hurricane. Max figured Georgie would need a whole hurricane to get clean.

Turning to the filthy Saint Bernard, Max said, "All right, Georgie, go to the back entrance there. Once the water starts, keep walking forward. And close your eyes so you don't get any soap in them."

Groaning, Georgie climbed to his feet and stared at the devices inside the car wash. "I don't know if it's safe."

"You'll be fine!" Rocky called. He and Gizmo had run over to the hoses and were jumping up and down in the spraying water. "You're about as big as a car, so that thing was made for you."

"If you say so." With his snout held low, the big dog padded slowly to the entrance of the car wash. High above him a small yellow sign read MAX. HEIGHT—7' 11" near a metal box with three glass circles on its front.

Max darted inside the booth and pressed the button next to BASIC WASH. Then he ran back outside to watch.

"Nothing's happening," Georgie said, taking a step backward. "Guess it isn't working."

On the metal box, one of the glass circles lit up red. A moment later, another circle flashed yellow.

Max wagged his tail. "It's working fine. When the light turns green, that means it's time to go. And then you can finally stop being the Mudlurker."

"You can do it, Georgie!" Gizmo barked.

The green light blinked on, and the car wash came alive as a heavy spray of water burst from the ceiling. At the same time a track began to move. That carried the cars through the machine, Max remembered.

But there was no such track for dogs, so Georgie just stood there, his sad eyes open wide at the machine-made storm.

"Think how good you'll feel!" Max barked.

"You'll be superhandsome," Gizmo added.

Rocky snorted. "Come on, big guy, it's just water. If we could handle that storm last night, you can handle this!"

Georgie took in a deep breath and closed his eyes. "All right," he bellowed. "Here I go!"

The big dog leaped forward, and Max ran to look through the window. Despite the mist, he could see the dried muck on Georgie's fur turning into dark, sludgy mud, which oozed down his sides and puddled on the concrete floor.

Then, with a squeak of valves, the water stopped.

"Is it over?" Georgie barked, his eyes still closed.

A few feet ahead, two tall white plastic tubes began to rotate. Streams of thick foam squirted from metal openings while the tubes twisted back and forth, sending the soapy froth flying.

"Keep walking forward!" Max barked loudly.

Soon, Georgie was lathered from snout to tail, making him look like some doggy version of the snowmen Max's pack leaders built in the winter.

Sputtering, Georgie ran forward. As he did, rollers covered with strips of cloth descended from the ceiling and walls. As the rollers spun, the cloths whipped and slapped at Georgie's sides.

Georgie yelped in surprise, but the rollers acted like a hundred hands holding washcloths, and the soap and mud flew off his fur in heaps. The rollers stopped after a few seconds, and Georgie trotted forward, only to be greeted by more bursts of water, scrubbing him clean.

As the machine died down and Georgie reached the exit, gusts of air blasted him, puffing up his fur. When he emerged, he looked like a whole new creature.

The former Mudlurker was now a giant, regal, stocky beast of a dog, a Saint Bernard whose pristine white fur was spotted with wide swaths of tan. "How do I look?" he asked.

Gizmo appeared next to Max, clean and soaking wet. She shook herself, barking excitedly. "I knew there was a real dog under there! No more Mudlurker. Now all your friends in Baton Rouge will be able to recognize you."

For the first time since they met him, Georgie wagged his tail and opened his snout in a doggy smile. Drool fell from his lips, but no one commented.

"Hey, Max, guess what?" Rocky called from behind them.

Max turned—and was met with a face full of foam from a hose held in Rocky's jaws.

The other dogs laughed as Rocky dropped the hose and wagged his spiky tail. "Your turn!"

Together, Rocky, Gizmo, and Georgie sprayed Max with the hoses, cleaning him of the filth from their long journey. Dirt and sand washed free from his fur and was carried in rivers to the drains.

The morning sky was bright and cloud-free, and the swamp swayed with a gentle breeze that smelled of wet dog fur and soap. The pounding water massaged Max's muscles, easing the pain from his fall the day before.

As the dogs continued to splash in the water, it was almost easy for Max to think that the worst was behind them and the rest of the journey would be carefree.

But Max knew the long road wasn't over yet and the day had only begun.

CHAPTER 11

THE FINAL STRETCH

With everyone clean and refreshed, Max shut off the hoses and led his three companions forward to resume their journey. Now that it was daytime, he could see the pit more clearly. The bottom, as he'd discovered the night before, was a murky pond. Fallen leaves floated atop the water. Mosquitoes and dragonflies darted from leaf to leaf, sending out gentle ripples. Debris jutted out from the pond—the hood of the sunken car Max had seen, streetlamps, hunks of concrete and asphalt.

The sinkhole seemed to stretch as wide as a whole city block. It was a good thing there hadn't been any people around when the ground had given way.

Leaving the car wash behind, the dogs walked single

file up the edge of the pit, back onto the overgrown highway that had been cut in half by the landslide.

And there, nestled in the underbrush, was one of the old woman's beacons.

"Guys, look!" Max said.

He barreled across the cracked road and skidded to a stop next to the orange-and-white barricade. Unlike the barricades back where the gators had set up their fake party, the colors on this one were still vibrant. The plastic amber beacon blinked steadily, and spray-painted on a nearby tree was an orange circle with a black X through it.

"Finally!" Rocky said. "Guess we didn't lose the old woman after all."

"I knew Georgie's trail would lead us to her," Gizmo added.

Max sniffed at the base of the spray-painted tree. The storm had cleaned the area of most smells, but he could just barely make out the swirling scents of a lab and flowery perfume.

Which meant it couldn't have been that long since the woman had been there. And since the beacon was past the sinkhole, she must have made it across the road before it collapsed.

"She was a nice lady," Georgie said. "I don't blame you for wanting to see her again."

"Well, we've never actually met her," Max said. "Or Belle. But our friends know both of them very well."

145

"You sure do take a lot on faith, Max," Georgie said. "Coming all this way to find a human and a dog you don't even know."

"I guess I do," Max said. "But doing *something* sure beats doing nothing at all."

"Not always," Rocky said. "You know me, big guy; if I can get out of *doing*, I'm a happy dog."

Gizmo giggled. "Oh, Rocky, think how bored you'd be if you'd never met Max and me! You'd still be all alone in a vet's office with no one to talk to but some wolves."

"Hey! I wouldn't be alone. I'd have all my kibble."

The sun rose higher in the sky behind them, and now that they were past the sinkhole, the swamp seemed less oppressive. The trees had begun to thin out, and between them Max saw dry ground instead of algae-choked water. Moss still hung in sheets from the trees, and grass and weeds rose through cracks in the road, but Max felt they were leaving the worst behind.

It wasn't long before they reached the top of a gentle incline, where a tall tree had collapsed across the highway. It lay at an angle, its branches and leaves leaning against the trees on the left side of the road. Its bottom was burned and blackened, perhaps snapped free by lightning.

The dogs dropped to their bellies and scooted beneath the leafy end of the tree. Branches scraped Max's back, like bony fingers digging into his fur and skin. For a moment his heart pounded, thinking the thing might fall and crush him.

He scrabbled his way from under the collapsed tree as fast as he could.

"Hey, Max! Come look!" Rocky was spinning in excited circles next to Gizmo and Georgie. Max bounded to meet them across the highway, where a smaller road veered off into the trees.

Just to the side of the small road was another of the old woman's beacons and another spray-painted orange circle.

"Look!" Rocky barked again. "The old lady must have gone this way."

Max trotted up to Georgie and wagged his tail. "See, we didn't even have to go very far and we're already almost out of the swamp."

Georgie nodded. "I guess I—" The Saint Bernard stopped speaking, his entire body going stiff. Max didn't know why—until a gust of wind brought him a scent.

Swampy, musty water. A stench like rotten fish and decaying meat.

And as he watched in horror, four dark, giant shapes slithered onto the road.

The monstrous alligators were here.

Georgie moaned and trembled.

Max backed away, until he bumped into Georgie's hindquarters. He started to tell the others to make a run for it—but two more alligators were creeping down the highway behind them.

Rocky and Gizmo yelped and huddled next to Max and Georgie.

As the dogs sat there, quaking in fear, the six giant lizards surrounded them.

The biggest alligator stepped forward, its jaws parted in a vicious grin.

"And so we meet again," the creature said in its ancient, soothing voice. "Once more walking through the swamp as if you own the place."

Though the sun still shone bright and cheery, the gators looked just as menacing as they had in the dark and rain. More so, Max thought, because now he could see every crack and line in their green-black skin. Everywhere Max looked he saw glinting teeth, shining black eyes, and scaled feet ending in sharp claws.

"I knew it," Georgie whispered. "It was a nice try, friends, but we were doomed once we came into this swamp."

"Don't say that!" Rocky yipped.

"There has to be a way out," Gizmo said. "There's always a way."

"Not this time," the lead alligator said. "Welcome to our party!"

The gators surged forward as the dogs barked and whimpered in fear.

Then the trees began to rustle.

First it was the leaves directly above the dogs' heads,

and then the canopies across the highway. Branches broke free and whipped to the ground, erupting into wooden shards. It was as though a great wind had risen up, except there was no wind at all.

High-pitched voices screeched and squealed and hissed. Startled, the alligators looked at the sky.

And Max heard a familiar voice squeak, "Run! Up the fallen tree!"

It was Hank the possum's youngest child!

Max didn't waste a moment. He nipped Georgie's side, then barked, "Come on!"

Together the four dogs raced past the ancient alligator toward the giant dead tree that blocked the road.

"No!" the gator bellowed, but they were past the creature in a blur.

The trees on either side of the road were swirling and swaying now; the rustling of branches joined in with the din of screaming animals. Dozens of glowing yellow eyes peered from the darkness.

"What's happening?" one of the alligators asked.

"Ignore it!" the lead alligator commanded. "It's just some trick! After them!"

"They're gonna get us," Georgie wailed. "They're gonna eat us up!"

"No, they're not!" Max barked. "Come on, Georgie! Keep yourself together! We're going to get out of this swamp!"

"But—"

Rocky yowled, "Come on, big guy, listen to the other big guy! There's no time to get scared!"

At the jagged base of the fallen tree, Max picked Rocky up by the nape of his neck and tossed the Dachshund onto the tree, then did the same for Gizmo. As the two small dogs scrabbled up the trunk, Georgie leaped atop the decaying wood with a massive thud.

"I don't know if I can do this!" Georgie barked.

"Yes, you can!" Max said. "Grab the tree with your claws and run up as fast as you can!"

The big Saint Bernard did as ordered, awkwardly shuffling along the tree trunk toward the branches. Max climbed up to follow him.

Moss and clusters of fungus grew in patches along the fallen tree, and Max did his best to avoid slipping. He clung to the rough bark, keeping himself steady.

The alligators huddled together, hissing at the dogs. Still the possums in the trees made a ruckus, confusing the beasts, who didn't know which group of animals to focus on.

Whipping its fat tail in annoyance, the lead alligator crawled on top of one of its followers and tried to climb onto the tree itself. But the lizard monster's legs were too far apart to get a solid foothold.

The alligator gnashed its teeth. "You dogs can't stay up there forever!"

Satisfied that they couldn't follow, Max stopped listening to the raging alligators and kept his attention on climbing the tree. All he could see ahead of him was Georgie's massive backside.

With each step, the snapping of tree branches and screeching possums grew louder, and the dead tree groaned and shifted ever so slightly, creaking from the excess weight. Max worried that it might collapse onto the ground.

The lead alligator was right: They couldn't stay up in the tree forever.

Georgie stopped suddenly, and Max almost barreled into him. He halted just in time, waiting as the bigger dog stepped gingerly to the side.

The top of the dead tree spread out into two thick branches, leaving a hollow just wide enough for the dogs to fit. Rocky and Gizmo already sat there, beneath a swath of moss that draped above their heads like an awning.

Max and Georgie settled in as best as they could. The tree bounced gently from their weight, but it held.

"That was close," Rocky said, panting. "Except now we're backed into a corner again."

Her eyes narrowed, Gizmo said, "I'm really starting to hate those gators. Why can't they leave us alone?"

"And what's with all the noise in the trees?" Rocky asked. "We didn't just escape one set of monsters to go into the hands of others, did we, buddy?"

"Ohhh," Georgie moaned. "We probably did."

"No," Max said, "it's the possums. I think they came to help us."

As if summoned, a small, ratlike head poked out from a nearby bunch of leaves. The young possum sniffed at the dogs with her pink nose, her whiskers twitching.

"Oh, you all heard me," she squeaked. "We sure are glad."

"Hi!" Gizmo said, offering a weary wag of her tail. "Where did you guys come from? Thanks for the help!"

The small possum scratched her chin. "Well, my papa felt real, real bad about his trick, so we been following you. We saw you get away from those monsters last night, and then when they was still after you today, my papa went and got all our aunts and uncles and grandpappies and grandmamas and cousins and even the babies. He said we gonna scare them good."

"And you all did a terrific job," Max said. He peered back to see the confused alligators still staring up at the shaking branches, even while the leader continued to try—and fail—to climb up the fallen tree.

"They're not going away, though," Georgie said. "We're going to be stuck up here forever!"

"Naw," the little possum squeaked. "The Mudlurker will come 'round some night, and then you can run away again."

Georgie's whole body seemed to sag. "But I *am* the Mudlurker," he said. "They've seen me now, and they'll know I'm just a dog."

"You're joking," said the baby possum. "The Mudlurker

152

is a big ol' thing made of mud, and its howls can make the ground swallow you up!"

"Trust us," Gizmo said. "This is the Mudlurker all cleaned up. Didn't you notice we left the Mudlurker's lair with one more dog than when we went in?"

Whiskers twitching, the small possum looked between the dogs. "I guess we done noticed," she squeaked, sounding confused. "But we didn't think much of it."

"Hey!" Rocky barked. "If the possums didn't notice, I bet the gators didn't, either. I have an idea." He looked up at the possum. "Can you get your family to shake the trees as hard as they can? And tell them to start screeching about the Mudlurker coming, too."

"I sure can!" she said, darting off into the leaves.

Rocky turned his attention to Georgie. "We need you to howl louder than ever before."

Georgie sniffed, sucking up a glob of drool. "I'm not sure I can."

"Of course you can, big guy!" Rocky said. "Here we are, four dogs in a tree with monsters waiting to eat us. You're far from your family and friends, and as long as we're stuck up here, you'll never get out of this swamp to find them. Doesn't that make you just want to howl?"

Georgie's eyes started to water. "Everything isn't fair," he blubbered.

The trunk beneath them started to quake, and all around, the canopy of trees began to sway as if caught in some unseen storm. Max could just make out the shadows of dozens of possums leaping up and down on the branches, sending the tree limbs bouncing.

"The Mudlurker be coming!" a deep possum voice screeched.

"The Mudlurker gonna eat up everybody!" cried a female voice.

More and more possums began to scream about the arrival of the Mudlurker, their voices rising in a terrifying shriek. Some tossed down twigs and branches onto the tough hides of the monstrous alligators.

At the base of the fallen tree, the gators started to back away. With dark eyes, they cast nervous glances at the trees and let out warning hisses.

"Boss," one of the gators said. "We need to go."

"Never!" the leader shouted, flinging itself at the tree trunk.

The force of the giant lizard's weight made the trunk quake beneath Max's paws, and the dead tree creaked in protest.

"It's now or never, big guy!" Rocky said to Georgie. "Let out all your feelings. Make sure those gators hear it!"

Still blubbering, Georgie tilted his head back. His chest rose as he inhaled a long, deep breath.

And then Georgie howled.

It started as a rumbling, then burst forth as a deafening, wailing "*Aroo!*"

It was a baying lament that swelled from deep within

the dog's belly to echo for miles in every direction. The sound became all that Max or any of the other animals could hear; wave upon wave of despair crashed into their ears and flooded their minds.

All of Georgie's loneliness and fear and sadness was in that one long howl. The emotions reverberated through Max's body and deep into his bones.

The possums went silent and still, in awe of the Mudlurker's cry. As they did, a single cloud drifted in front of the blazing midday sun, casting the road in shadow.

And the alligators panicked.

"The Mudlurker is here!" one bellowed. It whipped in a frantic circle, its long tail lashing against its companions' sides, but they didn't seem to notice. Their eyes were wide, and the sides of their low-slung bodies heaved.

"Run!" another gator shouted, skittering toward the trees. "The beast will swallow us whole!"

The monsters, once so confident, now turned tail and fled. They slithered and dashed into the woods, their large, dark forms disappearing toward the depths of the swamp.

The biggest alligator, the leader, hesitated at the base of the dead tree. But even it couldn't stand the noise. It crawled beneath the dead tree and raced back down the highway.

Georgie lowered his wide snout, his howl dwindling into a soft whimper. For a moment, the four dogs sat in the crook of the dead tree's branches, completely silent. The trees no longer shook, and none of the possums spoke. But they were still there, watching.

The cloud that had blotted out the sun drifted away, illuminating the road once more in cheery daylight. As it did, one tiny, squeaking voice yelled, "Wahoo!"

The possums erupted into cheers and laughter, and as the dogs watched, the creatures dropped to hang upside down by their tails, clapping their small paws and hollering congratulations.

"Oh, Georgie," Gizmo said. "You did it. You scared away the monsters!"

"I guess I did," Georgie said.

Rocky jumped up onto all fours. "See, big guy? Stick with us and we'll always find a way out. We're smarter than the average dog, you know."

Max wagged his tail. "That was good thinking, Rocky."

The dead tree's branches rustled, and Max looked up to see the small girl possum and her papa climbing toward them.

"Hank!" Gizmo cried. "It's good to see you!"

The large possum landed with a heavy thud among the four dogs, his whiskers twitching.

"Thanks for all you did just now," Max said. "You and your family saved our lives."

Hank scratched his jaw. "It wasn't nothing. It was really my baby girl's idea. She done said we owed you one."

"Oh, Papa, it was your idea, too, and you know it."

Hank ducked his head. "I guess so."

Rocky raised a paw. "Consider all our past differences erased. We forgive you for sending us to the gators, and we're friends now. Shake on it, buddy?"

The big possum blinked his beady eyes, then took Rocky's paw in both of his.

"I never been friends with no dogs before," Hank said. "You all ain't as bad as you smell."

"Oh, we smell?" Georgie said. "But we took a bath and everything."

Gizmo and the little possum giggled.

"You'd best git while you can," Hank said. "Them monsters always come back. Plus my cousin Gary said they seen more of those wolves coming up through the swamp."

"Thanks, Hank," Max said. "You keep your family safe, okay?"

Hank nodded. "That's what we be planning."

As Hank and his daughter waved good-bye, Max turned and carefully made his way back down the trunk of the fallen tree. Soon he, Georgie, Rocky, and Gizmo reached the base and leaped down to the road. Hank's family raised their tiny fists and cheered as the dogs trotted beneath them.

"Where to now?" Rocky asked.

Max turned toward the side road that led north. "We follow the beacon and get out of this swamp."

"Yay!" Gizmo said as she ran alongside Max. "Finally."

"You can say that again!" Rocky yipped.

Leaving the possums to their celebration, Max led the other three dogs down the side road. The beacon on the orange-and-white barrier blinked steadily, beckoning them forward out of the musty, overgrown, gator-filled swampland and one step closer to the old woman who—they hoped—had all the answers.

CHAPTER 12

THE CANINE POLICE

"So tell us, Georgie," Rocky said as the dogs walked down the center of the road. "How'd you learn to howl like that?"

The big Saint Bernard ducked his head. "Aw, it's nothing any dog can't do."

"Oh, I've known lots of dogs," Gizmo said, trotting to keep pace. "And none who could roar like that."

Georgie tilted his head. "Well, believe it or not, I was the smallest of all the puppies in my litter."

"No way!" Max said.

"It's true! The others got all the attention, so I had to fight constantly to feed and get played with. Eventually I just got so fed up that I plopped my tiny self in the dirt, raised my nose high, and let all the frustration out in one big howl." He chuckled. "You'd better believe I got a lot of attention after that. In fact, it was the reason the innkeepers at the beach adopted me and became my pack leaders. They knew if I ever saw anyone getting out of line, I'd howl, and they would come running."

"Sounds like you're one heck of an alarm system!" Rocky said.

Max wagged his tail and shook his head as his three friends continued to talk. After all the unpleasantness of the swamp, it was nice to finally be free and take a breather—even if there were still rumors of wolves afoot.

Then, Max saw them—a pack of large figures just down the road.

"Stop," he whispered, halting midstep.

His friends huddled next to him. Georgie trembled, whimpering.

"Who are they?" Rocky asked. "Are they wolves?"

Max sniffed the air. The wind was blowing in the wrong direction, so he couldn't get a good read on their scent.

"I don't know," he said. "Just be prepared to run."

The animals—seven in all—trotted side by side in a row. They marched in unison—everyone stepping forward at the same time in the same rhythm. Max had never seen anything like it.

As they grew closer, Max saw that the animals were all German Shepherds. Their coats shone in the midday sun as though the animals were freshly groomed, and their pointed ears were alert. Around each dog's neck

was a dark blue collar from which dangled a gleaming, star-shaped medal.

They weren't wolves, but Max didn't relax. He knew better by now than to trust an organized group of dogs without getting to know them first.

The largest of the seven dogs marched a few steps forward. His back and snout were deep black, and the rest of him was a red-tinged gold.

"Whoa there," the lead dog barked. "We saw you coming up the road. Where are you headed?"

"What's it to you?" Rocky asked.

"Rocky," Max whispered in warning. He took a step forward. "We're trying to get as far away as we can from the swamp. We don't want to cause any trouble."

Rocky darted in front of Max, growling. "The four of us just scared off a bunch of monsters back there. I'm not in the mood for any more animals getting in our way."

Georgie whimpered. Max looked behind him to see the big dog lying in the street, sniffling. And just beyond Georgie, Max saw why.

Five more German Shepherds had appeared from the nearby trees, coming to stand behind them.

"It's fate," Georgie moaned. "No matter what we do, we're stuck!"

Gizmo licked the center of Georgie's forehead. "It'll be all right," she said.

The lead dog cleared his throat, and Max turned to meet his eyes.

"I think you might be misunderstanding our intentions," the leader said. "We heard the Mudlurker, and we came to aid a fellow dog in distress."

"You knew the Mudlurker was a dog?" Max asked.

The German Shepherd nodded. "Of course. We've all heard the rumors about some giant underground beast, but we know a dog howl when we hear one. Right, team?"

A chorus of voices barked in unison. "Yes, sir!"

"The name is Julep," the leader said.

Gizmo came to stand beside Max and Rocky. "Well, we managed to escape the alligators with the help of some possums, but it's nice you came anyway! I'm Gizmo. This is Max and Rocky, and back there is our friend Georgie."

With his snout held high, Julep marched purposefully around Max, Rocky, and Gizmo to study Georgie, who lay in a depressed heap on the asphalt, a puddle of drool and tears forming beneath his wide jaw.

"I know," Georgie mumbled. "I'm the biggest mess you've ever seen."

"Actually," Julep said, "I was just thinking that you must be the famed Mudlurker. Only a dog as big as you could possibly produce so glorious a howl. It's a pleasure to meet the dog behind the legend."

"But he isn't the Mudlurker anymore," said Gizmo. "Now that he's not sad and alone, he's going to be himself again. Right, Georgie?"

Groaning, Georgie hefted himself up onto his paws. "No more Mudlurking for me," he said. "At least, I hope not."

"Well, I'm right sorry to hear of your retirement, sir," Julep said. "We spun many a tall tale about you to keep the worst of the swamp animals from trying to get into our town."

"Is your town close?" Max asked.

"Sure is!" Julep said. "And our lady is there, too. We would be delighted to escort you."

"A lady!" Rocky leaped in the air.

His tail wagging, Max darted forward. "Is your lady an old woman with a big hat?"

Julep nodded. "She came through some weeks back, and life has never been better. Do you know her?"

"Not yet," Max said. "But I can't wait to!"

Julep's jaws opened in a happy pant. "Well, let's get going. It sounds like you four are ready to get back to civilization!"

After a single bark of command, the eleven other German Shepherds formed a loose, protective circle around Max, Rocky, Gizmo, and Georgie. Then the four companions and their new guards started north down the small road.

It wasn't long before the trees began to thin out. Max spotted a few small houses abandoned among the fields. The farther north they walked, though, the bigger and nicer the houses became. One was painted a buttery yellow, and its curtains were patterned with red-and-purple flowers. Another was made of brick and dark wood, with a pair of rocking chairs on its porch.

Though the landscapes were different from the countryside where Max grew up, he couldn't help but be reminded of home. Something about the comfortable, lived-in state of the houses felt familiar.

Of course, now the grass was overgrown, and there was a silent darkness around each house. These homes were empty, just like Max's farm, which had once been alive with the sound of farmers wrangling the cows and the delighted screeches of Charlie and Emma. Now it sat silent, like the houses on this street.

It was a sad, distressing thought, and Max looked away from the empty homes. Ahead was Madame Curie's owner, and after they'd met her, they'd find Georgie's town, where Belle lived. Then maybe they'd even find Charlie and Emma, his pack leaders.

"You dogs seem so organized," Gizmo said to Julep as they walked. "And very well trained! Did you do this yourself?"

"No, ma'am," Julep said. "We were all once police officers in our great town."

Rocky narrowed his eyes. "That doesn't sound right. Only humans can be police officers."

"But it's true!" a female Shepherd called out.

The Shepherd behind her snapped, "Don't speak out of turn."

"Hey!" Julep barked. "I'm in charge; I give the reprimands. Got it?"

"Yes, sir!" barked the dog who'd snapped.

"May I speak freely, sir?" the female Shepherd asked.

Julep nodded. "Go ahead, Dixie."

Dixie left the circle of dogs and ran to join the group at the center. She was a little smaller than Julep, but she exuded just as much confidence as her leader. While her face was almost fully black, the rest of her body was the color of honey.

"A pleasure to make your acquaintance," Dixie said. To Rocky, she added, "I didn't mean to start a row with you. I just didn't want to be taken for a fibber."

"Well, you have to admit, the story seems a little farfetched," Rocky said.

Dixie shook her head. "It's true; I guarantee it. We were raised as puppies to be part of the K9 unit in this town. We worked side by side with the human officers of the law to sniff out criminals and keep every citizen safe. Once all the people left, we figured it was up to us to keep order."

"That's amazing!" Gizmo said. "We met some Dalmatians who were trained to be firefighters, so it makes perfect sense that there would be dogs brave enough to be police officers, too!"

"Why, thank you," Dixie said.

"Yeah, yeah," Rocky muttered. "I was wrong, I can admit it."

Ahead of them, Julep jerked to a halt and barked, "Stop! Perimeter, face out. Keep your noses high."

The circle of Shepherds did as they were told, and Dixie darted back to her place. The dogs in front kept staring forward, but the rest of them turned to face the side or back the way they'd come.

Max and his friends huddled together. "Oh, something bad is happening," Georgie moaned.

"What's going on?" Max asked Julep, but the leader of the police dogs didn't respond.

Max looked on either side of the road. They were well out of the woods, in a residential neighborhood. Unlike the houses on the outskirts of town, these were built close together, though they still had big yards. Remnants of people's lives could be seen—a tricycle nearly hidden by the grass, a tire swing, gardening tools near tangled rosebushes. The neighborhood had been abandoned so quickly that some people hadn't even closed their windows, and white curtains drifted on the breeze.

Once again Max's heart swelled with longing, but the sight of the empty homes couldn't be why the pack of German Shepherds had stopped. No, something was afoot.

Max spun in a slow circle, catching sight of another of the orange-and-white barriers with its flashing beacon. He sniffed at the air, hoping to catch the woman's scent—but instead he smelled something else.

Wolves.

"Officers!" Julep finally barked. "Have we determined the location of the smell?"

"Sir!" one of the dogs at the rear called. "The wolves are coming up from the south and the east, through the swamp."

"How soon do you reckon they'll reach the town limits?"

"Sir!" Dixie barked. "If they get past the alligators, they're bound to reach here within a day or two."

Julep nodded. "Well, we're safe for the moment. Let's get to the square, then it's back on patrol."

"Yes, sir!" the eleven Shepherds barked in unison.

"Sorry about that," Julep said to Max. "We have to be cautious. But there's nothing to worry about for now."

"Thanks," Max said.

As the group resumed walking, Rocky and Gizmo leaned in close to Max.

"Wolves!" Rocky said. "Can't we ever get away from wolves?"

"I bet you it's Dolph again," Gizmo said with a growl.

Max sighed. "Whoever the wolves are, we're still at least a day ahead of them. So let's just worry about finding Madame's pack leader. She'll be able to help."

The dogs didn't have to walk much farther before they reached a giant, open square meadow that was, to Max's surprise, recently mowed.

Bits of shaved grass and ragweed wafted off the lawn and swirled into Max's nose, tickling his nostrils. He sneezed, but not before he got a good whiff. It was a smell that was both fresh and irritating at the same time, an unusual mix that he hadn't inhaled since before the people were gone.

"We're here!" Julep announced. "Welcome to the town square."

It was as though the humans had never left. The road branched into a perfect square around the stretch of lawn. Tall metal lampposts rose from the clean-swept sidewalks, and benches were evenly spaced.

Stately buildings of red-and-tan bricks lined the square. On one, a blue-painted sign read POLICE DEPART- MENT. Next door was a firehouse with a gleaming red truck inside. Across the square was a post office, and next to it, a small courthouse.

On the great lawn, a bronze statue of a man in a funny coat and hat stood on a concrete pedestal. Behind the statue, in the center of the grass square, was a fountain that gushed crystal-clear water. Surrounding it were plots of flowers in full bloom, without a weed in sight.

And at the back of the square, opening up onto the lawn, was the biggest building of all. From its steepled roof rose a tower that was open on top to reveal a big brass bell. Above the doors, a sign read TOWN HALL.

Everything was pristine and perfect. Though no humans walked the sidewalks, the touch of human hands had clearly been here recently.

"All right, back to patrol!" Julep barked to his pack. "Except you, Dixie. Come over here."

"Yes, sir!" Dixie barked.

169

She raced over to join Julep while the other German Shepherds tore off in different directions to continue their job of protecting the town.

Julep nodded to Max. "I'm afraid that I must supervise," he said. "I leave you in the capable paws of Dixie. She'll take you to our lady. She's not very far."

"Thanks for everything," Max said, offering a friendly wag of his tail. "We appreciate you coming for us."

"Even though we didn't really need it," Rocky said.

"Rocky!" Gizmo scolded. To Julep, she said, "You've been great! I hope we see you again soon."

"I'm sure you will, little lady," the Shepherd said. "Do enjoy your stay."

With that, Julep galloped off toward the post office.

"Come with me," Dixie said. "It's near feeding time!"

She turned and raced onto the grass, and Max and the others followed. In seconds, Max's paws left the sidewalk and met soft, squishy grass and earth. He couldn't help but drop down and roll around on his back.

"Oh, these flowers smell wonderful!"

Max looked up to see Gizmo and Rocky tromping through the garden. Dixie watched, panting happily, as the dogs played. Even Georgie seemed to enjoy himself, standing ankle deep in the fountain and lapping up the water as it cascaded past his snout.

Max shook himself, then trotted over to rejoin the group. As he neared them, however, Dixie went stiff and spun to face the town hall. Gizmo did the same.

"Squirrel!" Dixie barked.

"Squirrel!" Gizmo echoed.

On the lawn near the fountain, a gray-and-brown squirrel stood frozen in place, its tiny black eyes fixed on the gang of dogs. Its fluffy tail twitched, ever so slightly. And then the squirrel raced off.

Max knew there were more important things to do than roll in the fresh-mowed grass and chase a squirrel. His orderly, Praxis-enhanced brain told him to focus on finding the old woman.

But instinct proved to be stronger. Without thinking, the dogs tore into a run. Georgie leaped out of the fountain with a splash, and Gizmo and Rocky left behind a flurry of soil and colorful petals. Max's hind legs kicked up a cloud of dirt and grass as he followed Dixie.

The squirrel squealed angry insults as it ran over the lawn, but Max couldn't understand its chittery words. Not that it mattered. That little fluffball needed chasing!

They zigzagged around the flower beds before circling back to the fountain. Realizing it couldn't lose its pursuers, the squirrel made a mad dash toward a white building near the town hall. The building was round, with open walls and a roof that rose to a point.

"It's going to the gazebo!" Dixie cried.

"Flank it, Rocky!" Gizmo yipped. "It's getting away!"

The Dachshund's legs were a blur as he tried to reach the angry squirrel. "I'm trying!" he yelped. "It's too quick!"

The squirrel reached the gazebo steps moments ahead of the dogs. It leaped onto a bench, then a railing, and finally scrambled up one of the posts. After another round of unintelligible insults, it vanished into the eaves.

The five dogs collapsed onto their bellies, all eyes on the hole through which the squirrel had disappeared. They panted and heaved for air.

And then, Georgie laughed.

It was a sound almost as loud as his howl, a deep laugh that burst from his mouth and enveloped the entire lawn in good cheer. His tail slapped the grass.

It was impossible for the other dogs not to join in, and soon all five of them were rolling on their sides, guffawing.

"I haven't had so much fun in a long time," Georgie said.

"Yay!" Gizmo cried. "I'm glad!"

Max nudged Georgie's side with his nose. "See? Everything is going to be all right. We're about to meet the old lady in the hat, and it won't be long before we're off to see Belle in Baton Rouge."

Dixie narrowed her eyes. "Did you say Belle? In Baton Rouge?"

"He sure did," Rocky said. "Why?"

Before Dixie could answer, a loud, metallic *bong* echoed above them.

Rocky scrabbled backward. "What was that?" he asked.

Dixie pointed her snout at the tower atop the town

hall. Another *bong* rang out, and Max saw the shining brass bell vibrate.

"When it's daylight, it rings on the hour, every hour," Dixie explained. "When it rings six times in the afternoon, that means it's feeding time!"

The dogs all looked up at the gleaming bell, counting silently. When the sixth *bong* reverberated through the streets, Dixie started toward the road that ran past the post office.

"This way," she said. Max, Rocky, Gizmo, and Georgie followed her.

"Say, Dixie," Max asked as he trotted at her side. "Why did you react that way when we mentioned Belle and Baton Rouge?"

The police dog's ears twitched, and she finally said, "It's just I've heard the name, is all. Some dogs 'round town must have spoken of her. You can ask them more, if you're curious."

"I think I will," Max said as they reached the sidewalk in front of the post office. Other dogs and cats slipped from behind bushes and out of darkened doorways, making their way to the sidewalk. Just like the German Shepherds, their fur was shiny and recently groomed. Each one wore a brand-new, brightly colored collar with a little silver tag dangling beneath it.

"Afternoon," a black cat said, nodding cordially at the newcomers.

"Afternoon to you, too, Minerva," Dixie said. "How are things?"

"Same ol'," Minerva yowled. "That little dog Beth Ann keeps trying to sleep in my foyer. I tell her she lives two houses down, but she always forgets, bless her heart. I try not to get too mad at her, though."

"Well, you just let me know if she causes any real problems, you hear?"

Minerva flicked her tail. "I can handle it, dear. But thank you for the offer." The black cat nodded once more at Max and his friends, then darted ahead.

Other pets soon surrounded the dogs, none apparently concerned by the new arrivals. In fact, they were friendlier than most animals Max and his friends had met, saying, "How do?" before breaking off to chat with their friends.

The parade of pets stretched in a line past a general store and a gas station before finally halting in front of a single-story building. The air was filled with gentle laughter and friendly conversation as the animals waited patiently for whatever was about to happen. Dixie motioned that they should do the same, so Max and his companions sat on the sidewalk, looking every which way, their ears alert.

Max focused on the building. There was a sign in the front window, but it was too far away to read. He could barely see a cartoon drawing of a dog and a cat. A vet's office? That would make sense, though he'd never heard of animals lining up to get in!

On the north side of the building, Max saw the front end of a large white van parked in a driveway. He also thought he could hear the sounds of a farm, which seemed strange—who would keep a farm in town? A quick sniff told him it was true, though. Over the musky scents of pet fur was the gassy stench of cows and pigs, goats and chickens.

"I can hear her!" a dog near the door barked.

All the pets fell silent. Max held his breath even as his heart pounded a happy beat inside him. Could this finally be it?

With a creak, the front door opened. A woman emerged wearing loose pants and a flowing blouse patterned with purple roses. Just like the beach animals had said, she had on a straw hat tied with a purple ribbon.

The woman knelt to scratch the ears of the animals on the porch, then stood up to survey her visitors.

Max could see her clearly now. She had a pale, wrinkled face with friendly eyes and white hair.

And when she smiled, Max knew for certain.

This was the woman in the photograph back at the laboratories where Praxis was made.

This was Madame Curie's owner, who would help reunite him with his family.

After all the dangers of the long road here, they'd finally found her.

CHAPTER 13

THE GOOD DOCTOR

The last humans Max had seen after everyone disappeared were the bad people back at the city near the riverboat. They'd been awful and cruel, and stunk of meanness. They were nothing like the family Max had been searching for.

So as Max watched the old woman stride down the front walkway with a small army of dogs and cats leaping happily around her feet, a joyous warmth flooded his insides.

Her caring and warmth were apparent as she bent down and scratched animals behind their ears and stroked their fur, offering gentle smiles and calm, soothing words of praise. Her scent—a human smell

of sun-warmed skin and flowery soap—wafted over the manicured front lawn of the vet's office, and with it came hundreds of memories of Charlie and Emma and the rest of his missing family.

Even though he wasn't sad, Max couldn't help but whimper as he watched the woman approach.

Cats leaped at her loose pants, meowing, "Pet me, lady!" and "No, feed me first!" One yowled, "You kept me waiting a long time. But I'll forgive you if you put food in my bowl right now!"

Dogs large and small spun in excited circles, their bodies trembling in uncontained glee, their tails a blur. They barked, "You're the best!" and "Pet my head, please!" and "Ball! I saw a ball! Want to play?"

"You're all so eager today," the woman said. She scratched the underside of a tawny cat's chin, and it closed its eyes in ecstasy. "I'll have food for you very soon. The livestock need tending first, my dears."

Next to Max, Gizmo danced from paw to paw, while Rocky leaped up and down.

"I can't believe it's a real, live person," Gizmo said. "And she seems so nice!"

"Oh, I could really go for a belly scratch," Rocky said. Looking up at Max, he asked, "Do you think she gives out belly scratches?"

Georgie chuckled. "She does give belly scratches," he said. "At least, she did to me. I never thought I'd see her again. I'm glad I came with you three."

Grass squelched beneath the old woman's white sneakers as she drew closer. Dixie sat at full attention, all professional.

Max considered leaping onto the woman and licking her face.

The woman paused a few feet from Max, Rocky, Gizmo, and Georgie, and a look of confusion briefly crossed her face.

"My, my, what have we here," she said.

Her voice was the sweetest, most beautiful thing ever to grace his ears, Max decided.

"You three are new." Her eyes falling on Georgie, she said, "And you, my friend, seem to have followed me from the beach."

She rubbed Georgie's head, then carefully held her hand out to Max, Rocky, and Gizmo. They sniffed it one by one, inhaling her perfect scent and absorbing her calm manner. Instinctively, Max licked her hand.

The woman smiled and wiped her hand on her pants. "You seem like friendly dogs, though much too skinny. And your fur…" She shook her head. "I'm Dr. Lynn, and we shall find out your names soon enough. A pleasure to meet you."

"You, too, Doc!" Rocky barked.

"Yes," Gizmo yipped. "Lynn is such a pretty name! I'm Gizmo, and this is Rocky."

"And I'm Max," Max woofed.

"Oh, you're chatty dogs, aren't you?" Dr. Lynn said.

"I bet you haven't heard a human voice in some time. Well, once everyone is fed, it's time for you three to have a checkup."

"Oh, a checkup?" Rocky said. "Well, maybe it will end with belly rubs."

Leaving the dogs behind, Dr. Lynn strode toward the backyard of the vet's office, where Max had heard the sounds of farm animals. Many of the waiting cats and dogs bounded after her. Some cast suspicious glances at Max and his friends.

"That was strange," Georgie said to Max, Rocky, and Gizmo as the horde of pets raced away. "You were talking like you knew what the old woman was saying."

Dixie looked at Max with narrowed eyes. "Yes, how did you know the word she spoke was her name? It takes the rest of us a long time to understand how humans say *sit* or *stay*, let alone figure out their names!"

"It's nothing, really," Max said carefully. "The three of us just... Well, we're a little smarter than the average dog."

Dixie scoffed. "Oh, you think you're smarter than us?"

Max said, "It's nothing like that. It's a long story, and it involves why the people left."

"There was this pig we met, on the river, see," Rocky said. "And an elephant."

"An ele-what?" Georgie asked.

"Big animal. Gray. Long nose and big ears." Rocky spread his front paws wide. "And when I mean big, I mean *big*."

Dixie rolled her eyes. "Never heard of them. But what do they have to do with being smart?"

"Well, they took us to this laboratory," Max said. "And they put us through a process that made it so we can understand human words and writing."

Dixie said, "That's impossible. Is this some sort of trick?"

"No!" said Gizmo. "We'd never do that to you after you've been so nice." She sighed. "Unfortunately, even though we can understand her, it doesn't seem like she knows what *we're* saying. I guess they didn't make a Praxis that let humans understand dog barks."

"But if you can understand humans," the German Shepherd said, almost to herself, "then that means you can be better police dogs than us." She met Max's gaze. "You have to take us to this lab."

"Uh, hold on, sister," Rocky said. "That place is miles and miles from here, in the complete opposite direction of where we're going."

Dixie stomped her front paw. "Then we can find a way to do it here!"

Max cleared his throat. "Um, maybe," he said. "But, Dixie, right now we need to be with Dr. Lynn—with the old woman. Thank you for guiding us through the city. Julep, too, and all of you police dogs."

"Julep!" Dixie barked. "Yes, I should go see Julep." She turned and ran back down the street.

"Why would an ele-what need a nose that long?" Georgie mumbled.

Rocky laughed. "Don't worry about it, big guy. You're not going to meet one anytime soon."

Though Max was concerned by Dixie's strange reaction to learning about their Praxis abilities, he had more pressing concerns. Dr. Lynn had returned from feeding the farm animals in the backyard. All the animals watched her in hushed excitement.

She unraveled a hose from the side of the building, then turned the spigot and filled a few dozen large, plastic bowls with clear, sparkling water. That done, she briefly disappeared behind the house and reappeared carrying a big bag of kibble. Surprisingly, all the dogs waited patiently as she scooped out servings, even though the pinging of food into the bowls made Max want to dive right into a meal.

The good doctor had these pets well trained.

Finally, Dr. Lynn filled the remaining bowls with kitty chow. When she was finished, she whistled, and the dogs and cats surged forward to lap up the water and crunch down mouthfuls of food. Georgie barreled forward to enter the fray without a single thought, until the only animals not eating were Max, Rocky, and Gizmo, who sat waiting on the sidewalk.

"Still waiting for me, I see," Dr. Lynn said as she strolled across the grass. "I'd have expected you to go for the food, but you three seem awfully obedient."

Behind her, the dogs and cats woofed and meowed as they shoved past one another to get their fill. Max wondered if a fight might break out, but any animal inclined to hiss or growl glanced at the old woman and calmed down.

Max's tail set to wagging again as the doctor rubbed the top of his head with one hand and the underside of his jaw with the other, and he almost collapsed to the ground with pleasure. He closed his eyes, enjoying every stroke of his golden coat, imagining Charlie and Emma were there to tousle his fur along with Dr. Lynn.

Fingers massaged his neck, and Max realized she was sifting through his fur. He opened his eyes to find the woman looking puzzled.

"Hmm, no collar," she said.

Max sighed as she pulled her hands away from him, then watched with longing as she scratched Rocky's ears. The Dachshund fell onto his side, exposing his belly. Dr. Lynn laughed and scratched his stomach, and Rocky's hind leg scrabbled at the air.

"Oh, yeah," Rocky barked. "Maybe up a little higher. Between the shoulder blades, too, if you don't mind."

But Dr. Lynn only shook her head at not finding a collar on Rocky, either. Gizmo received her own round of petting before the old woman stood up and crossed her arms.

"Not a collar among the three of you," she said. "Let's hope you either lost them or your owners decided to go high-tech." Backing away, she held out her hand. "Do you know *come?*"

With a nod from Max, all three dogs climbed to their feet and followed the old woman onto the lawn.

"Very good," she said. "Come! Follow me!"

She turned and walked toward the front entrance of the vet's office, glancing over her shoulder to make sure the dogs were behind her. Max decided he was not going to let the woman out of his sight.

"What's so special about them?" a slender gray cat asked, casually swiping a paw over its face. Nearby lay the black cat, Minerva, sunning herself after her meal.

"Oh, them?" Minerva asked, tail twitching. "I don't rightly know. They look all raggedy, though I'm sure they can't help it, being dogs. Bless their hearts."

Dr. Lynn led Max, Rocky, and Gizmo up the front walkway and onto the porch. They sat as she opened the front door.

Holding the door open, Dr. Lynn looked down at the three dogs and said, "After you."

Max nodded at her, then walked inside, followed by his two small friends. As they sat on the cool linoleum floor of the lobby, the old woman laughed.

"Aren't you three smart!" she said, offering Max another blissful scratch behind his ears.

The lobby was similar to the one at the vet's office back home. There were chairs lining the walls and a big front desk. Everything gleamed bright and clean.

While the three dogs waited, Dr. Lynn took off her big straw hat and tossed it on a chair in the waiting area.

She shook her head to let her white hair fall in soft waves to her shoulders.

"Back this way, my friends," she called as she walked past the front desk and down a hallway.

The three dogs followed her into an examination room. She carefully picked up Rocky and Gizmo to set them atop a metal table, then sat down on a stool in front of a computer.

Max studied the room. Like the front lobby, the surfaces glimmered beneath the fluorescent lights. There were counters and cabinets along two of the walls and a big metal sink. The acrid smell of bleach lingered in the air, along with the barest scents of other animals.

After so many months on their own, it seemed almost strange to be in the company of a human again. For the first time in ages, Max was able to relax and just be a dog. He'd almost forgotten what that was like.

Strange, yes. But also very, very nice.

"This might sound weird, but I'm actually kind of looking forward to this," Rocky whispered.

Gizmo giggled. "Me, too! Mostly I just want to feel her hands on my fur again. I'd almost forgotten what it felt like, to have a human."

The doctor spun on her stool and smiled at the two small dogs. "I hear you vocalizing; I know you must be bored. This won't take too long, I promise."

The old woman climbed off the stool, then picked up a device that sat next to the computer. It looked like a long, flat gray spatula with a screen that showed a bunch of red zeroes.

The woman waved the device over Max's back, just between his front shoulder blades. The thing beeped, and she lifted it up to look at the numbers.

"Excellent," she said, turning back to the computer. "Your owners put a microchip in your back."

"They did?" Max said.

"You have a chip in you?" Rocky asked. "Like a potato chip? How? Did you eat one?"

Max shook his head. "No! But even if I did, I don't think it would be in my shoulders."

Dr. Lynn ignored their barking and typed into the computer. The screen flashed, and Max could see a photo of himself next to a bunch of words.

"So you're Max," Dr. Lynn said. "Good name, Max. And you're from . . . Oh, my."

She peered down at Max.

"You've come an astoundingly long way, my friend," she said. "I wish I'd seen you walking about when I was up there weeks ago. You must be looking for your family, huh, boy?"

Max whimpered and placed his head on her lap.

"There, there," Dr. Lynn said as she petted the sides of his neck. "You won't be alone much longer, Max. I'm going to fix this mess I caused, one way or another."

Dr. Lynn stood once more, then ran the scanning

device over Gizmo's back and frowned when it did not beep.

"I guess you weren't chipped," she said. "For today, I'll call you Jane. It's a lovely name, yes? It's from Jane Goodall, a scientist like me who loves animals."

Gizmo wagged her tail and licked Dr. Lynn's hand. "Thank you! Jane is a great name."

Dr. Lynn laughed. "You like it! If you don't mind, Jane, I must turn my attention to your handsome Dachshund friend."

When the old woman scanned Rocky's back, the device beeped once more, and she returned to the computer. In seconds the screen showed a picture of a much fatter Rocky.

"Oh, you're Dr. Walters's dog!" she said. "I remember you." Turning back to the dogs, she added, "And Max, too. You were at the same kennel where I put up Madame. In fact, that's why I came through those parts. I was trying to find her."

"How sad," Gizmo said softly. "She doesn't know what happened to Madame."

"I think I'm glad we can't tell her," Max said.

Meanwhile, Dr. Lynn set about with the rest of the checkups. She began by washing the dogs one by one in the big basin, marveling at their obedience and intelligence as each of them calmly let her scrub them with the foul-smelling soap that kept the fleas away.

The car wash had rid them of some of the muck they'd crawled through, but there was nothing like a good, deep scrubbing, and Max soon felt cleaner than he had in ages. The woman ran a brush all through his fur, talking soothingly as she gently prodded his limbs, checking them for injuries.

"Ouch," she said as she discovered the recent cut on his forehead. "It looks like you hit your head. I'll put something on it to keep out the bacteria."

By the time Dr. Lynn was done with them, Max, Rocky, and Gizmo had never looked better. Max couldn't remember when Rocky's black fur had been so shiny, but Gizmo proved the real revelation. She'd been traveling for weeks or months on her own before Max and Rocky met her, so her tan-and-black coat was always a tangle of fluff. But now, every tuft and curl was in the right place.

"We all look so nice!" Gizmo said.

Rocky pranced in a circle on the metal tabletop. "Why, thank you," he said. "You look pretty amazing yourself."

Now that they were clean and their outsides all exam-ined, Dr. Lynn turned her attention to their insides. She pressed a cold stethoscope against their chests and sides to listen to their heartbeats and breathing, shone light into their eyes and noses, and lifted their lips to exam-ine their gums, teeth, and tongues.

Finally, she produced a long needle attached to a

small plastic tube. A syringe. Max winced, but he trusted Dr. Lynn, so he did not flinch as she approached.

"Sorry about this, Max," the doctor said. "It'll only prick for a second, I promise." She gently propped Max against her leg, prepared to grab him if he tried to run. Then, she stuck the needle into his skin and pulled back the plunger on the syringe, drawing his blood.

Letting out a breath, Dr. Lynn put a cap on the syringe and set it on a nearby countertop. She then did the same to Rocky and Gizmo, who both clenched their teeth and closed their eyes to make it as easy as possible for their new doctor friend.

Shaking her head in amazement, Dr. Lynn began to label vials for the freshly drawn blood.

"I have never once had a checkup go this smoothly," she said. "Not even Madame could get through one without squirming a little bit. I don't know if Dr. Walters was Jane's vet, too, but I'll have to find the man and learn his secrets."

Producing some more vials and bottles from the cabinets, Dr. Lynn said, "Now all we have to do is get your current weight, and we're done."

"Hey, down there," Rocky said, gesturing to a metal slab near the door. "That's probably the weighing machine, if I remember my other vet visits right."

Max wandered over to the machine while Rocky and Gizmo jumped off the table and onto the linoleum.

Together, the three dogs crowded around the slab and sniffed at it.

"I think you might be right," Max said.

Behind them, Dr. Lynn gasped.

All three dogs turned to face her. The old woman stood next to the examination table, a hand in front of her mouth.

"It's not possible," she whispered.

"What's wrong?" Gizmo asked.

Rocky's head darted from side to side. "Did we do something bad? Were we not supposed to move?"

Dr. Lynn stared at the dogs, then ran her hands back through her wavy white hair.

"Max," she said. "I need a ball from behind the front counter in the lobby. It's in a box with several other balls, but only two are red, and only one of those balls has little nubs on it. I need that ball. Rocky and Jane, you two stay right where you are."

Max barked and wagged his tail. While Rocky and Gizmo sat down in front of the scale, Max ran out of the examination room and back to the front desk in the lobby.

There, just as the old woman had said, was a cardboard box with several balls inside. There were plain blue, yellow, and green balls, and an orange one that had holes in its side to show a shiny bell in the center. Max nosed them aside until he saw flashes of red at the bottom of the box. One ball was smooth, and one was covered in dozens of nubby spikes.

Max grabbed the spiked red ball in his jaws, then ran quickly back into the examination room. He dropped the red ball at Dr. Lynn's feet, then sat down and looked up at her, tail wagging as he waited for her approval.

A smile spread across the old woman's face. "My, oh my," she said softly.

Crouching down, she scratched beneath Max's chin, then stared directly into his brown eyes.

And she said, "You three can understand me."

CHAPTER 14

HOW IT ALL BEGAN

Dr. Lynn collected bowls from another room and set out two each for Max, Rocky, and Gizmo, so all three dogs had their own portions of fresh kibble and water.

While they ate their fill next to the examination table, the doctor dripped a tiny amount of each of their blood onto glass slides, then viewed the red splotches under a microscope. She combined the blood with various chemicals, shaking them together and holding the vials up to the light. As she worked, she recorded her findings both in a notebook and on the computer.

The doctor worked in silence, so the room was filled with the crunching of kibble and slurping of water. Just as Max, Rocky, and Gizmo finished their meals,

Dr. Lynn closed her notebook and said, "I don't know how, but you three completed the Praxis project."

"Let's sit by her feet so she knows we're listening to her," Max said.

The three dogs sat side by side in front of the woman's white shoes. They looked up at her and offered a wag of their tails.

Biting her lip, Dr. Lynn looked at each of them. "I certainly didn't expect this. Did another human do this to you? Please bark once for no, twice for yes."

Max, Rocky, and Gizmo all barked once.

"Hmm," Dr. Lynn said. "But you were at the laboratory, right? Please bark once for no or twice for yes if you were at the laboratory."

All three barked twice.

Dr. Lynn sighed, reaching down to scratch behind their ears. "I was hoping there might be some other solution, but I see I still have my work cut out for me. A few more questions. Was it my dog Madame Curie who took you to the lab?"

One bark: *No.*

"Did you see Madame? Did you travel with her?"

Two barks: *Yes.*

"Then why isn't—" The old woman's hand flew to her face, covering her mouth. She asked, "Did you leave Madame behind?"

None of the dogs barked at first. Max's chest felt

tight, and his tail drooped. He finally barked twice to say yes.

"Did you want to leave her behind?"

No.

Dr. Lynn's hands trembled now, and her eyes watered. She took a shaky breath and asked, "Did Madame...pass on?"

Max whimpered and lowered his head. Rocky and Gizmo curled against each other, sniffling. They didn't have to bark in response. Max could tell that Dr. Lynn knew.

A tear fell down the old woman's pale, wrinkled cheek, then another. She looked up from the three dogs, not bothering to wipe away the tears.

"I'm so sorry," Max said. He rose and set his head on the woman's lap. "She was a very good friend. I miss her, too."

Absently, the woman rubbed Max's head, but she still stared off into the distance, lost in memory.

"This is so sad," Gizmo said. "She never got to say good-bye."

"I'm starting to wish we hadn't figured out how to talk to her, after all," Rocky said.

Max licked Dr. Lynn's hand, then nuzzled her leg with his head.

Shaking her head, the doctor swiped the back of her hand across her cheeks and eyes. She looked down at

Max and rubbed the sides of his head, offering him a sad smile.

"Something tells me that you loved Madame, too, Max," she said. "I wouldn't put it past her to send you to find me. I know she must have come looking for me, too, even if she never..."

Gently moving Max aside, Dr. Lynn climbed off the stool and began cleaning up the examination room. The dogs watched and listened.

"You know, I named Madame after one of my idols," she said, her back turned to the dogs while she placed the vials in a cabinet. "Madame Marie Curie was a brilliant scientist at a time when women were not so highly looked upon. Now I would never dare to compare myself to her, but the real Marie Curie and I have something in common." She looked at the dogs with serious eyes. "Her work led her to be fatally sickened by the radium that she discovered. And I myself am afflicted with the Praxis virus, which now lies in every animal in much of the country. My creation, which was meant for good, has instead done much harm. And it's up to me to fix it."

Dr. Lynn leaned back against the counters and crossed her arms. "I don't know who finished the Praxis process with you. Perhaps you stumbled upon it yourselves, or maybe one of our other enhanced animals helped you. I wonder, do you know the full story of why you're smarter now, and why all the people left?"

The three dogs each barked once for no.

"I'll tell you, then," she said. "You deserve to know why you were left behind. Your families never wanted this. You were not abandoned. You are still loved."

She crouched down in front of the dogs and petted them one by one. "They had no choice in leaving you, and even now they miss you. Do you understand? You *are* loved."

Max barked twice, then jumped up, hugging the woman with his paws over her shoulders and his head nuzzled into her neck. She put one arm around his side and pulled him close, then reached for Rocky and Gizmo. They sat there on the linoleum, beneath the bright fluorescent lights, embracing one another with their eyes closed.

Even though Max had often told himself that his family was waiting, that they wouldn't have left if they didn't have to, and that people didn't hate the animals, it still hadn't kept some doubt from creeping into his mind.

So to hear from a human, a person as trustworthy and kind as Dr. Lynn, that everything he'd hoped for was true—it made his heart swell. He ached with longing for his family, more than ever now. But knowing for certain that they missed him made the hurt not quite as bad.

Dr. Lynn let go of the three dogs and stood up, again wiping tears from her eyes. "All right, Max, Rocky, and Jane," she said. "I'll tell the story from the beginning.

But how about we go somewhere more comfortable first?"

Dr. Lynn exited the examination room with Max, Rocky, and Gizmo trotting at her heels. As she walked, the old woman pulled her hair back into a loose knot, and when they reached the lobby she collected her straw hat and placed it on her head. She grabbed a handful of toy mice from a basket atop the welcome desk and stuffed them in her pants pocket, then collected the box of balls that Max had dug through earlier.

That done, she led the three dogs back outside.

Evening had fallen, and the sky was streaked orange and pink. Golden twilight stretched long shadows down the pristine streets of the small town, and sparkling fireflies glittered and darted through the air.

Most of the town's dogs and cats lounged on the lawn in front of the vet's office, grooming themselves or chatting. Some of the younger dogs wrestled near the empty food dishes, watched over by narrow-eyed cats.

As soon as they saw Dr. Lynn, all the pets snapped to attention.

"She's back!" shouted a small dog that seemed more fur than animal—its coat hung down to its feet. A Lhasa Apso, Max recalled.

"Is it playtime?" a brown-furred mutt asked, its tail wagging.

Excitement flowed like a wave through the crowd

of animals. The cats tried to act nonchalant as they stretched and opened their mouths in wide yawns—but Max could see the excited glint in their eyes.

Two of the police dogs paced along the sidewalk, keeping watch over the crowd. Max didn't recognize either one by name—Julep and Dixie must have been patrolling elsewhere.

"All right, all right," one of the Shepherds barked. "Keep calm, friends."

"Anyone who oversteps their bounds spends a night in the kennel," the other Shepherd called out. "We don't need another incident like with Porky."

An enormously fat, striped tan cat flattened his ears. "That was an accident. And the name is *Porgy*."

Max, Rocky, and Gizmo sat down on the porch as Dr. Lynn took in all the animals with a smile.

"Looks like you have been waiting patiently," she said. "You definitely deserve some new toys!"

She reached into the box and tossed a ball into the crowd. A giant shape—Georgie—leaped up and caught it in his jaws. He bounded off toward the street, chased by several of the bigger dogs.

Dr. Lynn tossed another ball, and another, until her box was empty and all the dogs on the lawn were racing off to play. Then she set down the box and reached into her pockets. The cats approached now, and she tossed the fake mice at them one by one. Some of the cats tossed their toy mice in the air, to dash wildly after them and then pounce, while others were content simply to chew on the little furry things.

The two German Shepherds came to Dr. Lynn, wagging their tails. She scratched beneath their chins, then produced two bone-shaped doggy biscuits from a pocket. "You two did a wonderful job of keeping the peace," she said as the police dogs gobbled up their treats. "If I see your human partners, I'll be sure to tell them how well trained you are."

Turning back, Dr. Lynn whistled. "Come on, Max, Rocky, and Jane," she called. "My temporary home is just up the street."

One of the German Shepherds narrowed his eyes at Max. "Where is she taking you?"

"We don't know," Max said. "She just wants us to follow her."

"Don't go too far," the other Shepherd said. "Julep wants to talk to you."

Max nodded. "We won't. Don't worry."

The two dogs didn't say anything further, just glared.

"Yeesh, what's with them?" Rocky asked as they continued up the sidewalk.

Max shook his head. "You saw how Dixie acted when she learned we could understand humans. They must consider it a big deal."

"Well, it is a big deal," Gizmo said. "I don't blame Dixie for wanting to talk to humans, too."

"Yeah," Rocky said. "But I hope it doesn't lead to

anything bad. Just think, if dogs like the Chairman knew about Praxis, they'd get even more power hungry than they already are. Who knows what these police dogs might do now that they know about it?"

Gizmo's tufted ears drooped. "Oh, but they seem so nice. I hope they stay nice."

An iron gate creaked, and the dogs looked up to find Dr. Lynn had led them to a big home surrounded by a tall black iron fence. The fence enclosed a huge lawn with twin weeping willows.

The dogs followed the woman along the stone pathway between the flowing, swaying willows. Hidden behind one of the trees was a green lawn mower.

"You should have seen how this town looked when I arrived," said Dr. Lynn. "Grass as tall as my waist." She shook her head. "I suppose that's what it will return to when I move on, but I hope it looks lovely for a little while longer."

They reached the front porch and climbed its steps. The porch stretched around the entire first floor of the house, which was covered with white shingles and seemed much fancier than any house Max had ever been in. Even the rocking chairs next to the front door seemed lush.

Dr. Lynn opened the front door and ushered the dogs into a wide foyer with a polished, dark wood floor and a staircase. To the right was a comfortable sitting room. A couch and two chairs were arranged on a red rug in front of a fireplace. The furniture reminded Max of the time he was taken with Charlie and Emma to visit a couple of elderly humans. Their couches also had carved feet and plush velvet padding, and even though the old couple were otherwise very nice, they made it clear that if Max climbed atop the furniture he'd be a *very bad dog*.

Dr. Lynn didn't seem to have any such concern, though. She patted the cushions on the couch and let Max, Rocky, and Gizmo jump up and get comfortable, then kneeled in front of the fireplace to light a fire. A tall clock ticked in the corner.

Wood crackled, and the crisp scent of smoke swirled through the room. Dr. Lynn stepped back, then sat on the couch. Warmth washed over Max as he lay down on his belly and set his head on the old woman's lap. Rocky and Gizmo crawled over Dr. Lynn's legs. Then they, too, rested their snouts on her thigh.

"Nice place, isn't it?" Dr. Lynn said. "I figure since no one's around, they wouldn't mind if I indulged in a bit of luxury. I do pride myself on leaving my surroundings better than I found them."

She sighed. "So, my dears, you should know about Praxis. It's the reason we've all found ourselves here.

"Many years ago, my partners and I sought to create cures for mental illnesses in humans, as well as birth defects and accidents that damage the brain. Through our tests and studies we created a synthetic virus that had no harmful effect on animals, but when exposed to certain conditions—like radiation or electricity—would mutate to create new, healthy brain cells. It was incredible."

Dr. Lynn chuckled. "I know you three are smarter now, but is any of this making sense?"

Max licked the woman's hand. "Some of it," he said. "But there are lots of words I haven't really heard before."

"Hmm?" Dr. Lynn said. "Well, I can't tell if that's a yes or a no, so I'll take it as a maybe. To put it simply, my partners and I found a way to use a virus to heal brains, but only in animals. The side effect was, of course, smarter animals."

Looking back into the flames, she continued. "We gathered test subjects from many species. Most were kept at our laboratory, but we did have a dolphin named Nixie that we kept at a facility down south. I wonder what's become of her."

Dr. Lynn shook her head. "Anyway, we found that if we infected the animals with the virus and then exposed them to the second part of what we'd come to call the Praxis process, the animals' intelligence would increase by leaps and bounds. They could understand human speech and writing, even if most could not speak or write themselves. It was astounding.

"The only problem was that Praxis either wouldn't cause any noticeable change in humans, or it would give them horrible side effects. Eventually, I gave up on ever achieving our original goal. I retired to a new home—near where you lived, in fact. I thought Praxis was over, but then . . . the worst happened."

Gently pushing the dogs aside, Dr. Lynn stood up and paced in front of the fireplace. The orange light cast flickering, dancing shadows. Sorrow and guilt creased her face.

"Somehow, in spite of all our safeguards, the virus escaped our facility. Carried on the wind, it began to infect many animals. Since Praxis doesn't hurt animals, we thought everyone was safe.

"But then the virus began to spread in new ways. As though they'd sensed it happening, birds in all the affected areas migrated south. Soon after, some people whose animals were infected became infected themselves, and they fell very ill. It wasn't long before the cause was traced to our lab and our experiments. And since no one could know which animals were infected, the only answer seemed to be to abandon all the animals and evacuate until a solution could be found.

"Some have said we should . . . get rid of all the animals, but my colleagues and I convinced them it wouldn't help, that there was no way to track down every infected animal. The only answer is a cure, which I intend to find. As I mentioned before, I myself am infected with the Praxis virus. Luckily, prolonged exposure doesn't change anything, which means I am free to work with you animals. Still, I will get sick eventually. Which is why I need to solve this problem as soon as possible."

Dr. Lynn met the dogs' eyes one by one. "I think you three might have helped me through a stumbling block. I still have tests running in the vet's office, but if I'm right, after the Praxis process was completed, you were rid of the virus. That means this is curable. There is still the matter of figuring out how to eradicate the virus without making all animals abnormally smart— that would certainly lead to chaos!—but thanks to you, I am closer than ever to saving the people and bringing them home."

Gizmo's ears perked up. "Did you hear that? We *are* cured. That means our families will be safe with us!"

"Even better," Rocky said. "The doctor said she can cure *everyone*. That means everything can go back to normal."

"Normal," Max said wistfully. "I'm not sure what normal is anymore."

Rocky waddled across the couch cushion and licked Max's nose.

"It means, big guy, that I go back to sleeping on a doggy bed, fat and happy. And you can run all over your farm with your pack leaders again."

Dr. Lynn gave a slight groan. "It sounds like you three are just as excited by the cure as I am," she said. "It will be some time yet before I know what I'm dealing with. Perhaps we should get some sleep."

She smiled at the three dogs. "If you think this room is nice, you'll definitely enjoy the bedroom."

Once the flames had died, Dr. Lynn led the three dogs up the stairs and into the master bedroom. There, atop a high, plush bed, all four of them lay down to sleep. Max could hardly believe how much had happened in one day—from messing around in a car wash to fleeing from alligators to finding Dr. Lynn.

It seemed a lifetime since Max had last curled next to a human, and it felt so wonderfully right. He wanted to lie there forever, inhaling her pleasant scent and feeling her hand run absently through his fur.

Max sat in the gazebo in front of the town hall. It was a beautiful day, with bright blue skies and a few wispy clouds. Birds trilled in the trees, and though he couldn't see them, he could hear the talking and laughter of human families eating a picnic lunch.

Next to Max, Dr. Lynn sat in a flowing floral dress, smiling beneath her wide-brim hat as she scratched Max's ears. Rocky and Gizmo cuddled together on her lap, and Georgie lay at her feet.

It's starting, Dr. Lynn said, her voice crystal clear even though her lips did not move.

A parade of animals marched down the street in front of the square. There was a dainty Poodle leading a pack of ragged, happy dogs, followed by a swarm of cats mewing at the top of their lungs. On their backs they carried a pillow atop which mottle-furred Raoul stood tall and proud.

The subway dogs came next, blinking in bewilderment at the bright light, then a marching band of rats wearing matching red coats with gold epaulets, singing a silly rhyme.

The parade went on, an endless stream of all the animals Max had met on his journey. There were the dogs of the Corporation with Madame and the growling Chairman. The riverboat dogs danced and twirled, raising a cheer to a triumphant Boss, who was held aloft on a plush gold doggy bed. The zoo animals made an exotic display, and the beach animals were there, too, music bursting from their radio.

The possums flipped and flew over one another, a prelude to the stately police dogs, dressed to the nines in formal navy coats and black caps.

Dr. Lynn rubbed Max's head. *Here comes the big finish,* she said. *Pay close attention.*

A grand float appeared, and the square was filled with gasping *ooh*s and *aah*s. It appeared to be a cloud brought down to earth, trailing wisps of dew. Dogs of all shapes and sizes looked up at the lone figure who stood proudly atop its highest peak. It was a Collie, her head held high and her fur glimmering in the sun. A gold scarf was tied around her neck and flowed majestically as the float moved down the road.

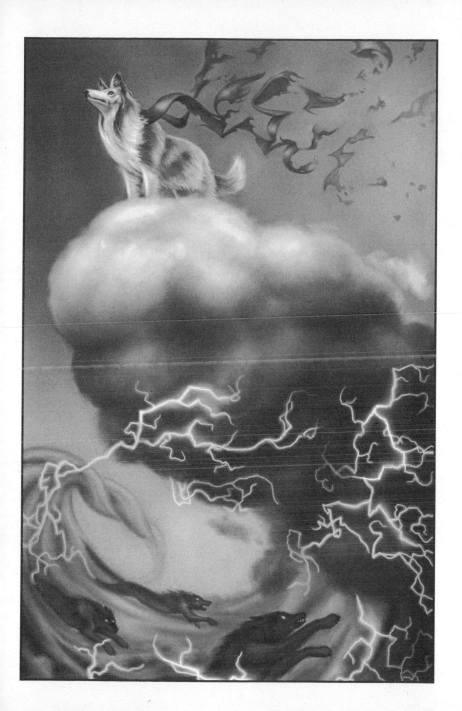

There she is, Georgie said. *Good ol' Belle. I can take you to her.*

Max was about to respond—but as he watched the float reach the end of the street, something changed. The once-white cloud had darkened to gray, and flashes of lightning arced within.

"Something is wrong," Max said.

Good ol' Belle, Georgie said. *Everyone just loves her.*

Great gusts of wind whooshed through the street, picking up the gold scarf around Belle's neck. The scarf shredded into tatters and tore away.

The stormy float turned the corner, and Max could make out several wispy shapes behind it. Some looked like wolves with glowing red eyes. Others, Max couldn't recognize at all.

"What does it mean?" Max asked.

Everything will be all right, Dr. Lynn said.

Everyone just loves Belle, Georgie repeated as the unseen humans' laughter grew louder.

Please find her, Boss's voice sounded.

A crack of thunder echoed through the perfect summer sky.

Max awoke.

It was dark in the bedroom. A cool breeze blew in through the open window, raising the lacy white curtains. One of the shutters had opened and had slammed against the wall—the sound Max had heard in his dream. Rocky and Gizmo snored nearby on the bed.

But the space where Dr. Lynn had lain was empty.

Max's heart began to pound, until he heard the door creak behind him as Dr. Lynn slipped back into the room.

"Oh, Max," she whispered when she saw him awake and watching her. "It's true, my friend. What happened at the labs cured you. I can save everyone." She scratched behind his ears, her eyes glimmering.

"I'd almost given up hope," she said.

"Me, too," Max admitted. And though his words had come out as a bark, she seemed to know what he'd meant. She leaned forward and gently kissed his forehead.

"I have something for you," she said. "And for Rocky and Jane." She crawled into the center of the bed and sat down. She gently shook Rocky and Gizmo until the two small dogs opened their eyes.

"What is it?" Rocky said. "I was sleeping over here."

"Did something happen?" Gizmo asked.

Max shook his head. "She says she has something for us."

Dr. Lynn picked up Rocky and set him gently on her lap. Producing a red collar, she attached it around Rocky's neck.

Rocky yipped and wiggled, trying to escape. "Whoa, I don't need a collar! I never have, and I never will!"

"Hold on, Rocky," Dr. Lynn said in a soothing voice,

even as her strong hands kept him in place. "This is very, very important. I know you don't like it, but I need the three of you to wear these."

"But why?" Rocky said with a whine.

Dr. Lynn finished clasping the collar around Rocky's neck, then set him back down next to Gizmo. "These collars have GPS devices attached. That means that no matter where you go, I will be able to track you. If you remove them, then I won't be able to find you. Understand?"

Max barked twice for yes.

"We already found *her*," Rocky grumbled. "I don't see why she needs to find us."

"Oh, Rocky," Gizmo said. "She knows what she's doing. Besides, I think you look very handsome with your new collar!"

Rocky ducked his head. "Yeah, yeah. Thanks."

Dr. Lynn quickly attached a green collar around Gizmo's neck, then a blue one around Max's. Max wasn't entirely pleased with his, either—it rubbed his fur. He hoped he'd get used to it soon.

The old woman fell quiet for a moment, then said, "I'm afraid, friends, that we have to part ways for now."

Max stiffened. He stared at Dr. Lynn, not wanting what he'd just heard to be true.

Dr. Lynn smiled sadly. "I know you came all this way to find me. And I wish I could spend more time with you. But it's urgent that I take the results of your blood tests to a special lab where my colleagues are working to find a cure, and if I take you with me..." She shook her head. "Many people are afraid of animals now, and even though it's not your fault, they blame dogs like you for what has happened. I don't want you to get hurt."

It made sense. Max remembered the three-ringed symbols that people had spray-painted in places where there were animals.

But the idea of losing the warmth and comfort of the first kind human they'd found in months made Max want to curl up into a ball and whimper.

The three dogs watched sadly as Dr. Lynn stood and walked out the bedroom door. Max and his friends followed her, trailing behind as she left the house and made her way back to the vet's office. Max saw a German Shepherd patrolling in the distance, but most of the other pets seemed to have turned in for the night. Some of the dogs and cats lay on the lawn and roof of the vet's office, snoring peacefully.

Dr. Lynn collected several boxes from the vet's office and loaded them into her white van. Max saw stacks of the orange-and-white barriers inside, ready to be laid out. The old woman also hefted out bag after bag of kibble and kitty chow, which she stacked in piles on the lawn, then filled all the empty bowls with water. Just as she had at the beach, she was leaving behind enough food for the animals to get by for a few more weeks, at least.

With her van all packed up, Dr. Lynn slammed the back door shut, then turned her attention to Max, Rocky, and Gizmo. "Remember," she said, smiling sadly, "you must keep your collars on. I'll leave a trail of beacons, so you'll always know where I'm going. I can't bring you with me in my van, but that doesn't mean you shouldn't stay close so that when I can collect you again, neither of us will have to go very far."

Kneeling down, she petted the three dogs one by one. "I'm not abandoning you. This will all be over soon. We'll see each other again, my friends."

She stood and climbed behind the wheel of the van. A moment later the headlights flashed on, and the engine grumbled to life. Max trembled as the van's tires crunched over the gravel driveway and turned onto the street.

"Oh, I'm going to miss her," Gizmo said softly.

Rocky darted in front of Max and Gizmo. "Why are we sitting here? Let's follow her! If she gets too far ahead, we might lose her! I don't trust these collar things."

Max longed to chase after the van, to find some way to open the back doors and sneak inside. Instead, as he watched the red taillights grow smaller, he said, "I'm going to miss her, too. But you heard what she said. It's too dangerous for us to go with her. There are more bad people who might hurt us."

"I can't believe people would do that," Gizmo said. "It seems so mean."

"Yeah, well, some humans can be mean," Rocky grumbled. "So what do we do now? Do we stay here and wait for her?"

Max shook his head. "We still have a promise to keep," he said, remembering his strange dream about the Collie on her parade float. "We have to go to Baton Rouge and find Belle. We made a promise to Boss."

"Oh, yeah," Rocky said. "And that's west, right?"

Gizmo sat next to Rocky. "Yes, it is. And I bet there's lots more animals who would like to know there's a cure coming. Lots of animals who would be less scared knowing their humans will be coming back soon."

"Exactly," Max said. "For now, we should get some more sleep. Tomorrow, we're back on the road."

The three dogs found a soft patch of ground on the vet's lawn. Max knew he sounded confident and in charge to his friends, but he couldn't help but ache inside.

It's almost over, he told himself as he drifted off to sleep. *The people will come home soon. Then everything will be back to normal.*

The words were only slightly comforting, but enough to ease him toward dreams.

Until a breeze carried a familiar musk past his nose.

Max snapped to attention and raised his head.

"Wolves!" he barked.

CHAPTER 15

A RISING FEAR

Rocky and Gizmo stiffened, their snouts raised as they, too, smelled the nearby stench of mangy, desperate wolves.

"Oh, no," Gizmo said. "I think the smell is coming from behind the vet's house. Isn't that where the farm animals are? We have to help them!"

His black fur bristling, Rocky shook his head. "We need to find the police dogs. They're supposed to be on patrol to keep the wolves away. Some job they did."

A concerned *moo* echoed from behind the vet's house, answered by the snort of a pig. The animals back there were starting to sense that something was wrong. Any minute now they would panic.

Max lowered his head and whispered, "We need to

move fast. I'm going to run up the road and find a police dog. You two wake any dogs and cats you can find and spread the word to the other pets to hide. We'll meet up at the farm pens."

"You got it, big guy," Rocky said.

"Please be quick!" Gizmo added.

The two of them darted across the grass to the nearest dog, a fat, wrinkled Pug who was snoring loudly. As Max ran toward the square, he heard the Pug sputtering and groaning.

Max galloped down the street, searching for one of the German Shepherds. The glow of the streetlamps revealed the shadowy figures of cats and dogs asleep on stoops and beneath bushes.

Just as Max neared the square, a glint of gold caught his eye. A large dog was walking around the base of the gazebo. The shine of gold was from the star on the dog's collar.

"Hey!" Max barked. "We need help!"

The Shepherd's pointed ears stood at attention as Max barreled toward her. "Whoa there," she said. "What's the problem?"

"It's wolves," Max said. "We smelled them near the vet's office. My friends and I will try to alert the other pets, but we don't know the town like you do."

The police dog stepped into the lamplight. "Are you certain? We've been patrolling all day because of those wolves. I don't see how they could have slipped past us."

"Well, they have," Max said. "Please find Julep and let him know. Tell him Max sent you."

"Understood." The police dog nodded curtly. "Go get your friends and try to stay out of sight. Leave the handling of the wolves to us trained professionals."

"Of course," Max lied.

The police dog ran toward the town hall. Max spun on his heels and raced back up the street to the vet's office, where barks and yips and yowls were growing louder by the second. By the time he reached the sidewalk, a half-dozen pets were awake and arguing with Rocky and Gizmo on the dark lawn.

"Don't listen to them," the black cat Minerva drawled. "I've lived here my whole life, and there are no wolves in the area, not a one. The notion is absurd."

Fat Porgy glared at Rocky and Gizmo. "You dogs are just trying to cause trouble—I can tell. I never liked you sort."

In the center of the lawn, Rocky paced in a frantic circle. "Well, I don't really like you much, either, bub. But we're trying to keep you from getting eaten by wolves."

The long-furred Lhasa Apso tossed its snout in the air, sending its fur whipping back. "The only thing in these parts that wants to eat pets is gators," it said. "And gators *never* come into town. Not even since the humans left."

"I dunno, Darlene," the squat Pug said to the Lhasa Apso. "There's some strange smell on the wind, and

216

the cows are starting to raise a fuss." The mooing had indeed grown louder, and Max could hear the squawks of chickens.

Stepping forward, Max let out a harsh, commanding bark. The cats on the porch hissed and backed into the shadows, while the four dogs—Darlene, the Pug, and two Golden Retriever puppies who had been sniffing at the mound of kibble bags—snapped to attention.

Rocky sighed in relief as he saw Max padding over the lawn. "Glad you're back, buddy," he said.

"Did you find the police?" Gizmo asked.

Max nodded, his attention on the other animals. "Listen up," he barked loudly. "Julep and the other German Shepherds are on their way, but none of you is safe here. You need to hide and tell the others to do the same."

Minerva rolled her green eyes. "I already told your little friends: There aren't any wolves! You dogs are all just so terribly *dumb*." She cleared her throat. "Bless your hearts."

Max growled and took a step forward. "So you're willing to risk yourself and your friends just because you don't like dogs?"

"I do as I please," the black cat said, then licked a paw and swiped her face.

The crunching of stiff paper met Max's ears, and he turned to see that one of the Golden Retriever puppies had climbed the mountain of kibble. "Why's all these bags here?" the puppy asked. "There's food in them. I can smell it."

"Where's the old lady's van?" the other Golden Retriever called out.

"Hey," the Pug barked. "The little 'un's right! The van is gone!"

That got everyone's attention. "Did she leave?" the boy Golden Retriever puppy asked.

"Of course not," Minerva spat.

"But all the other people left us!"

Darlene, the Lhasa Apso, whimpered. "She wouldn't do that to us, would she?"

Growling, Rocky asked, "Why won't they listen?"

Gizmo nuzzled Rocky's side until the Dachshund calmed down. "We have to keep trying," she said.

Max started to speak, but the terrified squeal of a pig echoed through the night air. He didn't stop to think. As he raced around the side of the vet's house, he called back, "Do whatever you can to get them to safety! I'll handle the wolves for now!"

"Got it!" Gizmo called after him.

Max galloped behind the vet's office. The light next to the back door cast a pale yellow glow. He could see a big metal shed at the end of the yard, the darkened woods behind it. Inside the shed were the cows, four in total. He could barely make out a calf in the shed, resting on a mound of hay.

Here, a white fence divided the yard into four areas.

Aside from the cows' space, there were three smaller pens holding three goats, two pigs, and several chickens. Each pen contained a large supply of food.

One of the pigs stood on all fours, quivering and struggling for breath. The other lay on her belly and looked up at Max with worry.

"I'm telling ya, Lucy, I saw something," the standing pig said. "It was dark and covered in fur, and oh, its eyes."

Lucy snorted. "I believe you, Ricky. I do. But are you sure it wasn't one of the dogs from town? They've been spending a lot of time here lately."

"I saw it, too!" a high-pitched voice warbled.

The speaker was a brown-feathered chicken. It scratched at the dirt with its talons, then waddled to the fence.

The chicken's head bobbed up and down. "It looked wild," it squawked. "If it was a dog, it surely wasn't anyone's pet. I don't trust dogs, especially not ones from the swamp!"

Ricky moaned. "Oh, see, Lucy, it's true. Something is wrong!"

Max cleared his throat and stepped into the light from the back porch.

Terrified clucks rose up from the mesh-lined chicken coop. "Lettie Mae, get inside, girl!" one of the chickens cried from their small home. "You're gonna get ate!"

Ricky shoved himself into the back corner of his pen,

his trotters digging into the dirt and hay. "It's back! I told you, Lucy, I told you!"

"Shh," Max said, stepping closer. "I'm not here to hurt you. I'm a normal dog. See?"

The two pigs timidly approached the front of their pen, as did Lettie Mae. Another chicken bravely took a few steps outside the coop.

"You're just a dog after all," Lucy said. "We're scaring ourselves for nothing."

"Actually, there is something in the woods," Max said quietly. "But I'm here to help, and the police dogs are on their way."

Lettie Mae ruffled her feathers. "Are we in danger?"

"Not with me around," Max said. "But I need you all to keep quiet and act like nothing is happening. If you panic, the wolves might stop trying to be stealthy and attack."

"Wolves!" Ricky said, trembling. "I've heard of wolves. They're big and bad!"

Lucy nudged her partner with her snout. "You heard the dog. We have to keep quiet."

"What's happening?" one of the goats bleated. "Is there something new to chew?"

A gust of wind rose up from the north, and the stench of manure and the tickling scent of hay swirled into Max's nostrils—followed immediately by the musk of wolves.

"Tell the goats what's happening," Max said to the

pigs. "And the cows, too." To the chickens, he added, "You ladies should keep inside."

"Don't have to tell me twice," one chicken clucked.

While the chickens crowded inside their coop and the pigs whispered warnings to their fellow barn animals, Max crept silently toward the trees behind the metal shed. One cow, sturdy with brown and white spots, watched him with big, concerned eyes as she lapped up water from her trough.

Reaching the side of the shed, Max dropped to his belly. The grass here was high, and smooth pebbles bit into his flesh. Behind him the farm animals were silent, though he could hear their hooves as they paced restlessly.

Max lay there, taking in shallow breaths. He felt silly, like a cat waiting to pounce on some unsuspecting rodent, but walking out in the open was just going to alert the wolves and make them run to some other part of town—or, worse, attack Max head on.

He didn't have to wait long.

If he hadn't been listening so intently, he might never have heard the soft, padding footsteps, carefully avoiding twigs that might crunch and give them away.

Two shadowy figures stepped out of the line of trees. One was a terribly thin, lithe wolf covered in patchy red-brown fur. Its head seemed narrower than those of the wolves Max had met before, but there was no mistaking the wildness in its yellow eyes—or the sharpness of its fangs.

Max had to fight to contain a frustrated growl upon seeing the other wolf.

It was Dolph.

Dolph, who'd burned down Rocky's home, right after the humans had disappeared. Dolph, who'd stalked Max and his friends through towns and cities, who'd killed poor Raoul, who'd attacked the riverboat home of a bunch of innocent, frightened dogs.

Dolph was relentless in his search for Max. For some reason, the beast couldn't rest until he'd finished off Max, once and for all.

And now Dolph was *here.*

The gray wolf stood larger than his red wolf companion, far worse for wear than when Max had seen him last. He was so thin that Max could see his ribs, and new wounds had joined the three white scars on his snout. A bald patch on his side revealed pale, tender flesh where the fur had been burned away. On the opposite side of his body were two red slashes that had only recently scabbed over, and he now walked with a slight limp.

Dolph's companion sniffed the air, but the breeze still flowed from the north, so Max's scent wasn't reaching the wolves.

"There's no one about," the wolf said. "Let's take the food."

Dolph glared at the smaller wolf. "We must be sure, Rudd. Trained, well-fed dogs patrol the streets. I have also heard rumors of a human in this place."

Rudd snorted. "I do not fear dogs or humans," he spat. "I fear nothing!"

Rounding on the smaller wolf, Dolph snapped his jaws. Rudd flinched but did not back away.

"Look at me," Dolph demanded. "See the wounds that dogs and humans can inflict. See the blood drawn by the monsters of these woods." He took a threatening step toward his companion. "Do you see?"

Snarling, Rudd said, "I see."

"And do you remember that were it not for me taking these new wounds, your other pack members would not have lived to join me?"

"I remember."

"You know my strength, then," the wolf leader growled. "You know I am smart."

"Yes, Dolph. But I still don't understand why we do not get ourselves a cow."

"We lack the strength," Dolph said. "We would be able to take down only one of the cows, and the rest would stomp us beneath their hooves."

"The pigs or chickens, then," Rudd said. "They are smaller."

"No," Dolph said. "I have thought it through. Because of the fences, we would not be able to take our meat away. The patrolling dogs would descend, and we would have to battle."

"Your plan is beneath us," Rudd growled.

"It is the only option we have," Dolph snapped. "We

are starving. We have no choice but to"—the gray wolf spat out the next word—"*negotiate*. We must ask the dogs to share their food."

Rudd shook his head. "How can we do that? The dogs will not trust us."

Dolph looked away into the shadowy trees. "I came this way following my enemy. *Max*. Despite our past, he might help me."

Max stiffened. The last thing he expected was for Dolph to ask for help. Not after all he'd done.

"Max," Rudd said. "A sheltered house pet. Many of us do not believe he is as dangerous as you say."

Dolph lowered his voice. "I would never have believed it myself, had I not seen him in action. He is the worst enemy we wolves have. He is also our only hope to stay alive."

It had to be a trick, Max thought. Maybe the wolves had smelled him there after all.

But both animals looked beyond starving and were covered in fresh wounds. Maybe the wolves had run afoul of the gators, too.

Despite his anger at Dolph, and all the anguish and horror the wolf had put him through, Max felt nothing but pity. The wolf's eyes, once defiant, seemed faded and sad. If Dolph, the leader of the pack, was in this condition, then how bad were the other wolves?

Max swallowed and made a decision. After all the compassion and care he'd seen Dr. Lynn give to others and to him, it felt wrong to not do the same. And maybe, if he helped, the wolves would leave the pets and farm animals alone, and would finally stop chasing Max, Rocky, and Gizmo.

Max climbed to his feet and took a few cautious steps out of the darkness. Dolph noticed him immediately and went stiff.

"Hello," Max said softly. "I heard what you said. I want to help."

Before Dolph could respond, the red wolf beside him snarled. "Meat," Rudd cried. "I am so hungry. I must eat the meat!"

Jaws open wide to tear into Max, Rudd leaped.

CHAPTER 16

A TEPID TRUCE

Max didn't have time to move.

Dolph bellowed, "Rudd, stop!" But the smaller wolf didn't listen.

Rudd flew toward Max, his teeth aimed at Max's neck, his claws stretched forward.

Then, from Max's right, a black-and-copper blur soared through the air and collided with Rudd's side midleap. The two animals smashed into the metal shed with a heavy, resounding clang, then thudded to the ground. From inside the shed, the calf bleated in terror, followed by the moos of the startled cows.

Hackles raised, Max bared his teeth. He watched as the red wolf struggled to get up, but the other creature was larger and sturdier. A blue collar and gold star revealed Rudd's attacker as a police dog. Max recognized the black snout and red-tinged body at once.

Julep.

The leader of the police dogs towered over Rudd, his mouth pulled back to show his teeth.

"Let me go!" Rudd spat. "I must feed!"

"Not a chance," Julep drawled. "Simmer down, wolf, or you're not going anywhere." Glancing at Max, he added, "You all right?"

Relaxing slightly, Max said, "I am. Thanks for coming."

Behind Max came the startled cries of the chickens, pigs, and goats, followed by more moos from the cows. Dozens of paws beat a heavy rhythm into the yard.

Max turned to see Dixie and five other police dogs running to join their leader. Next to them ran Rocky and Gizmo.

"So it's true," said a female police dog as the pack formed a half-circle around Julep and the angry, snapping wolf. "There were wolves in the woods. How did we not know this?"

"We were spread too thin," Julep said. "And we were not as prepared as we should have been. We will run new drills starting tomorrow."

From under the police dog, Rudd howled, "You speak as if I am not here. Fear me, dog!"

Julep swatted the wolf with his paw. "Hush."

Reaching Max, Gizmo leaped up and hugged him around his front leg. "You're okay!" she said. "I heard all the noise and knew I should come."

Rocky scrabbled backward, his eyes on the woods. "Big guy, it's Dolph! He's here!"

All the police dogs turned to look into the shadowed trees. Dolph still stood there, tall and defiant.

Growling, Dixie stepped toward the scarred creature. "Do not attempt to enter our town, wolf," she said. "We will not let you harm the animals under our protection."

Dolph glared at the line of Shepherds and snorted.

Julep carefully stepped off Rudd. He nipped at Rudd's side, and the red wolf howled before running back to Dolph, his tail between his legs. Julep barked, "You heard the officer. You are not welcome here."

Dolph roared, the sound sudden and loud. Max jerked in surprise, and the farm animals squawked and squealed.

Rounding on Rudd, Dolph lashed out with his claws, drawing a line of blood from the wolf's snout.

"Control yourself!" he bellowed as Rudd cowered. "If our numbers were not so small, I would exile you for your actions!"

"Sorry, Dolph," Rudd gasped.

"Take your problems somewhere else!" Julep commanded.

Dolph hesitated until his eyes met Max's.

229

"Julep, wait," Max said. "Rudd acted on his own. His alpha, Dolph, came to ask for help."

Dixie growled. "Why would we help wolves?"

Max shoved through the line of German Shepherds to face Dolph. Instinct screamed at Max to run, or fight, to take down the wild animal before he could do any harm. Even in his weakened state, Dolph still looked fearsome and dangerous.

But Max's thoughts returned once more to Dr. Lynn, and to Boss, and Raoul, and Madame Curie—all the leaders who'd put others before themselves. Maybe if Max had never been blasted by Praxis he wouldn't have considered being compassionate, though he hoped he would.

He had to help.

"Do I have your word," Max said slowly, not looking away from Dolph's face, "that if we let your pack through and give you some of our food, you will eat and leave without harming anyone?"

Dolph's body trembled, and his lip twitched, as if holding back a snarl. Through clenched teeth, the gray wolf said, "You have my word."

"What are you doing, buddy?" Rocky asked. "This is Dolph we're talking about! He's been trying to kill us for weeks now!"

Max sighed. "I know, Rocky. But look at them. They're starving. It would be cruel to let them die."

His whole body quivering, Rocky backed away from Max toward the stern, silent Shepherds.

"I don't care!" Rocky howled. "That other wolf just tried to attack you, big guy. There's no way we can trust them."

"Dolph tried to stop him," Max said.

The wolf leader nipped at Rudd's side, and the red wolf flinched and slunk deeper into the shadows.

"He will be punished," Dolph said.

Rocky raised his snout. "Nope, no way. Your pack tried to *eat* us," he said. "Gizmo, you remember. He called you Bite Size!"

The terrier darted her head back and forth between Rocky and Dolph.

"I think I agree with Max," she said finally. "We should help them."

Rocky's eyes went wide. "What? Are you crazy?"

"Oh, Rocky, don't be so dramatic," Gizmo said. "*Smell* them. They smell of fear and pain. We have to help." Wagging her tail, she looked at Dolph. "And maybe we can finally come to some sort of peace."

Dolph did not reply. He glared at Gizmo, then averted his gaze.

Max lowered his head to lick Rocky's side. "It'll be okay. And if things do go wrong, I'll protect you."

Sighing, Rocky dropped to his belly and set his head on his paws. "Fine, I guess. As long as they leave us alone."

Someone cleared his throat, and Max looked up from Rocky to see Julep towering over him, a tense, grim shadow.

"You might be forgetting," Julep said, "that you are not the one in charge here."

Max ducked his head. "I'm sorry, Julep. I don't mean to overstep. It's just—"

"I heard all you said," the police-dog leader said. "Come with me." To Dixie, he added, "You, too. The rest of you, keep an eye on these wolves."

Julep turned from Max and brushed past his officers to head back toward the animal pens. Max glanced over his shoulder at Dolph, then followed.

Julep, Dixie, Max, Rocky, and Gizmo huddled by the white fence that surrounded the barnyard. Before anyone could speak, one of the cows mooed loudly.

"We are all in such a state," she said, her brown eyes wide with fear. "What is happening? Are there really predators?"

"Don't fret your pretty head, Buttercup," Julep said to the big animal. "Just go back into the shed. We're taking care of it."

The cow looked uncertain, but Julep offered her a reassuring wag of his tail. Once Buttercup was out of sight, Julep's tail went still.

"What's this I hear about you lot being able to understand human talk?" he asked.

Max blinked in surprise. "What does that have to do with the wolves?"

Dixie burst out, "You mentioned it earlier! Something about pixies or taxes."

"Praxis?" Gizmo asked.

"Yes! Praxis!" Dixie said. "It seemed crazy, but you said it let you talk to humans."

"I hardly believed Dixie's story myself," Julep said. "But then I got reports of the old woman taking you to the big house, and some said it seemed like the three of you were conversing with her."

"I still don't understand why you're bringing this up now," Max said.

Dixie rolled her eyes. "Don't you see? An animal who can truly understand humans, not just a few simple commands, would be the best companion any human could hope for."

Julep nodded. "Our K9 force would be able to work with our human officers better than ever before."

Max asked, "But what about the wolves?"

"I see what they're getting at," Rocky said. "Clever. They know we want to help the wolves, and we need their permission to do so. They're going to make us give them what they want before they'll help."

"Is that true?" Max asked.

Julep sat down and scratched his ear. "It sounds like a reasonable trade to me."

Dixie's tail was a blur. "It sure does. You're going to tell us how to get this Praxis, aren't you? You have to!"

Gizmo growled. "I can't believe you police dogs wouldn't help just to make sure the town pets don't get hurt."

"It's all right, Gizmo," Max said, nuzzling her side.

Meeting Julep's eyes, he said, "Fine. Once the wolves have been fed, we'll tell you how to be changed like us."

Rising to all fours once more, Julep wagged his tail. "I knew you would make the right choice."

He marched back to his line of police dogs, who sat watching Dolph and Rudd. The others trailed behind.

"All right, wolf," Julep barked. "Gather your pack. We will let you eat."

"Kibble!" Dixie added from behind him.

Julep cleared his throat. "We will let you eat *kibble*. Everything—and everyone—else is off-limits. Understood?"

Dolph nodded. He growled a command at Rudd, and the smaller wolf nodded before darting back through the trees.

For a moment, the alpha wolf met Max's eyes. Max hoped to see thanks in them, but he couldn't tell what Dolph was thinking.

Then Dolph disappeared into the darkness to collect the rest of his pack.

While they waited, Julep sent one of his force to alert the remainder of their team. He returned moments later with ten more dogs. The canine police stood evenly spaced in two lines, forming a path through the grass.

Max, Rocky, and Gizmo sat watching the trees. The cows, chickens, pigs, and goats huddled together, bleating and mooing and squawking among themselves. None could sleep.

Then, finally, the underbrush rustled, and the wolves emerged.

Dolph's pack was fewer than it had been back near the riverboat, only about ten total, and many of the faces Max had seen there were now gone. In their place were a half-dozen new wolves who looked similar to Rudd—slightly smaller in stature than the gray wolves, with reddish-brown fur.

With Dolph in the lead, the wolves kept their heads and tails low as they slunk between the lines of German Shepherds. They were all so skinny they seemed little more than bones and flesh, and their fur was patchy and sparse. Some bore scars and wounds like Dolph, though none were scarred as severely as their leader.

Though Rudd averted his eyes, a few of the other wolves cast defiant glances and bared their teeth at the police dogs. All it took was a growl or a bark from one of the Shepherds, though, and the wild beasts fell back in line.

The chickens gasped as the wolves passed by, most of them darting inside their coop. Max saw Ricky the pig faint into an unconscious, hairy pink heap.

But the wolves made no attempt to attack the livestock. As the police dogs marched alongside them past the vet's office, the wolf pack remained in two orderly lines.

"Come on," Max said to Rocky and Gizmo as Dolph's wolves and their police escorts disappeared from view. "Let's go around the other side and catch up."

In the vet's driveway, they found several pets still arguing among themselves: the Lhasa Apso, the Pug, Minerva the black cat, the boy Golden Retriever puppy, and, surprisingly, Georgie.

The Saint Bernard sat away from the other animals on the grass. His head drooped as he watched them bicker, a puddle of drool forming at his feet.

"I'm telling you, she'll be back!" Minerva yowled, her tail flicking in annoyance. "There is no use going after her."

"But Dee and Zee said walking the roads was no trouble at all," the Golden Retriever puppy said. "They said the walk from Baton Rouge was fun!"

Minerva swiped a paw at him. "Walking for miles out of doors is no fun!"

"Hey, leave him alone," the Pug said with a growl.

"What if she doesn't come back?" yipped the Lhasa Apso, Darlene. "We need her!"

No one noticed Max, Rocky, and Gizmo at first— until Georgie's tail thumped heavily against the ground, and he bellowed, "There you are!"

"Georgie!" Gizmo said. "How was your evening?"

The big, drooping dog came to meet them. "It was good! I met some other dogs from Baton Rouge who know stuff about Belle." Lowering his voice, he asked, "Is it true? Did the old lady in the hat leave?"

Max nodded. "It's true. But—"

"What?" Minerva yowled.

"Oh, no!" Darlene moaned.

The Golden Retriever puppy spun in a frantic circle. "We gotta go find the lady!"

Before Max, Rocky, or Gizmo could say anything, they found themselves surrounded.

"Did you see where she went?"

"You made her go!"

"How are we supposed to eat?"

Max backed away, trying to figure out whom to answer first.

But he didn't have to. New, musky smells filled the yard, and all the animals went still. The procession of wolves had arrived.

As they saw Dolph's pack slink onto the lawn, the animals' voices rose once again—this time as yowls and yips of fear.

"Wolves," Georgie gasped. "Oh, no."

"Don't worry, big guy," Rocky reassured him. "They'll be leaving soon."

As the pets stood frozen, the police dogs formed a circle around the stack of kibble bags in the yard.

"Can we feed?" Dolph growled.

Julep nodded at the wolf leader. "One bag. Just one. Have at it."

And the wolves turned into a blur.

They swarmed the mountain of dog food. Dolph

opened his jaw wide and wrenched into the bag as though biting into fresh kill. Yanking his head back and forth, he tore a hole, letting the kibble cascade free.

Though the police dogs remained firm and stone still, all the pets watched with wide eyes as the starving wolves attacked the food. They nipped one another's sides, clawing and fighting their way into the pile of kibble with snarls and growls. Sharp teeth flashed, and their yellow eyes seemed to glow in the dark. Only Dolph, as pack leader, ate without being bothered.

Then, it was over. Satiated, the wolves fell back, leaving nothing behind but the shredded remnants of the kibble bag.

"That's it," Julep barked. "You're done. We will escort you back to the woods."

Huffing, their eyes still frenzied, the wolves formed a line. All except Dolph.

The wolf leader limped toward the driveway, his pale eyes narrowed. As he reached the circle, two of the police dogs blocked his way.

"Max," Dolph snarled. "I must speak to Max."

"You heard Julep," one of the dogs barked. "Back in line."

"It's fine," Max said. "I'll speak with him."

From the sidewalk, Julep nodded, and the police dogs parted to let Max through, Rocky and Gizmo behind him.

"Is your pack well fed?" Max asked.

Dolph ignored the question. "We are not done," he said.

Max shook his head, certain he'd misheard. After he'd made sure the wolves wouldn't go hungry, he at least expected a thank-you.

"I don't know what you mean," Max said.

Dolph barked, "Yes, you do, mutt. We have unfinished business. We will leave now, but I will not stop my pursuit of you."

"That's not fair!" Gizmo barked at Dolph. "We helped you! Why won't you leave us alone?"

Dolph glared at her but said nothing.

Rocky gently nudged Gizmo's side. "They're wolves," the Dachshund said. "I told you, we can't trust them."

Growling, Dolph met Max's eyes. "I am not unreasonable. We will leave this town alone, since they gave us food. We have no quarrel with them. You also helped me feed, and though it does not erase your past misdeeds, it is enough that I will give you a day's head start— beginning at dawn."

The wolf put out a paw, but the police dogs moved in, and he pulled back.

"You'd better leave this place first thing in the morning, Max," Dolph said. "Once our strength is regained and we can feed ourselves in the natural way, we will come for you, stronger and faster than before."

Max trembled. His heart pounded.

Just as finding Dr. Lynn hadn't ended his journey,

this small truce hadn't ended the wolf's crusade against him. Dolph was unrelenting. No matter what he went through, he always got back on his feet and continued his quest to destroy Max.

Max could have roared at the wolf leader or tried to fight him and catch him off guard. Instead, he said, "All right, Dolph. Just as long as we have your word you'll leave this town alone."

"You have it," Dolph spat.

The wolf leader turned and limped back to his pack. As the police dogs lined up to escort the wolves to the trees, Dolph's voice rang out. "See you soon, Max," he cried. "See you very, very soon."

CHAPTER 17

UNWELCOME

Everyone sat still and silent as the German Shepherds escorted the wolves out of town.

Then there was chaos as the assembled pets realized what a narrow escape they'd had. Darlene yowled in unbridled panic, then collapsed in the grass, her eyes covered.

The Pug barked, "What do we do? We need to do something! What if they come back?"

One of the Golden Retriever puppies asked Minerva, "So, do you want to stay here now, kitty?"

In answer, Minerva hissed and spat, lashing out with her razor claws, narrowly missing the pup's face. He whimpered and ran off to where his sister sat with a few other young dogs.

Rocky and Gizmo huddled next to Max, ignoring the panicking pets and whispering to each other about Dolph's betrayal. Georgie melted into a large, tearful puddle in the grass.

All Max could think about were Dolph's parting words. The wolf hadn't even seemed angry, really. He'd been calm, almost rational, as if no longer seeking Max's death out of rage, but from another deep, hidden emotion.

"What's all this?" a dog barked. It was Julep, who was marching past the mound of kibble bags with Dixie.

Minerva darted through the grass. As soon as she reached the two police dogs, she hissed. "How dare you," said the black cat. "How dare you!"

"How dare us what, Miss Minerva?" Julep asked.

Minerva snapped her tail. "You know what! Your pack just escorted a whole herd of wild beasts through our town. Those creatures could have attacked me." Fur bristling, she added, "And I bet they have my scent now, too. They'll be after me for sure."

Dixie stepped around the cat and nosed Darlene until the Lhasa Apso lowered the paw covering her eyes.

"We have it under control," Julep said as Dixie nudged the other panicked animals into paying attention. "If we hadn't helped those wolves, they might well have attacked us. Now that their bellies are full, they're much less likely to come back."

The Pug blinked. "Um, didn't that wolf say that he'd be going after Max here?"

"He did," Darlene yipped. "I heard him clear as the town bell. Those dogs led the wolves here; then they scared off the old lady."

"Hey!" Rocky barked. "We didn't do any of that."

"It's true," Minerva said. "Everything was fine before these mutts appeared."

A puppy whimpered. "Why did they do that to us?"

"They have to leave," Darlene wailed. "Right now, Julep. Make them leave!"

"Enough!" Julep bellowed.

The German Shepherd stalked forward, glaring at each of them. Dixie stood on the gravel, watching silently.

"You all go home and sleep," Julep said. "My officers and I will get this straightened out. Get."

"But—" Minerva yowled.

"I said get!"

Grumbling among themselves, Minerva and the other animals left the lawn and disappeared down the darkened street. Julep and Dixie watched them go while Max, Rocky, and Gizmo huddled together on the grass. Georgie lay nearby, depressed and blubbering.

When the pets were out of sight, the police dogs came to sit in front of Max and his friends.

"Seems you have some explaining to do," Julep said.

"Several of my officers swear they saw the old lady drive out of town, and seeing as how her van is gone, I'm inclined to believe them."

"We didn't make her go away," Gizmo said. "We would never do that. I can't believe the things that cat was saying about us!"

Julep chuckled. "I trust you, little lady. But we still need to know what happened."

"And you're supposed to tell us about Praxis!" Dixie added.

"It's all right, Gizmo," Max said with a sigh. "They have the right to know what happened."

Max started with everything Dr. Lynn had told them about the virus and what it could do. He explained that Dr. Lynn left to continue working on the cure that would let all the people come home. Georgie confirmed that she'd helped groups of animals like this before.

But of course what the two police dogs wanted to know most about was Praxis.

So Max explained about the laboratory: the white room that blasted electricity, and Gertrude the pig, who oversaw everything with an elephant nicknamed the Mountain. He provided directions to the lab as best he could.

Dixie trembled with excitement. "That doesn't sound too far," she said. "How long will it take us?"

"You really don't want to go back that way," Rocky

said. "It took us weeks, and we barely made it here in one piece!"

"And won't you be leaving the town unprotected?" Gizmo asked.

Julep paced back and forth on the lawn, while Dixie watched him, waiting for her leader to speak. "Here's what I think," Julep finally said. "We almost let wolves slip through today because our patrols weren't as good as they ought to be. Fact is, without the human officers we're not as well prepared to protect this town as we should be. Being smarter would help a lot." He looked at Gizmo. "But you're right, we can't leave the town unprotected."

"But Julep!" Dixie barked. "We have to go—we just have to!"

Julep raised a paw. "Now hold on. Let me finish. What I was going to say is that we'll leave most of the K9 team here to keep things orderly. But you and I will go to this lab and find this pig."

Dixie was practically dancing. "Oh, this is great! I can't wait to leave!"

"Let's see how she feels a week from now," Rocky muttered to Gizmo and Max.

Clearing his throat, Max rose to his feet. "Well, good luck on your journey. I hope Praxis is everything you want it to be. If it's all right with you, my friends and I should sleep. It's been a long day."

Julep nodded. "Of course." The Shepherd started

to walk away, then looked back at Max. "But Max, the other pets might be right. I don't blame you for the old lady leaving, but there's no denying the wolf pack is after you. As long as you and your friends are in town, we aren't safe. You have to move on first thing. Got it?"

Max's stomach felt hollow as Dolph's words echoed through his mind once more. He looked down at his two small, exhausted friends, who were already halfway asleep. They hadn't even had a full day to spend in this town. It seemed so unfair.

But they had no choice.

"We understand," Max said softly. "We'll leave first thing in the morning."

Max lay on the rough floorboards of the front porch, in a darkened corner that shaded him from the glow of the streetlamps. Despite being so tired, he slept in fits and starts, opening his eyes several times to discover it was still night. The gentle snores of his friends wafted across the lawn together with the grunting of farm animals and the chirping of crickets.

Finally, after hours of battling for sleep, Max rose to all fours. He opened his jaws wide and blinked his heavy eyes, then trotted down the porch steps and onto the front walkway.

The air was thick with moisture that clung to the blades of grass and to Max's fur. In the east, Max saw pink and orange seeping into the sky. Dawn was almost here. Which meant he and his friends needed to get out of town.

Yawning, Max went to the huddled pile of tan-and-black fur that was Rocky and Gizmo and nosed their sides until they woke up. Then he did the same to Georgie.

The big dog scrambled to his feet. "What is it?" he asked. "Are the wolves back? Or is it the gators?"

"Shh," Max whispered. "No, we're still safe, Georgie. It's dawn, though. We need to leave."

Georgie's head drooped so low that his long, floppy ears almost touched the ground. "Oh, yeah. That."

Rocky and Gizmo were already tearing into one of the bags of kibble. Max couldn't help but notice that the shreds of the bag the wolves had devoured still littered the front yard. Whole patches of the lawn had been clawed up.

Dolph's words came back to Max again, but he couldn't succumb to fear, not now. He needed to focus on the next leg of their journey.

Kibble poured free from the bag the two small dogs had bit into, and they leaped back, tails wagging, as they watched their prize pool over the grass. Rocky said, "That's the stuff. Beef flavor!"

"Good choice," Gizmo said, then stuck her snout into the pile.

"We need to eat quickly," Max said. "We may have found Dr. Lynn, but we still need to find Belle. We made a promise."

Georgie's head rose from the kibble. "Oh, that reminds me," the big dog said. "Last night I told you I met some dogs from Baton Rouge." Georgie cleared his throat. "Well, they had some things to say about Belle that you should know."

Max nodded. "All right. We'll talk to them before we leave."

Max joined Georgie, Rocky, and Gizmo in eating kibble, then the four of them lapped up water from one of the many bowls Dr. Lynn had filled. Bellies full, Max asked Georgie to lead the way.

They walked by the home where they'd had those brief, wonderful hours curled up with Dr. Lynn. Max stared longingly through its wrought-iron fence as they passed, wishing he were still inside in front of a flickering fire, his head resting on the woman's lap.

The collar she'd placed around his neck bit slightly into his skin, but Max decided he liked having it. As long as he wore it, she could find them again.

And as long as he wore it, he wouldn't forget that the end of his journey was close.

As they passed tall, stately homes, Max saw the shadows of dogs and cats just waking up from where they'd slept on grass or beneath bushes, on porches or atop eaves. At the end of the street, where another road ran north to south, Georgie stopped walking. They stood on what was once a playground. Grass rose up taller than Max, hiding swings and the lower portion of a slide.

Dr. Lynn hadn't ventured here with her lawn mower. They'd reached the town's outer limits.

"This is the place," Georgie said, gesturing toward the big brick house on the corner. It was the same as every other house on the street—several stories tall with a white-painted porch. A picket fence surrounded the yard.

Georgie nosed past the gate, which squeaked on rusting hinges, then held it open for the others. "Around back," he said.

Inside the yard, Max caught scent of several dogs—and heard them barking excitedly.

"Good catch!"

"Watch it, it's coming for you!"

"Woo-hoo! Did you see the air Jay got?"

Max peered around the corner to see five medium-sized dogs racing through the backyard, their tongues hanging out, looking like they were having the time of their lives. One of them had a bright green Frisbee in his mouth, which he released with a snap of his neck. The neon disk soared through the air until one of his companions caught it in her jaws. The other dogs laughed and barked in approval.

They were nearly identical, slightly smaller than Max, with shaggy black fur that covered most of their bodies. They had white fur on their bellies and chests and in a stripe down their foreheads. Their ears were pointed and alert, their yellow eyes open wide in excitement.

Border Collies, like the puppies at the beach!

"Georgie!" one of the females cried. "Did you come back to play?"

"Hi, Em!" he barked back. "Afraid not. I brought my friends I was telling you about, the ones who are looking for Belle."

The mood in the backyard changed in an instant. The dog with the Frisbee let it drop to the grass, and the five Border Collies stared at Max, Rocky, and Gizmo.

"Brr," Rocky muttered. "Is it just me, or did it just get chilly out here?"

"It still feels warm to me," Max said.

Gizmo chuckled nervously. "I think he means how they're acting, Max. But maybe they're just shy. Let's go say hi."

Max, Rocky, and Gizmo trotted across the grass. The Border Collies still stared, silent.

Georgie cleared his throat. "These are the dogs from Baton Rouge," he said. "Dee, Jay, Kay, Em, and Zee."

Gizmo wagged her tail. "Wow, you came all the way from Baton Rouge. How brave!"

"Not really," the male named Jay said. "It's not that far."

Rocky tilted his head. "Why did you leave? Were you looking for your people?"

The dogs glanced at one another. "We don't really have any people," Em said. "I mean, the people who raised us were just looking to sell us off. They never had a chance, though."

"Then why did you come here?" Max asked.

251

Em licked her lips, then sighed. "Well, we weren't taking too kindly to the way our neighbors were acting, the way they were forming packs and making demands. So we decided to head out on our own." She asked Max, "Why are you looking for Belle, anyway?"

"We made a promise to a friend of hers who is no longer with us," Max said. "An old Australian Shepherd named Boss. He wished for her to know that he didn't abandon her on purpose."

The Border Collies gasped.

"Oh, Boss," Dee said. "We liked him. I can't believe he's gone."

Sniffling, Kay hid her head in Zee's fur. Zee licked her reassuringly.

"You've come a long way for Boss," Em said, fighting back her own tears. "And Belle should rightly know what happened to him. Just...be careful."

Max remembered his dream of the animal parade and Belle's stormy float. Something told him finding the Collie wasn't going to be as easy as he'd hoped.

"Why should we be careful?" Max asked. "Boss told us Belle was known as the nicest dog in the city."

"Yeah," Rocky said. "He made her sound absolutely perfect."

"Oh, she was," Em said. "All I know is, things changed after the people left. Belle changed. Just please." The Border Collie met Max's eyes. "Be very, very careful."

CHAPTER 18

ALMOST THERE

Despite the Border Collies' warnings, Max asked for directions to Baton Rouge. Em begrudgingly agreed to aid them and scratched a map in the dirt.

"Thanks so much," Max told the Border Collies. "This is a big help."

Em ducked her head. "I hope so. And I hope when you find what you're looking for, you don't get hurt."

"I don't think any of us wants that," said Rocky.

With their path memorized, the dogs said their good-byes. Max was ashamed to tell the others that for a moment he'd considered not going after Belle. His dreams lately had seemed almost prophetic, and the most recent seemed to say something was wrong with Belle.

But images of Boss came back to Max, of the old dog lying near death on the shore of a mighty river, saying how sorry he was never to see Belle again. So Max, Rocky, Gizmo, and Georgie followed the Border Collie's directions out of town.

The rising sun burned away the mist, revealing a blue sky dotted with clouds. The swamp was far behind them now, and the air carried with it no real animal scents save for rabbits, mice, and squirrels hiding in the underbrush. The four dogs chatted about what they'd do when reunited with their families.

Like the others, Max enjoyed being clean and well fed. For the first time in a long while, the journey to find his people felt pleasant. By midday they discovered a gas station that hadn't been ransacked by other animals. They ate their fill from a bag of kibble and lapped up water that had pooled in a sink behind the checkout counter.

Evening began to fall as Max led them down a wide road between huge parking lots filled with all types of vehicles. Numbers were painted on the car windows, and Max guessed they were passing some sort of car store.

Max was wishing that he and his friends knew how to drive—imagine how easy getting around would be!—when Georgie barked excitedly. "Look!" he bellowed. "I know those buildings. That's Baton Rouge!"

Craning his neck, Max saw the silhouettes of tall buildings to the north.

"Em and the other dogs were right," Gizmo said. "We didn't have far to go at all."

"Maybe not," Rocky said, sizing up the skyline, "but this road is heading west. The city is north."

Max trotted up. "We just need to find the road that takes us in that direction, like in Em's map."

"This way!" Georgie barked, loping into a car lot. "I bet I can find it!"

As the other dogs watched in surprise, the giant Saint Bernard leaped onto the hood of a silver truck. Then Georgie howled. Though as loud as the wail of the Mudlurker, this howl was different, less desperate, speaking of friendship and hope.

Max, Rocky, and Gizmo stood in front of the truck, looking up at Georgie in awe. The howl seemed to last forever, but finally he lowered his snout.

Georgie angled his head to the side, waiting. Max, Rocky, and Gizmo glanced at one another, confused.

And then a distant howl pierced the evening sky. Another joined in, and another, each one echoing from the north. Soon they heard several barks, and Georgie nodded. Thumping his tail against the top of the truck, he looked down at his friends.

"The dogs say there's a shortcut up ahead. We just have to find a tunnel, go through it, and then we'll be on our way to the farm where I was born."

"That's amazing!" Gizmo said as Georgie leaped

down into the parking lot. "How did you know they would answer you?"

"A lot of us grew up together," Georgie said. "We used to practice call-and-response like that for fun. It sure came in handy today."

Rocky said, "What are we waiting for? Let's go find this tunnel!"

Georgie looked at Max, who said, "This is your hometown, so you lead the way."

The big dog didn't need to be told twice. He bounded forward through the maze of dusty, dirty cars to a tall chain-link fence. There they found a rusted gate that was easy to shove open for all four dogs to slip through. Next, Georgie led them through a field, periodically raising his fleshy snout in another howl. Every time he did, a bark would echo through the night sky, and Georgie would change their course slightly.

"This way," he woofed, disappearing into a small grove of trees.

Seconds later, Max heard the Saint Bernard let out a startled cry.

"Georgie!" Gizmo yipped, darting ahead. She, too, vanished into the trees—and then cried out as well.

"What's going on?" Rocky shouted. He barked, "Are you all right? Answer me, Giz!"

"We're fine!" Gizmo's voice rose up. "But there's a steep drop just past the trees. Watch your step!"

Rocky sighed in relief. "You first, big guy. If I slip on the way down, you'll give me a soft landing."

Max chuckled. "Glad to be of service." Carefully, he walked between two of the tall trees, taking each step slowly. All he could think about was his tumble into the massive sinkhole.

Finally, Max raised his left paw in the air—and when he tried to set it down, there was nothing. "Right here is the drop-off," Max said.

"Got it," Rocky said.

Max stepped forward once more, this time prepared. And then, the dirt crumbled beneath his paws.

"Whoa!" Max cried.

The dirt and pebbles beneath him cascaded, and Max had no choice but to run as fast as he could, his legs splashing into an ankle-deep stream of water.

Panting, Max turned to find Georgie and Gizmo rolling in the water to clean the dirt off their fur.

"That wasn't so bad." Rocky waddled casually into the ditch, having followed Max's path. "Just have to maintain your balance."

Gizmo jumped to her feet and shook herself, sending water flying through the air.

"Yeah, yeah," she said as she splashed through the water to Rocky's side. "You were prepared!"

Georgie hung his head. "Sorry about that. None of the dogs mentioned that drop. But—we're here!"

Max looked past Georgie, hoping that *here* meant the city. But what Georgie was referring to was the tunnel, a giant concrete pipe built under a hill, big enough for a car to drive through. The ditch was an extension of the pipe. Max had never seen one quite this big.

The tunnel was dark and smelled of moldering plants and rotten food. The stench was almost like that of the swamp, and Max half expected to see one of the gators step out of the darkness.

"So, that's our shortcut, huh?" Rocky said. "Your friends don't know any other routes, do they, Georgie?"

Georgie's face drooped. "No. Did I do bad?"

"Of course not!" Gizmo said. "I'm sure it'll be fine. The dogs wouldn't have sent us here if it wasn't safe. Right, Max?"

Max felt uneasy. After all the terrors they'd faced, why should he be scared of what lay ahead? They'd come this far, he reminded himself. They just had to hold on a little longer.

"I'm sure it's fine," Max said. "Let's just get through it so we can find Belle."

Reassured by Max's show of confidence, Rocky, Gizmo, and Georgie fell in line behind him.

A dead tree lay half in the ditch, and a rusting shopping cart lay on its side. Max wound past the debris, crinkling his nose. At least the tunnel was so big they wouldn't have to brush up against the slimy walls.

It was not quite pitch-black in the tunnel—moonlight

streamed in from the far end—but it was dark enough that they had no choice but to walk forward blindly and hope nothing was in their way.

They were about halfway through the tunnel, with the patch of light at the other end growing steadily larger, when Max felt something brush past his ankle. He stopped, his heart pounding.

"What is it?" Rocky whispered. "Is something wrong?"

"Oh!" Gizmo yipped before Max could answer. "I felt something."

The skittering of claws echoed through the tunnel, followed by dozens of tiny splashes. Shadowy shapes popped out of a crack in the wall up ahead.

"Oh, no," Georgie wailed. "I did do bad. I heard the directions wrong and led us into a trap!" Blubbering, the giant dog spun away from the group, as more of the creatures appeared in the tunnel.

Hissing voices rose up to join the skittering and splashes in a roar like the swelling ocean.

Hundreds of tiny, beady eyes seemed to glow red. In the dim light, Max could barely make out sharp snouts and long, hairless tails.

"Rats," he gasped.

"Rats!" Rocky yipped, sounding excited. The Dachshund nipped Georgie's tail to get the sobbing dog's attention and said, "Hey, big guy, don't freak out. I can handle this."

"Do it, Rocky," Gizmo barked, her tail wagging.

The hissing rats surrounded the dogs in an endless sea of gray-and-black fur. Clearing his throat, Rocky barked loudly. "Oh, great and wonderful rats! You have outsmarted us lowly, worthless dogs. Truly you are the most magnificent of all creatures." Ducking his head, he said, "I, Rocky, bow before you in respect. I am most definitely not worthy."

The hissing stopped, replaced by gasps.

"Could it be?" one rat squeaked.

"Is it him?" another asked.

"It's Rocky! He's here!"

The mass of rats began to chatter excitedly. "I love you, Rocky!" one screamed. "Aaah! I love yoooou!"

Sniffling, Georgie whispered, "What is going on?"

Overhearing him, one of the rats said, "Don't you know?" he asked. "Rocky is legendary! Our cousin Longtooth up north spread word of how amazing he is!"

Max remembered Longtooth very well. Rocky, Gizmo, and Max had fled into a darkened subway tunnel in the Chairman's city after being chased by dozens of feral, crazed dogs. It was there they'd encountered an army of rats who'd taken refuge from the Chairman's Corporation.

But Rocky had managed to sweet-talk the rats and their leader, Longtooth, and they'd escaped unharmed. Longtooth had said he'd spread word of the dogs to his fellow rats, but Max hadn't expected the message to travel this far south.

Puffing up his chest, Rocky said, "Didn't we tell you, Georgie? I'm famous!"

Gizmo giggled. "Oh, hush."

The rat who'd spoken to Georgie cupped his paws around his snout. "This is no place for Silver-Tongued Rocky and his Less Impressive Friends!" he squealed loudly. "To the junkyard!"

"The junkyard!" roared the crowd.

And as Max watched in amazement, the swarm of rats parted in the middle, clearing a path through the tunnel and leading the dogs one step closer to Belle.

CHAPTER 19

THE JUNKYARD KING

The army of rats swarmed on either side of the dogs, like a living, welcoming black-and-gray carpet.

As they splashed out of the fetid tunnel and into the fresh night air, the rodents began to sing.

"*The dogs went wild and tried to make us their food,*" half of the crowd sang.

"*But great King Longtooth thought that very rude!*" the other half replied. The rats climbed up a hill to a road, still singing.

"*In darkened tunnels, an epic battle raged.*"

"*The subway dogs went wild and then rampaged!*"

Soon they were on a flat street again, following the singing rats north toward the darkened city.

"We planned a last stand against mutts both small and stocky."

"Then out of the darkness came the Silver-Tongued Rocky!"

A great cheer rose up from the swarm of rats. Max couldn't help but laugh at their sheer enthusiasm. They were on the outskirts of the city now. The rats led the dogs down a side street, and Max was stunned to see cars of all sizes and colors stacked into mountainous piles up ahead. The shadow of a giant crane could be seen towering in the sky behind the piles.

A tall chain-link fence surrounded the field of piled cars, with spirals of razor-edged barbed wire glittering dangerously on top. At the end of the street, above an opening in the fence, an arched sign read ED'S JUNKYARD AND FINE ART, though someone had started to paint the three-ringed symbol as a warning over the sign.

The rats finished their song as they surged into the junkyard. *"Rocky praised our greatness and our rule of the tunnels dark."*

"And then he returned to the world above, with one last rallying bark."

All the voices joined together. *"And then the subway rats came to rule again, all thanks to the words of Rocky, our Silver-Tongued friend!"*

The rats' voices rose once more in tinny, screeching cheers, echoing through the junkyard. Max couldn't imagine how many creatures must live in the place.

"They really love you," Georgie said in awe. "But why did you help rats in the first place?"

"It's a long story," Rocky said. Puffing out his chest, he added, "All that matters is that now I'm some rat folk hero! I bet these guys will take us right to Belle." Rocky looked up at Georgie. "It pays to be famous, doesn't it, Mudlurker?"

Max realized a few of the rats were listening in on the conversation.

"Shh, guys," he whispered. "Let's see what's up ahead before we start celebrating, okay?" They went silent as they wound through the maze that was the junkyard.

Directly across from the gate was a dingy, old school bus, a run-down version of the bright yellow bus that used to pick up Charlie and Emma each morning. Only this bus had no wheels; instead, it sat on large cinder blocks. Someone had painted a mural of flowers and leaves on the side, and wild plants sprouted through the open windows.

To the right was a ramshackle building, but the rats didn't take the dogs that way. Instead they surged to the left, where the walls of cars grew so close together that humans would have to walk through in single file.

As they slipped through the narrow passages, Max realized that the junkyard was more than it seemed— the place was an absolute treasure trove of *stuff*. Metal lamps on tall poles illuminated the so-called junk as insects swarmed around the glowing lightbulbs.

The dogs were led past old ovens with open doors revealing rusted interiors coated in black. Rats watched the dogs from inside, whispering as they ate from dented tin cups.

Around another corner they found piles of box springs surrounded by pillars of stacked tires. Straw and shredded cloth and chewed-up foam had been used to make little nests in the springs, and Max could see baby rats sleeping inside. Larger rats stood watch atop the tires.

There was neat stuff tucked into every nook and cranny. A gum-ball machine as big as a car. A toy robot with metal claws. Brass lamps with spiraling poles. An old-fashioned bathtub with clawed feet.

Max couldn't imagine why anyone would throw this stuff out. Luckily the rats seemed to think the same thing, and they'd made their homes on every spare bit of junk they could find.

In fact, as they wound through the maze, Max saw hundreds of rats, all standing alert, murmuring and pointing at the dogs. It seemed strange that rats, of all creatures, would be so in awe of a Dachshund—but Max had to admit he'd experienced many strange things during their journey.

After one last bend in the maze, the rats led Max, Rocky, Gizmo, and Georgie through a car at the bottom of one of the stacks of automobiles.

"Whoa," Rocky said as he took in the new location.

"Oh," Gizmo whispered in awe. "It's so...pretty."

Panting, Georgie wiggled himself through the window frame an inch at a time. "What's out there?" he said. "Where are we?"

"I'll go see," Max said. "You're almost through, Georgie. Just keep wiggling."

Max shoved himself through another car window and discovered what had impressed his friends.

The rats had led them to a hidden clearing within the towering walls of cars. Strands of white holiday lights were strung high, illuminating the clearing in a twinkling glow.

Across the open area was a silver trailer, a sleek, futuristic thing. More of the glittering strands were strung up above the trailer's door and windows. Max saw the cords stretching down to a small machine that hummed and sputtered.

But the trailer and lights weren't what had impressed Rocky and Gizmo. Max saw five statues taller than even the trailer, made entirely of junk. Two were strange, abstract shapes that twisted and looped toward the night sky. One was a man, hunched over with one hand on his back and the other holding a cane. Another was of a woman sitting on a rocking chair, holding a bouquet of flowers. There was even a dog, one paw raised, tongue hanging out.

Each statue had been created from trash. Max saw wrenches and screwdrivers welded together to form hands, inverted umbrellas and layered nuts and bolts making the bouquet, coiled wire forming a coat of fur. Max was astounded that all these normal items could be put together to create something entirely new.

Max was so taken by the sculptures that he almost didn't notice that every last inch of space inside the clearing was filled with rats. They sat patiently, whispering and staring at a table and two chairs next to the front entrance to the trailer.

"Oof!"

Max turned just in time to see Georgie fall face-first into the dirt beneath the car window. He spat out a mouthful of slobbery dust, then blinked in surprise as he, too, took in the scene.

"Wow," the big dog said. "Who would waste all that junk on such ugly statues?"

"I like them!" Gizmo said. "It's...art."

The whispering of the rats grew louder and then fell into a sudden hush. There seemed to be some sort of commotion beneath the trailer.

As Max watched, three rats appeared from the shadows, carrying what looked like a small red pillowcase. They scurried up the chairs and then jumped onto the table.

Two of the rats grabbed the top corners of the pillowcase and stood on their hind legs, as though holding a curtain. The third rat raised a paw.

"May I present," it pronounced, "the one and only, the astounding and amazing, the enlightened and effervescent, our king, Flicktail!"

The rats swirled away the pillowcase-curtain with a flourish. To Max's surprise, a large white rat appeared, wearing a gold thimble on his head.

Now all the rats rose up into a cheer as Flicktail placed one hand against his chest.

"Oh, my people," he said. "Oh, how you *do* go on. I don't deserve it."

This only caused the rats to cheer louder.

Flicktail clutched his enormous pink belly and laughed with glee. The three rats who had introduced him lifted a plastic yellow bucket onto the table. Max saw that the inside was filled with a small pillow.

Flicktail plopped backward into his bucket throne. He said, "I hear we have special guests! Do come forward, please. I am delighted to meet you!"

Max glanced down at Rocky. "How about you lead the way?" he asked.

Rocky pranced forward. "But of course."

Gizmo followed Rocky, then Max, and then Georgie. The rats shouted out greetings. One baby, clinging to its mother's back, tried to mimic Rocky's distinct waddle.

"Calm down, Wildrump. I'm trying to see!" the mother said.

"I gotta practice, Mama," the baby rat squeaked. "I wanna be just like Silver-Tongued Rocky when I grow up!"

"So adorable," Gizmo whispered.

As the dogs neared the table, Flicktail clapped his paws together.

"Silver-Tongued Rocky," he said. "You are as dashing a dog as I've ever seen. Did you enjoy our song about you? It's been all the natives have wanted to sing around these parts for ages." He laughed again.

Rocky sat back on his hind legs. "Yes, sir, King Flicktail. I enjoyed it a lot. Longtooth said he'd spread word of us, but I never expected anything like this!"

"You're the best, Rocky!" a rat cried out from the crowd.

Flicktail laughed again. "Oh, you darling dog, you have no idea how much your words rallied the rats! If it weren't for you, we might not have dared make this junkyard our kingdom." Flicktail stood and raised his claws. "Give it up again for Rocky, my people!"

The assembled rats let out a great hurrah, the squeaks and chirps piercing the night sky.

"And you!" Flicktail cried, pointing one claw at Gizmo. "You must be the brave and gracious Gizmo. Truly our songs haven't done your beauty justice." Looking at Max, he said, "And with the golden fur and giant size, you can't be anyone but Max, Fleet of Foot and Bold of Heart."

"You've heard of us, too?" Gizmo asked.

"Of course!" Flicktail cried. "You're Rocky's sidekicks, after all."

Rocky chuckled. "Oh, definitely."

"This is Georgie," Max told the rat king. "He's a friend of ours that some know as the Mudlurker."

Flicktail looked Georgie up and down. "Never heard

of him," he said. "No matter! Any friend of Rocky is a friend of ours. And Rocky and his friends should not have to sit on the ground."

The crowd rustled, and Max looked to his right to see three brown couch cushions winding between the towering metal statues. They were being carried on the backs of dozens of rats, who plopped them side by side in front of the dogs, just beneath the table.

"Sit," Flicktail urged. "Are you hungry?" Before any of the dogs could respond, the king called out, "Bring our guests sustenance!"

Now four plastic mixing bowls were carried across the clearing to be set before the dogs. Two contained fresh kibble, and the others sloshed with water.

"Wow," Max said, curling up on one of the cushions. "Where do you get all this food?"

"I don't know," Flicktail said, sounding bored. "My rats just bring it to me."

"Sounds good," Rocky said as he climbed onto the second cushion next to Gizmo.

Georgie took up the final cushion, and all four dogs ate and drank. Above them, Flicktail gnawed on a chicken leg.

"So tell me," Flicktail said, "what brings Rocky and his friends to our neck of the woods?"

Gizmo offered Flicktail a wag of her tail. "Well, it's a long story, but we're in Baton Rouge to find a dog."

Flicktail tossed his half-eaten chicken leg aside. "Oh? You didn't come to see me?"

"Not really," Gizmo said. "But we're glad we met you anyway!"

The rat king twitched his whiskers. "So who's this dog you seek?"

Max said, "We're looking for a Collie named Belle."

Some of the rats gasped. Flicktail jerked up, his red eyes wide.

"Belle?" he squeaked. "You don't want to see her."

"Why not?" Max asked. "We promised a friend we'd track her down, and he told us she was the nicest, kindest dog in the whole city."

Flicktail crossed his arms. "Well, your friend must have known another Belle. No, I wouldn't recommend you go to her."

"Hey," Rocky said. "You forget, I'm the Silver-Tongued Rocky. What's a lone Collie gonna do to me?"

Flicktail looked at Rocky, his tail snapping back and forth. Finally, the rat king laughed. "You know, Rocky, we've sung the same songs of you for so long that I'm eager for something new. Tell us a story about your journey since you last saw Longtooth."

"Well..." Rocky said. "I'm not sure we have time, your kingliness."

"Of course you do!" Flicktail cried.

Encouraging shouts rang out from the crowd.

"Please, tell us a tale!"

"More of your heroics!"

"Marry me, Rocky! Never mind that yappy dog!"

"Hey," Gizmo said.

Rising from the cushion, Rocky said, "All right, I suppose I can tell you a story, since it means so much to everyone."

The Dachshund marched importantly to the nearest chair, leaped atop it, then hopped onto the plastic table, which trembled from the force of his landing. Flicktail had to cling to his throne, but the rat king laughed in delight once more.

"Listen all, and listen well," Rocky barked. The assembled rats leaned forward, watching the Dachshund in rapt silence. "I come to you with a tale of danger and intrigue," Rocky continued. "One that starts on the dark waters of a raging river, where we discovered a giant boat full of ghosts and dogs like us..."

Rocky regaled the crowd with their adventures alongside Boss on the riverboat, in the zoo, and at the laboratory. He fudged a few details—in this version, *he* was the leader, he didn't get lost on the monorail, and he carefully made no mention of Praxis—but their incredible story was more or less the same.

The rats gasped at the revelation of the bad humans, laughed at the antics of the zoo animals, and recoiled in horror at Rocky's vivid account of the wolves.

But Gizmo fidgeted anxiously on her cushion, and Max knew what she was thinking.

The rats had been gracious, but the four dogs were so close to Belle now. And Dolph was still after them. Unless they left soon, the wolves would catch up to them.

"The boat went up in a blaze," Rocky said, nearing the end of his story. "My courage saved the helpless riverboat dogs from certain death!"

"Amazing," Flicktail whispered.

Rocky added, "Sadly, we did lose Boss that day. He will go down in history as second in bravery only to me. His last words to me were a request to find his lost love. A romantic to the end."

Max heard some of the rats sigh.

Raising his head once more, Rocky wagged his spiky tail, nearly slapping Flicktail's bucket throne. "And that, my dear rats, is the tale of how I saved the riverboat dogs and became one of the most fearless animals in the world. Almost"—he winked—"as fearless as all of you."

The crowd went wild. They leaped up and down, cheering and clapping. One rat was so excited that he tumbled off the trailer. He got up, shook his head, and then resumed cheering.

"Amazing!" Flicktail repeated, leaping off his throne. "Oh, the songs we will sing; I can already hear the lyrics! *Something-something-something* Boss, *something-something-something* loss!" He clapped in glee. "Rocky, please tell us another!"

"More!" shouted the crowd.

Rocky shook his head. "I'd love to," he said. "However, it would risk blowing your minds too much."

Flicktail rubbed his paw along Rocky's back. "Oh, but I insist." Gripping a clump of the Dachshund's black fur, he added, "I really, really insist."

Gizmo jumped to her feet. "And I have to insist that we go. You have been wonderful, but we came all this way for Belle. We should go to her."

Letting go of Rocky, Flicktail peered down at the little terrier.

"I already told you that Belle is not someone you want to meet," he hissed. "And I find the idea that you don't trust me quite rude. Terribly, terribly rude."

The cheering died down. In the sudden, eerie quiet, all Max could hear was the humming of the generator and the buzzing of insects around the tall lamps.

Max swallowed and said, "We don't mean to be rude. It's just that the wolves Rocky told you about are still after us. And no matter how Belle may have changed since the people left, we promised Boss we'd find her. I hope you understand."

Flicktail leaned back. "Oh, I understand," he said. "I understand that you are delirious in your exhaustion. Look, the big one can't even keep his eyes open."

Georgie peered up between slitted eyelids. "What about me?" he asked. "I'm awake."

"Nonsense!" Flicktail said, his tail snapping once more. "You four must sleep here, and we can resume the stories once you're well rested. If any wolves come by, they will be no match for my people. You *will* sleep here, won't you?"

Max could tell his words weren't really a request.

They were an order.

The swarm of rats had grown even larger, and Max was suddenly very aware that they were surrounded. The rodents pressed up against the cushions and dangled from the statues. Their beady, glittering eyes seemed to pierce directly into Max.

He shuddered.

Rocky silently jumped down from the table and curled up on the cushion next to Gizmo. As he did, Flicktail settled into his throne once more.

"You are our guests," the king said. "The rules of hospitality around my kingdom of junk state that my guests cannot leave until I say the party is over. And trust me, my guests. We have much more to do before I say we are done."

CHAPTER 20

THE SCRAP TUNNEL

Though his body was flooded with adrenaline, Max had no choice but to shut his eyes and feign sleep as the hundreds—if not thousands—of rats watched.

What felt like moments later, a wet nose nudged Max's snout and he opened his eyes to darkness. The lights in the clearing were all out.

A shadowy figure loomed above Max, and he thought it might be Georgie, until he realized the cushions next to him still contained three sleeping dogs.

"Who's there?" Max whispered, still half asleep.

The figure stepped forward, and Max saw it was a weary-eyed dog, its coat made up of tangled ringlets of dingy white fur.

"Hello," the dog replied. "You're the leader, right?"

"If you mean of the dogs here, then yes," Max said. "Who are you?"

The dog climbed onto the cushion and put his snout very close to Max's ear. "Sorry to cramp your space," he said in a hushed voice. "But I don't want to wake the rats. The name is Whitey."

"I'm Max." Tilting his head, Max asked, "Do you live in the junkyard?"

Whitey nodded. "If living is what you can call it. The rats keep me penned in the consignment shop up front, thinking they run the place. Which I guess they do. They came and took a bunch of my food earlier today, so I followed them, and that's how I found you."

Max gasped. "The rats keep you locked up? Did they do that to your fur, too?"

Whitey shook his head. "Naw, I always looked like this. My pa was a Labrador, but my ma was a Poodle. The people called my brothers and sisters and me Labradoodles."

Max almost laughed. "Labradoodle, huh? That's an interesting name."

"Well, I like it fine," Whitey said. "But, Max, there's no time to talk about that. I've been thinking how to get out of here for ages, and once I heard the other dogs barking and howling directions earlier tonight, I figured it was a sign to make my move. I can take you with me, if you want."

Max peered around him in the darkness. The rats were out of sight. But that didn't mean they were gone.

Turning back to Whitey, Max asked, "Aren't the rats going to try to stop us?"

Whitey shook his head. "Their hootenannies go till late at night and start right up again in the morning. But for a few hours they shut off the lights and go to sleep." Climbing off the cushion, Whitey added, "Trust me, Flicktail may act nice to you now, but when it comes down to it, he's going to look out for himself."

Glancing up at the empty table, Max said, "Yeah, I got that idea." He rose to his feet, then leaned down and licked Rocky's and Gizmo's heads. Yawning, they opened their eyes.

"What's going on?" Rocky asked. "Is it story time already?"

"No," Max said, "we're getting out of here."

"Oh, good," Gizmo whispered. "No offense, Rocky, but I don't really want to be trapped by a bunch of rats, no matter how much they worship you."

"Nah, me, neither," Rocky said. "It was fun at first, but being famous is kind of exhausting."

Max shook the Saint Bernard. The giant dog opened his eyes and said loudly, "Is it time to eat again?"

All four of the other dogs shushed him at once. "We're making a break for it, Georgie," Max whispered. "This dog is Whitey. He lives here in the junkyard, but the rats keep him penned up. He's going to show us a way out."

The Labradoodle sniffed Georgie. "You're the howler!" he said. "I think I heard a friend of yours barking nearby."

Georgie's eyes went wide. "Near here? Let's go! I'm so ready to see my friends again."

Gizmo raised a paw. "Nice to meet you, Whitey."

"Same," Rocky said. "Lead the way!"

The curly white dog trotted through the clearing, keeping to the shadows. "The rats have guards posted at the real exits, but there's a passage through the junk, though it'll be a tight fit for Max and Georgie."

"We're right behind you," Max whispered. "Let's talk only if necessary. The last thing we want is to alert King Flicktail!"

Silently the dogs walked single file to the northernmost stack of vehicles, where Whitey went to a car at the base of one of the towers. He sniffed the trunk, then raised a paw and smacked the little metal circle where a key might fit.

With a creak of rusty hinges, the trunk opened. "This way," Whitey whispered, then jumped inside.

Max followed just in time to see Whitey crawling belly-first through a hole in the trunk that led into the backseat. Max wiggled through the hole, the metal rough and cool against his stomach, the smell of mildew washing over him. The fabric on the cushions inside was torn free to reveal stained yellow padding and splotches of black mold.

Holding his breath, Max followed Whitey into the front seat. Rocky and Gizmo quickly followed, though Georgie needed some help fitting through the opening.

Whitey continued on and Max bounded after him, through the shattered windshield and then into a car that faced the opposite direction. Luckily, there were no more trunks to navigate. Instead, Whitey led them through a makeshift tunnel made of cars—in one window, over old seats, and then out another window.

They were just getting their rhythm when Max hefted himself out of a truck window and found himself facing a wall.

"Over here," Whitey whispered.

Looking up, Max saw that the wall was actually the front of a big, square van. Max leaped into a cabin with two seats on either side of a small aisle. The aisle led to a beaded curtain that separated the rest of the van from the driver's seat.

The strands of the beaded curtain clacked against one another as Whitey darted through. Max started to follow when he heard Gizmo gasp.

"Oh!" she cried. "An RV."

"A what?" Max whispered.

The little Yorkie didn't answer. Instead, she brushed past the curtain, and Max ran after her.

It was dark in the RV, but Max could make out the shadows of what looked like a small, cramped house. There was a counter and sink and tiny refrigerator on one side, a table on the other, and a couch opposite a TV with a smashed screen.

Gizmo stood in the center of the aisle, frozen.

Max carefully stepped over fallen, rusted skillets and a shattered coffeepot, then gently nudged Gizmo's side.

"We have to go," he said.

Gizmo shook her head, eyes watering.

"Oh! Sorry." Sniffling, she looked away. "It's just that this is a lot like the RV my pack leaders had. The same one they took me in when I saw that squirrel and jumped out the window and got left behind."

"Did you think . . . ?" Max started to ask.

"No," Gizmo said. "For a second I thought I smelled them. But it was just my imagination."

"I understand," Max said.

Sniffing one last time, Gizmo offered Max a doggy smile. "I'll be fine. Let's keep going!"

Reaching the back of the RV, they nosed through another beaded curtain, then leaped onto a lumpy mattress. While Gizmo jumped out the back window after Whitey, Max checked that Rocky and Georgie were keeping pace, then climbed out of the RV after Gizmo.

But instead of another vehicle, he found himself landing on concrete, and realized they were inside a large pipe, like a smaller version of the tunnel they'd come through earlier. Several of the pipes had been laid end to end through the junkyard. Once more walking in single file, the dogs raced through the pipes. Whitey stopped at the edge of the final one, panting for breath, with Gizmo right behind him. Max slowed his gait as he approached.

"Something wrong?" he whispered.

Whitey looked back over his shoulder. "Nothing's wrong. Yet. But we need to climb, and it's going to make noise. The good news is this is the last hurdle. Once we're at the top, we're home free. You ready?"

"Yes!" Rocky and Gizmo said.

"I think so," Georgie mumbled.

Max nodded. "Lead the way."

Whitey nodded back. Beyond the Labradoodle, Max saw what looked like metal rods rising up into a hill with weird plastic shapes on either side. He realized the poles were the inner supports of giant, plastic signs, the type that hung above restaurants and gas stations, and that the signs had all been stacked into one big mound.

Whitey stepped forward, and immediately the metal groaned. Something cracked, and the structure shifted. Taking a deep breath, Whitey said, "No going back now." And he was off.

Max watched in awe as Whitey carefully stepped from pole to pole, climbing up toward the night sky.

"Be careful when you follow," Max whispered to Gizmo. "If you think you can't make it, I'll help."

"Got it," she whispered back. "I'll tell Rocky."

Max stepped onto the first metal support, then pressed down, hoping it would hold him. It seemed solid enough, so he stepped forward with his other paw. The poles and signs wobbled beneath Max's feet, and the junk seemed to whine and moan, complaining with each step. Behind him he heard Gizmo and Rocky moving carefully from pole to pole, and then a loud groan as Georgie started to follow.

They climbed slowly, steadily, and silently. The pads of Max's paws hurt terribly, but he refused to give up. They were almost free.

And then, when Max was only a few feet away from the top where Whitey waited, the plastic sign next to him cracked and broke loose from its supports. It tumbled down through the darkness, smacking against the junk pile and clanging against metal. Finally it landed on an asphalt lot far below, shattering into pieces.

A second later, a squeaking rat voice rang out. "What was that noise?"

Another called, "Something is moving in the signs!"

Someone shouted, "Rocky is gone! The dogs are trying to leave!"

All around them, the lamps on the tall wooden poles snapped on, illuminating the junkyard in hazy orange light. The air was filled with the hisses and squeals of angry rats.

"Come on!" Whitey barked from above.

Max didn't need to be told twice. He leaped up, frantic to reach the top of this man-made mountain. At last he climbed onto a stack of tires, then spun to watch his friends.

Gizmo had been right on Max's tail, and she scrambled up next to him a moment later. Rocky had a tougher go of it, but the squat dog made a wild jump and landed belly-first atop the tires.

That left Georgie. Howling in fear, the Saint Bernard bounded up the makeshift steps. As he leaped out from between a sign showing a yellow shell and one emblazoned with two gold arches, his hind legs shoved the shell sign off balance.

And with a shriek of metal and plastic, the pile of signs began to collapse.

"Come on, Georgie!" Gizmo barked.

"Almost there, big guy!" Rocky called out.

Georgie did not stop, barreling up the signs as they shifted and trembled beneath him. The stack began to give way, and a great flurry of noise rose up as signs tumbled down the pile in an avalanche of junk and broke apart on the ground. "Out of the way!" Georgie bellowed.

Max leaped to the side as Georgie jumped out of the wreckage. He soared through the air, flying over Gizmo's and Rocky's heads before landing in a heap on the tires. Not a second later, the entire pile of signs gave way, thudding to the ground and throwing up a cloud of grime and dust. The rats below squealed and darted out of the way.

"Come on!" Whitey cried.

Max turned and found that the stacks of tires ran all the way up against the barbed-wire fence, high enough for the dogs to leap safely over the razor wire. Though the stacks trembled and quaked, they were too tightly packed together to give way. The dogs were almost to the fence when the first rats reached the top of the tires.

"Please don't leave us, Rocky!"

"You're our guests, and our guests can't leave until we say!"

"We need you here!"

Max didn't stop to think. He could see the horizon clearly now, and the tall, shadowy buildings of Baton Rouge were closer than ever. Galloping to the edge of the mountain of tires, he leaped over the razor wire.

He soared through the air, and for a moment he thought they'd been led astray, that beyond the fence was some cliff, and he was falling to his doom. Then his paws met hard earth, and he rolled over and over through a field of grass until he came to a stop.

Aching and gasping for breath, Max forced himself to his feet. Nearby he heard *oof*s and thuds as his friends made the terrifying leap.

"Everyone okay?" Max barked.

"Yes!" Gizmo yipped.

"I think so," Rocky answered.

"We're fine, too!" Georgie answered for himself and Whitey.

And though he hurt all over, Max shouted, "Let's go!" and barreled forward into the field, his friends beside him.

As they neared the main road, Max dared one look back.

Standing atop the pile of tires, surrounded by rats, stood King Flicktail. And though the rat wasn't giving chase, he did not take his red eyes off Max as the dogs ran to find Belle as fast as their legs could carry them.

CHAPTER 21
THE DECAYING MANSION

It was dawn. As they tore past lot after lot, Max half expected King Flicktail and his rats to burst up from the sewers and overtake them, joined by Dolph and his pack. But thankfully there were no signs of rats or wolves.

So far.

"Where," Rocky said between pants, "are we running?"

None of the others answered him. Whitey and Georgie had taken the lead, with Max following closely behind. Now the dirty Labradoodle looked up at the big Saint Bernard.

"I swear I heard someone barking around here," Whitey said. "Do you know who might live here?"

Georgie sniffed the air, then raised his snout and howled, just loudly enough to alert anyone nearby.

Moments later, the sound of barking echoed from farther north. When Georgie heard it, his tail wagged. "We're close!" he told the other dogs. "This way!"

With renewed energy, Georgie galloped forward up the street. The dogs followed him past a post office, through a garbage-strewn alley, and onto a smaller street that led into a suburban neighborhood. The houses were small, built on a single level, with faded, peeling paint.

Georgie howled again. This time the response was much closer. He led the dogs around one more corner, to the entrance of a large brick building.

The place was several stories tall, with concrete steps rising from the sidewalk. Twin lion statues guarded either side of the entrance, and in the dark interior Max could make out shelves of books. A sign above the doors read LIBRARY.

Georgie bounded up the steps, then proceeded to sniff the concrete landing and the wooden benches and garbage cans in front of the doors. Max saw a little slot on the wall next to the doors, under the sign that read BOOK RETURN.

"Hello?" Georgie called as the others crowded behind him. "Is anyone there?"

A shadow passed in front of the book-return slot. Max stiffened, wary—but when the creature stepped into the light, he saw it was just a small brown mutt with ragged fur and a friendly expression.

"Georgie?" the dog asked. "Is that you, old boy?"

"Fletcher!" Georgie bellowed.

His eyes alight with glee, the Saint Bernard practically tackled the smaller dog, licking her all over.

"Georgie Porgie!" Fletcher squealed, laughing. "I thought that was you howling last night, but when you didn't show up in town, I figured we were wrong."

The big dog stopped his licking. "Well, the tunnel everyone howled about turned out to be full of rats, and they kind of took us hostage. But we're okay now!"

"Rats, huh?" Fletcher asked. "The world's gone crazy, my friend. But I'm just so glad to see you—we assumed you'd left for good!"

"I thought so, too," Georgie said. "My pack leaders took me to a beach inn, but after they disappeared, I had no one to talk to but a bunch of lazy pets, and they all wanted me to take care of them. I tried to be good and help all of them, but none were truly my friends. I got so lonely, especially after being trapped in that swamp...."

"Wow, you were in a swamp?" said Fletcher, her eyes wide.

Max cleared his throat. "Sorry to interrupt. I'm Max, and these are my friends Rocky, Gizmo, and Whitey."

Fletcher sniffed at Max, then brushed past him to take in the scents of the others. Satisfied that none of them seemed dangerous, the mutt, who was not much bigger than Rocky or Gizmo, leaped atop one of the benches, then onto the back of the lion statue.

"Nice to meet you," Fletcher said, observing them from her new perch. To Georgie, she said, "These guys follow you from that beach place?"

"Oh, no," Georgie said. "They helped me, actually. If it weren't for Max, Rocky, and Gizmo, I'd probably still be the Mudlurker, alone in a broken shop in the swamp. And without Whitey, all of us would still be at the junkyard, trapped by rats."

Fletcher shook her head. "Mudlurker? Junkyard rats? This story of yours is getting crazier by the minute, Georgie Porgie."

"We'd love to tell you all about it," said Gizmo, "but we've got wolves after us—"

The mutt's fur bristled. "Wolves?"

"—and we really must get to Belle before they catch up."

Fletcher went rigid. "Belle?"

Rocky sighed. "Yeah, Belle. You have a bad habit of repeating everything we say as a question."

Max nosed Georgie's side. "Now that we found one of your friends, maybe you could take us to Belle's home. It's near some puppy farm, right?"

"Happy Paws," Georgie and Fletcher said at the same time.

"It's been a long time since I've been here," Georgie admitted. "I don't recognize much except the big buildings downtown."

"What about you, Whitey?" Gizmo asked.

The dingy junkyard dog lay near one of the trash

cans. "I'm afraid not," he said. "I'm sure it's around here somewhere, but I've never much left the junkyard, though the rats talk about Belle a bit."

Rocky rested his head on his front paws. "What do we do now? Just walk and hope we stumble on her?" He looked at Fletcher. "Unless you can give us directions?"

"But why do you even want to find Belle?" Fletcher asked. "Do you know what's been going on?"

"Well, we heard from our friend Boss that she was known as the nicest dog in Baton Rouge," said Max.

"She was," Fletcher said.

"But the closer we've gotten to here, the stranger everyone acts when we say her name." Max tilted his head. "I figure she must have gone sad and angry at being abandoned, but a lot of dogs have. Surely if we just talk to her and tell her what we know about her lost friend, she'll find some peace."

"Belle used to be a sweetheart," Fletcher said. "Happy Paws was built near her pack leaders' property, so she would wander over to play with the puppies. All the Happy Paws pets knew her. Sometimes she and Boss would sneak out and walk into town to say how do. Even the humans found it charming."

Fletcher shivered. "But she went bad after the people and Boss left. She couldn't handle how everything had changed, and she holed herself up in her mansion. Then she started appearing from the shadows at night, growl-ing something fierce and stealing food. I hear she gathered some of the angriest, meanest dogs from the city to come stay with her. There's a whole gang up there now."

She finished, "And that's why you shouldn't go anywhere near Belle. If there really are wolves after you, then forget about her and find someplace where you'll be safe."

Scratching behind one of his curly, floppy ears, Whitey said, "Sounds reasonable to me."

Georgie said, "I had no idea things got so bad with her. That's really sad."

Max could tell by Rocky's and Gizmo's worried, weary looks that they were both questioning whether they should finish this mission.

Besides, Boss was dead. How would he even know?

That last thought came to Max unbidden, and as soon as it drifted through his mind he shuddered. Memories of Dr. Lynn came back to him, along with the words she spoke.

You are loved.

After all the pain, worry, and heartache, that simple phrase had meant so much.

No matter how bad Belle had gotten, she deserved to know the same thing.

"Thank you for the warning, Fletcher," Max said. "I really appreciate your concern. But we made a promise, and we came a long way to fulfill it. If you can't lead us to Belle, at least send us in the right direction. We won't ask you to put yourself in danger."

"Are you sure, Max?" Gizmo asked.

Rocky climbed to his feet. "He's sure. Besides, we survived a swarm of gators. Packs of angry dogs are old news!"

"Well, you can't say I didn't warn you," Fletcher said. "I guess I can figure out some directions."

"I'll go with them, Fletcher," Georgie said. "I sort of know the roads."

Rising up from beside the garbage can, Whitey stretched his legs. "Yeah, I think I'd like to see this place, too, if you don't mind me tagging along."

"Of course not!" said Gizmo.

Fletcher sighed. "So I suppose I'm going to look bad if I'm the only dog who doesn't come along?" She shook her head and leaped down from the statue. "Fine. Besides, Georgie Porgie and I have a lot of catching up to do."

"Thanks for this," Max said.

"Yeah, yeah," Fletcher said as they reached the sidewalk. "But I ain't going past the front gate. Once we get there, it's up to you."

The morning sky had grown gray and turbulent, the clouds writhing and swirling like an angry ocean. The air was damp and warm. Fletcher took the lead with Georgie at her side, the two of them reminiscing about old times. As they shared stories of what they'd been up to, Whitey trotted just behind them, listening and occasionally piping in with some joke. Rocky and Gizmo followed him, and Max brought up the rear.

The six dogs padded through the neighborhood where Fletcher lived, following a road that led west. Max spotted a few other dogs in the yards, but they seemed skittish at the sight of a pack. He could smell their anxiety and fear, and he could tell this wasn't the first time they'd hidden from a roving group of canines.

It wasn't long before the neighborhood gave way to great stretches of land surrounded by ornate iron fences with pointed tips on every spike. Inside each fenced-off area, Max could see tall, gangly trees and large, stately white homes.

"Boss lived there," Fletcher called back as she gestured at one of the big mansions with her snout. "It's one of the more modest manors, but he didn't seem to mind." Max could see the front porch and the rocking chairs where Boss must have lain at his pack leaders' feet, Belle beside him. Then he pictured Boss, injured on the riverbank after Dolph and his pack had been defeated, imploring Max to find Belle.

Dolph had played a large part in why Boss wasn't here himself.

Max tried very hard not to think about the wolf leader, but he was still after Max and his friends. Surely Dolph would be close by now.

Max was going to keep his promise to poor Boss and

find Belle—but he also needed to put much more distance between the single-minded wolf and his friends.

Fletcher came to a stop at the end of Boss's yard. "Belle lives over there," she said.

"Where's the gate?" Rocky asked.

Fletcher waved a paw. "Up ahead some. But this is as far as I go. You can probably find the way in on your own."

"I'm sure we can," Max said. "Thanks, Fletcher. We appreciate all your help." He turned to Georgie. "You've been a great help leading us here. But the wolves aren't after you, and who knows how dangerous it is up ahead. If you want to stick with Fletcher, find more of your friends, and go somewhere safe, I'd understand."

"Oh," Georgie said, glancing between Max and Fletcher. "I actually thought I could come with you to talk to Belle. In case you needed help," he added. "Unless you don't want me."

"Of course we do!" Gizmo said.

"Yeah," Rocky said. "You've been great to have around, Mudlurker. But we know how you get in situations like this. After all you've been through, big guy, you deserve a break."

Georgie parted his lips into a doggy smile, and a big drop of drool plopped to the dirt. "Thanks so much. I'm going to help, though. You're my friends now, and I always help my friends."

"Georgie Porgie!" Fletcher cried.

Georgie lowered his head and licked her forehead. "Don't worry. I'll be fine."

Whitey cleared his throat. "If it's all the same to you, I think I'll wait out here with Fletcher," he said. "I've got a bad feeling about this now that we're so close."

"That's fine," Max said. "We'll be quick. If either of you two senses any danger, though, don't be afraid to run." He started forward, with Rocky, Gizmo, and Georgie following behind.

The land beyond the iron fence was dense with trees, and everything inside was shrouded in dingy gray darkness. Blankets of moss hung like clothes on a line from the high, leafy branches, swaying gently in the breeze.

"Here we go," Max told his friends.

"So far, so good," Rocky said.

Side by side, the four dogs padded through the open gate and started down the road. Despite the overgrown grass and dead leaves, everything seemed normal.

But the farther they walked, the stranger things became.

At first it was just a distant, rotten stench, like a Dumpster full of old food. Max was mostly used to that smell by now.

Then he caught sight of a gazebo half hidden by the trees. It looked as if someone had chewed through the supports on one side of the small building, and the roof was on the verge of collapse. Max swore he heard the skittering of giant claws, but saw nothing.

Then Max forgot all about the gazebo. The driveway circled a once-grand fountain at the entrance to the mansion, and every last bit of blacktop was taken up by bags of trash. Giant black and white garbage bags were piled on top of one another and shredded by desperate, vicious claws and teeth.

Mounds of rotted, decomposed food spilled forth from holes in the bags. Old newspapers and banana peels and plastic bags floated in a fetid pool that swarmed with a thick cloud of flies.

The smell was so terrible that Max felt he could almost *taste* it. His eyes watered, and it was all he could do not to gag.

"Why is there so much garbage?" Rocky asked.

"It was never like this before," Georgie said.

Gizmo shook her head in disbelief. "So someone dragged these bags here on purpose? Why?"

Max turned back to the piles of trash. "It doesn't matter. We need to keep going."

"But, Max, buddy," Rocky pleaded. "I might pass out."

"We can do it," Max said. "Just hold your breath and run!"

Taking in a deep, gulping breath, Max galloped forward, not waiting another second. He ran around the piles of garbage bags to the steps that led to the mansion's entrance.

It was hard to focus on the mansion with all the garbage to distract him, but Max could tell that it was at least four stories high and painted white. Tall pillars rose up from the main porch that surrounded the building.

Reaching the top of the stairs, Max gasped for air. The stink of garbage still wafted around him, but it wasn't quite as bad as below.

Seconds later, Rocky, Gizmo, and Georgie joined him on the porch. The enormous wooden door was ajar, revealing a deserted foyer beyond. Next to the door were two wicker chairs, both knocked on their sides, the weaving slashed and frayed. Mounds of dirt were everywhere, and the windows were cracked.

Max padded toward the front door, hoping to catch some scent of Belle, but all he could smell was the festering trash heap behind him.

He shoved the massive door, and it opened inward, creaking on its hinges.

"Hello?" Max called out.

He stood in the doorway, his friends behind him, waiting.

Max took a step inside, then another. It was dim in the foyer, but the open door and the broken windows offered enough light to see by.

Just opposite the door was a wide stairway that rose

up to a landing above. Set next to the entryway was a painting, shredded by claws, of a woman. To Max's right, he saw a living room. The furniture was covered in white sheets, spotted with ashy paw prints. There was a fireplace filled with soot, the rug in front of it burned black.

"Belle?" Max called louder. "I'm a friend. I've come to speak to you."

By now, Rocky, Gizmo, and Georgie were crowded behind Max in the foyer. None of them spoke.

Max cleared his throat, preparing to call out again— when he heard paw steps from the landing above.

A regal Collie was standing at the top of the stairs. Her fur was caramel-colored, as fluffy and clean as if she'd just come from a doggy salon. A great crest of white fur ran up her chest, and her pointed ears were high and alert.

She looked like any other dog, except that someone had tied a floral bedsheet loosely around her neck. It fell over her back and dragged behind her on the floor like some makeshift cape. Max remembered the golden cape she'd worn in his dream, and how it had shredded to pieces.

"Visitors!" the dog barked. "In my home. I always do delight when strangers come calling. It happens so rarely in these dark days."

"Are you Belle?" Max asked.

The Collie raised her snout. "Of course. Who else would I be?"

She spun in a slow circle, her cape flopping stiffly against the floor.

"Do you like my outfit?" she asked. "I do so love to be fancy on a cloudy day." Meeting Max's eyes, she added, "And what about my home? Isn't it splendid?"

"Um, yes," Max lied. "Your home is very nice."

Belle danced down the steps, tossing her head back and forth to some unheard rhythm.

"Of course you think so," she said. "Everyone does."

Leaping off the bottom step, she came to stand nose to nose with Max. "And that's a very good thing, since now my home is your home, too."

Behind Max, Rocky, Gizmo, and Georgie, the giant front door slammed shut. They spun to see two thin, mangy brown dogs standing in front of it, their eyes narrowed and their teeth bared.

"Welcome to my mansion," Belle said. "Make yourselves comfortable. You'll never leave here again."

CHAPTER 22

SOUTHERN BELLE

◆

Max, Rocky, Gizmo, and Georgie stood in the dusty, dim foyer and stared at Belle in shock.

Belle's tail twitched in a halfhearted wag. "I see you have no complaints. So many of the dogs whom I've invited to live with me protested, and it was simply dreadful."

"Stupid dogs," the female mutt growled.

"They didn't know a good thing when they saw it, Lady Belle," the male mutt added.

The two brown dogs were the same height as Max, but they were a mix of so many different breeds that their features were a mishmash. There was a manic glint in their brown eyes, the same glint Max saw in Belle's stare.

Rocky was the first to find his voice. "Uh, Belle, lady,

we were just coming to visit. Nice digs and all, but we really can't stay."

"Nonsense!" Belle barked loudly. "No one is allowed to leave me. You came inside, and so now you must stay forever."

Swishing her sheet, the Collie turned to the two mutts. "When are Romeo and Beadle back with food? Our new friends will want to eat."

"They left a few hours ago, Lady Belle," the female said. "They should be back anytime now."

"Do you mean kibble?" Gizmo asked.

Belle looked down her snout. "Of course not. The bags. You've seen them. Out front." Darting forward, she pressed her nose directly against Gizmo's face. "So many treats inside those bags. We feast here."

"Oh," Gizmo said. "Those bags."

With a twinkling laugh, Belle pranced backward. "You are a darling young miss, aren't you? There used to be so many little dogs like you, but they all went away. Everyone went away."

"Belle—" Max started to say.

The Collie laughed again, louder this time, and began to pace in front of the four dogs.

"Yes, everyone went far away, with no thought of me." She looked at the group. "So you must stay. Perhaps we can wrap sheets around you, too. Though I see you already wear adornments."

Belle brushed in close next to Max and sniffed at the

collar around his neck. "I had a collar once," she said. "It was old and had a sparkly crystal on it. But this smells new. It smells *human*."

Max refused to show fear, even as the two mutts by the door raised their lips into snarls at the mention of the missing people.

"These collars were given to us by a kind woman not two days ago," Max said. "That's part of the reason we came here, Belle, to give you good news. Your pack leaders and all the other humans didn't want to abandon you. They had no choice. They still love and miss you, and it won't be long before they'll be able to come home."

"Lies," Belle hissed. "My pack leaders left me without a word. Meanwhile I saw other humans taking their pets with them. Those pets were wanted. I was not."

Memories came back to Max, of Boss explaining how Belle had watched as his pack leaders had tried to sneak away with him. That must have been what she meant.

"And it's not just the humans!" Belle howled. "All of my so-called friends in town do not come to visit me. The puppies from Happy Paws ran away, too. And B—" She stopped short of saying the Australian Shepherd's name. "I had to form a new family. I had to go to the sewers and pounds and I found my mutts, who are happy to live in such luxury. Aren't you, Blanche and Devereaux?"

"Yes, lady," the two mutts growled in unison.

"Tell her about Boss, buddy," Rocky whispered.

Belle's ears twitched. "What was that?" she asked.

Max stepped forward. "We didn't just come to tell you about the humans," he said softly. "Belle, we met Boss. He wanted us to—"

"No!" Belle screeched. The Collie turned into a golden blur as she raced upstairs, her makeshift cape whipping behind her. Without turning around, she said, "Never say his name. His betrayal was the worst of all. The thought of him makes me ill."

"Belle, please let me finish," Max said.

The sad, lonely Collie turned slowly so she could look down the wide staircase at Max, Rocky, Gizmo, and Georgie. She wagged her tail. "I forgive you," she said. "You didn't know any better. But you must never speak that terrible name again."

Georgie looked to Max, head drooping. "I don't think this is going like you wanted."

"Not at all," Max whispered.

Next to him, Max sensed Rocky trembling in barely contained anger. Before Max could do anything, the Dachshund waddled forward, head held high and defiant. He stood on the bottom step and looked up at Belle. "Look, lady, we were just trying to make you feel good. Even though everyone we met lately, including the local rats, said you went nuts, we thought we'd help you anyway. If you aren't going to listen, we've got things to do."

Belle shook her head. "But you can't leave."

Rocky sniffed. "Who's going to stop us? You and these starving dogs?"

Belle snarled. "Yes," she spat.

On some unspoken command, the two mutts Blanche and Devereaux roared and leaped toward the dogs. Rocky yipped and hid behind Max. Gizmo barked back, even as Max forced her behind him with his front paw.

"No!" Georgie bellowed.

His voice was so deep and loud that it practically made the walls shake. Georgie closed his eyes and shouted, "Leave them alone!" Only he dragged out the last word, raising his voice until what burst from his jaws was an ear-shattering howl.

The despairing, desperate howl of the Mudlurker.

Belle scampered up the staircase, practically trip ping over her sheer. But her two mutts turned their bared fangs at Georgie.

Georgie spun himself toward the dark, musty-smelling archway. He stopped howling just long enough to shout, "Get out while you can!"

Blanche and Devereaux made chase, their claws clattering over the floor as they barreled after Georgie. In seconds the three dogs were gone, disappearing into the darkness.

"We have to go after them!" Gizmo cried. "They might hurt Georgie!"

"He'll be fine," Rocky said, scrambling toward the

door. "He's ten times their size. Let's do what he said and get out of here!"

"No!" Max barked.

Both small dogs stopped in their tracks and turned to look at him.

"Who are you saying no to, buddy?" Rocky asked. "Me or Gizmo?"

"Both of you," Max said. "We're finishing what we started. We have to go after Belle and tell her what Boss said."

"But she's crazy!" Rocky yowled. "She's been eating garbage and taking dogs prisoner and making them her slaves!"

Gizmo ducked her head. "I kind of agree with Rocky, Max. I feel terrible for her, but I don't see what we can do."

Max turned to his friends, his face stern. "Think of all we've seen," he said. "Everywhere we've gone, animals like us have felt unloved and abandoned, and because of that, some have done terrible things. Remember Dandy-claw back in the Enclave? He wasn't trying to be mean on purpose."

"Well, he was," Rocky muttered.

"He wanted to feel safe," Max continued. "To keep his friends safe, too. He just didn't know the best way to do it. But he tried," he went on, pacing in front of the steps. "And so did Raoul and the house of cats, Boss and Captain on the riverboat, the animals at the zoo, the beach pets, everyone back in Julep's town, and the possum family in the swamp. Even the Chairman just wanted life to make sense again, though he went about it in the worst possible way."

"I'm not sure what you're getting at, buddy," Rocky said.

"I think I understand," Gizmo said. "No matter what the animals we met have done, it's been mostly for the same reason—to try to feel like their lives aren't scary, even though everything has changed."

Max nodded. "Exactly. That's why Belle is acting the way she is." Looking between his two friends, he said, "Remember that cat Possum?"

The two small dogs nodded.

"She was convinced that we should all just give up. But when I told her there might be a cure and that the people could come home, she had hope again. It's the same way we felt when Dr. Lynn told us our people still loved us."

Max turned back toward the stairs. "I think that's what we're meant to do until we see Dr. Lynn again. We're meant to keep hope alive so pets don't give up. Belle has changed a lot since the people left, but we've *all* changed a lot."

"Of course," Rocky said. "We can read words now!"

Chuckling, Max said, "Exactly. But who we were before is still in there, and the same must be true for Belle. We need to give her hope again."

A howl echoed distantly, followed by mad barking.

Gizmo gasped. "Oh, no, Georgie!"

"Belle is the only one who can call off the mutts," Max said. "Let's go find her as fast as we can."

"Right behind you!" Rocky said.

The trio raced up the staircase as Belle's voice rang out. "Help me! They're going to attack me! Come save your lady!"

The three friends followed Belle's voice down a long, dark hallway. Dog droppings lined the walls, and dead potted plants lay on their sides atop mounds of dirt and shards of porcelain. At the very end of the hall, a pair of double doors were open wide onto a grand room filled with gray daylight. As the dogs raced closer, Belle's voice grew louder.

"This isn't how it was supposed to go," the Collie cried out. "Beasts rampaging through my home, spitting fiery lies. Come to me, my pets! Come save your Lady Belle from these bad dogs!"

Max ran through the doorway first and caught sight of Belle on a balcony outside a pair of ornate glass doors. A warm, damp breeze carried with it the mingling scents of chlorine, decaying leaves, and yet more garbage. Belle's makeshift cape swirled behind her in the wind.

Belle had been calling to her pack of mutts outside, but as soon as she saw Max, Rocky, and Gizmo, she darted back into the grand room and curled up beneath a coffee table.

The walls here were lined with floor-to-ceiling shelves filled with books and metal artifacts. At one point, Max imagined, the room must have been some grand sitting area. But many of the books on the lower shelves had been tossed to the floor, their pages torn to bits and their leather covers gnawed into slobbery messes. Piles of leaves coated the balcony and the floor in front of the ornate doors.

"Belle," Max said as he padded quietly toward the trembling Collie. "Please listen to what I have to say."

"Don't you come closer," Belle said from beneath the low table. "My pets are on their way. They will punish you for your lies. And then you will learn to be my pets, too."

Downstairs, the halls suddenly filled with barks and growls. Dozens of footsteps thudded, climbing the stairs.

"She's not joking!" Rocky said. The Dachshund slammed against one of the hall doors, making it creak on its hinges. Gizmo joined him, and the door shut.

Belle stuck her head out from beneath the coffee table. "Help!" she howled. "Your lady is in here!"

Max glanced back to see the shadows of at least six dogs bursting through the dark, trash-filled hallway. Rocky and Gizmo worked to shut the other door, but it didn't seem to be moving.

They were cornered. Max looked back to Belle, meeting her frightened eyes. He needed to get through to her. But that would never happen if he and his friends got hurt.

"Out of the way," Max called to Rocky and Gizmo, and he leaped with all his might against the door. He bounced right off it and fell to his side.

Something was jamming it in place, some doorstop, but nothing he could see. The barks kept growing louder, the footsteps more thunderous, and he caught a flash of the first mutt at the door.

"Come on!" Max shouted, already running toward the balcony. "We're cornered!"

"We're going to jump off the balcony?" Gizmo asked.

Rocky sniffed the air. "Smell that chlorine, Gizmo. Looks like we're going for a dive into the pool, just like old times."

Reaching the leaf-covered balcony, Gizmo laughed. "You almost sound like you enjoy it!"

As her pack swarmed through the entrance to the sitting room, Belle wiggled out from beneath the coffee table. "Don't you dare!" she called after Max, Rocky, and Gizmo. "You aren't allowed to leave!" To her pack, she ordered, "Get them!"

Rocky didn't hesitate. His legs were a blur as he took a running start to the edge of the balcony. Leaping between rails, he shouted a triumphant "Hiiii-*yah*!" A second later came a splash.

Side by side, Max and Gizmo leaped as well; for a moment, the world was nothing but warm, suffocating, humid air. Seconds later, Max's belly smacked hard against frigid cold water and he was enveloped by a great splash.

Rocky had been right—this wasn't their first time taking a wild leap into unknown waters. Following the bubbles from his nose, Max swam to the surface. Gasping for air, he kicked with his hind legs and paddled until he reached the ledge of the pool.

It took all of Max's strength to heft himself out of the water and onto the dry concrete. Water glugged in his ears, but with a shake of his head he could hear again—and immediately he could tell that every dog in and around Belle's mansion was barking at the top of its lungs.

Max spun around. Rocky and Gizmo were close by, shivering and staring at something on the opposite end of the pool. Max turned to see what his friends were looking at.

He felt a hollow open in his stomach.

The pool was a rectangle, with its short end facing the house. The long sides were bordered by overgrown bushes. The only escape was through the doors to the house behind Max—which were shut tight—or the opposite end of the pool, which opened up to the backyard.

And that's where six of Belle's mutts stood, blocking the path. They had herded Georgie, whimpering and afraid, to the pool's edge.

"I told you!" Belle called from the balcony. "You must learn your lesson for making me feel so terrible."

Max's mind raced. He could try to get back into the house, but he didn't know how he'd get the doors open, and once inside it would be a maze of halls to navigate, not to mention more of Belle's mutts.

Plus, going inside would mean abandoning poor, brave Georgie. But trying to take on six dogs with only Rocky and Gizmo as backup seemed much too dangerous.

Once more, Max found himself cornered.

Before Max could react, he saw the mutts by Georgie go stiff and smell the air. The hedges lining the pool began to rustle, and low growls pierced his ears.

Another scent quickly joined the stench of chlorine and garbage, and despair rushed over him.

The musk of wolves had enveloped the yard surrounding Belle's mansion.

Dolph·was finally here.

CHAPTER 23

A VERY NICE THING

The wolves appeared in the yard behind the six mutts: half a dozen red faces and four gray, ears flattened and teeth bared, led by Dolph, who was scarred and still limping.

Confused, Belle's mutts simply stood there, not knowing what to do. Max couldn't move.

He wasn't hurt. Not physically, anyway. But inside his Praxis-enhanced brain, a war raged.

He'd spoken so proudly to Rocky and Gizmo about looking for the best in all animals, even their enemies. About how all anyone needed was a little bit of hope, and things would be okay. That even if someone seemed dangerous, offering help was the right thing to do.

But here was Dolph, the deadly, vicious wolf. Max

had done the right thing for Dolph, hadn't he? And what did he get for it? A stronger enemy.

He'd tried to help Belle, and now he was cornered with nowhere to run, even though he was so terribly close to seeing his family again.

He'd tried to help Dandyclaw and the Enclave, only to be turned upon. Same with the Chairman and his Corporation, and Gertrude and her laboratory.

Max watched the ten wolves move ever closer to Belle's mutts and Georgie, and he grew sadder and sadder. Even though Praxis supposedly had made him smart, he thought maybe he was just a dumb dog after all.

"Max," Gizmo said, nudging his side. "Max, we have to do something, we have to—"

The wolves attacked.

They leaped toward the six brown-furred mutts, jaws open wide, teeth grazing the thin dogs. Yelping in terror and tucking their tails between their legs, the mutts raced past the wolves and into the yard, disappearing from sight.

The wolves followed, howling and snarling. All except Dolph, who looked past Georgie, still cowering next to the pool.

Directly at Max.

Then Dolph ran out of view, chasing after the mutts as well.

"This is our chance, buddy!" Rocky yipped. "Come on!"

Max didn't know what to think. Silently, he followed his two small friends around the lip of the pool toward

Georgie. As he did, he heard Belle's voice echoing from deep within the mansion.

"Stay away from my pets!" she cried. "I need them!"

Max, Rocky, and Gizmo reached Georgie's side. The big dog was clearly frightened, but he didn't seem to be hurt.

"You all right, big guy?" Rocky asked.

"I think so," Georgie said. "I was hoping you would have already escaped, though."

"And leave you behind? Never!"

Max peered around the hedges. The howls and barks from the wolves and dogs echoed through the mossy trees, but he couldn't see them in the vast, overgrown backyard.

"We're going to leave," he announced to his friends. "We need to find Fletcher and Whitey, have them help get Georgie somewhere safe, and then we need to run away while the wolves are distracted."

"What about Belle?" Gizmo asked. "You said—"

"It doesn't matter," Max snapped.

He looked up at the balcony where Belle had stood moments before. He wished so desperately that he'd had just a little more time to speak with her.

"All the other animals were right," Max went on. "She went bad. Let's just go before Dolph comes back."

No one said anything as Max padded off the concrete surrounding the pool and into the tall grass of the backyard. From the sounds of it, the wolves and mutts were fighting farther away, but Max crept slowly and carefully, ready for the next horrible surprise attack from Dolph.

Instead, as the four dogs rounded the line of hedges and headed toward the front side of the house, Max saw Belle.

The Collie spun in frantic, terrified circles next to the house. Her flowered sheet flowed around her, almost as lovely as she must have wished. Catching sight of Max, Rocky, Gizmo, and Georgie, Belle sobbed, then darted away toward a section of the yard that was hidden behind tall white walls.

"She's so sad!" Gizmo said. "We have to talk to her."

"Gizmo—" Max started, but Gizmo was already off through the overgrown grass.

"Is that a good idea?" Georgie asked.

"Probably not," Rocky said, "but Gizmo is Gizmo. She trusts her instincts, even if it sometimes means running full on into danger." He wagged his tail. "That's what I love about her."

Reluctantly, Max followed Gizmo's trail, his eyes darting around to make sure that no wolves or mutts were nearby. He sniffed the air, but all he could smell were the piles of garbage in the front driveway.

Deeper in the walled garden, Max could hear someone crying and Gizmo's soft, soothing voice.

Quietly, Max led Rocky and Georgie through the overgrowth, avoiding the thorns on the rosebushes, until they came to an open area. An empty birdbath sat near a round metal table, with two iron chairs on either side.

Sitting in one chair, wrapped in her cape, was Belle. On the opposite chair sat Gizmo.

"They're gone," Belle whimpered. "All my pets are gone. They'll never come back for me. I will be alone forever."

"Oh, Belle," Gizmo said. "That's not true. You have so many people who love you. Hardly a day has gone by where we haven't met some animal who talked highly of you—or at least, of how you were before the people left."

"Then why do you want to leave?" she wailed. Casting her watery gaze on Max, Rocky, and Georgie, she asked, "Why won't any of you accept my invitation to stay?"

"Probably because it wasn't an invitation," Rocky said. "It was an order."

Belle swiped her flowery cape over her snout to hide her face. "No one stays because they want to," she whispered. "Not even the dog I loved more than any in the world would stay with me."

"Boss?" Gizmo asked.

Belle's head shot up, and her sheet fell free. She trembled. "I said never to—"

"Well, we're going to say his name anyway, lady," Rocky interrupted, leaping up on the chair next to Gizmo. "Boss sent us to find you."

Belle narrowed her bushy brow. "I don't believe you."

"It's true!" Gizmo said. "Right, Max?"

Max blinked. He met Belle's eyes and nodded.

319

Sighing, Belle waved a paw and said, "But if what Boss had to say was so important, why didn't he just come tell me himself?"

For a moment, no one spoke.

"Well?" Belle asked.

"Boss...passed away," Gizmo said softly.

Belle's entire body went stiff and her eyes opened wide. She opened her jaw as if to say something, but no words came out.

"He was a hero," Rocky said. "He fought to save a whole boat full of dogs. Without him, they would have been killed. He was so brave."

"He was always so brave," Belle whispered.

With a whimper, Gizmo leaped down from her place next to Rocky and then up onto the chair next to Belle. Gizmo continued, "He wanted you to know that he never meant to leave you behind. He didn't know what his pack leaders were doing when they took him, and he dreamed every day after that about coming home to find you. He longed to run through the tall grass with you again and play in the old pond, and he also wanted you to know he loved you very, very much."

The Collie's eyes began to water, and she shut them tight.

"It's like Max was saying to us," Rocky whispered. "We all deserve to know that we're loved. The people are coming back soon. Boss may be gone, but your pack leaders will come home for you."

"You promise?" Belle said softly, her eyes still closed.

"Of course," Gizmo said.

"Definitely," Rocky said.

Blinking her eyes open, Belle met Max's gaze.

"What about you?" she asked.

Max was thinking so many things that he couldn't decide what to say. As he tried to form the right words, gravel crunched in the garden behind him and Georgie.

And Dolph's smell met Max's nose.

Max spun on his heels. It was the last thing he wanted to do, but he would fight if he must. No matter how confused and upset he was, he would never let a pack of wolves hurt any of his friends.

But Dolph was alone.

The large, scarred wolf limped forward, his pale eyes wary.

"Where is your pack?" Max asked with a growl.

Dolph snarled. "They're still chasing off those crazed mutts. You're welcome."

"You're welcome?" Rocky repeated, his eyes wide. "For what? Stalking us all the way to Baton Rouge?"

"No," the wolf said. "You're welcome for saving you from this dog's pack."

Max shook his head, confused. "Aren't you here to settle our feud? Isn't that what you said when we last saw you?"

Sighing, Dolph paced back and forth over the weeds and gravel.

"Trust me, Max, the last thing I expected was to be saving your hide. But you helped my pack. I felt I still owed you a favor." He met Max's eyes. "Besides, if anyone is going to take you down, it will be me, not some gutter dog."

"So you helped us," Max said slowly, "because I helped you."

Dolph snarled once more. "Yes. It's not hard to understand." Turning his back on the dogs, the large wolf limped toward the exit. "But don't expect any more favors, Max. We're even now."

And with those parting words, the wolf leader was gone.

"What a pleasant guy," Rocky said. "I really wish he'd come around more often."

"Really?" Georgie asked.

Rocky chuckled. "No, not really, big guy. I was just being sarcastic."

From her chair, Belle sniffled, her eyes watery with tears. Gizmo licked the bigger dog reassuringly.

"So that's it, then," the lonely Collie whispered. "Boss is gone forever, and the wolves chased away all my new friends. I have nothing left for me at this mansion."

Only an hour before Belle had seemed crazed. *Bad.* But in the end she was still the same nice Collie whom Boss had loved.

Max's sworn enemy had helped him, all because he had shown him some bit of mercy and kindness. Belle had regained her senses, all because Gizmo and Rocky took the time to treat her with respect and kindness.

Max couldn't deny there was a lot of danger in the world. Not all animals or people were kind. But looking at Belle now, a flame relit within him. He had to believe that most animals could be good if given the chance.

Wagging his tail, Max trotted across the gravel to Belle and licked her snout.

"This isn't it for you, Belle," he said. "The people *are* coming back. We will be with our families again."

"But what am I supposed to do until then?" Belle asked.

Ducking his head, Georgie said, "Maybe you could stay with me and my friends."

Max, Belle, Rocky, and Gizmo all looked at the big dog.

"You'd do that for me?" Belle asked. "Even after my pets chased you?"

Georgie offered her a droopy, slobbery smile and a wag of his tail. "Sure! I think anyone would go mad in this mansion. We can find a nice place where we can keep each other company."

Belle offered a wag of her tail back. "I think I'd enjoy that. It seems like it would be a nice thing."

"A very nice thing," Gizmo said, nodding in agreement.

Together, Max, Rocky, Gizmo, Belle, and Georgie left the enclosed garden and walked side by side through the overgrown grass until they reached the road that led to the front gate. The stench of the garbage behind them—a smell that spoke of Belle's sadness and despair—was replaced by the fresh scents of the nearby yards. By the time they reached the gate, the moody clouds above were fading, burned away by the afternoon sun, and the garbage bags were completely forgotten.

As Dolph had promised, the wolves were long gone, and so were the mutts. Waiting right where they'd left them, however, were Fletcher and Whitey.

"Who is this vision of loveliness?" Whitey barked as the dogs approached.

Belle held her snout high and tossed her head back and forth to send her floral cape fluttering in the midday breeze.

"Flattery will get you everywhere," she said. "I'm Belle."

"Oh," Whitey said with a wag of his tail. "It seems the stories of your demise were greatly exaggerated."

"Georgie Porgie!" Fletcher cried.

The small mutt bounded forward, then leaped at Georgie's side, sniffing and licking him.

"Are you okay?" she asked. "We heard barks and howls, and whenever the wind shifted there was this awful smell. I was so worried!"

Georgie laughed. "I'm all right. No one can hurt the Mudlurker."

Shaking her head, Fletcher *tsk*ed. "Mudlurker. What

a thing to call you." Sizing up Belle, she added, "So what's the deal with her?"

"I asked her to stay with us until the people come home," Georgie asked.

"Is that okay?" Belle asked. "I don't want to intrude."

Fletcher tilted her head. After a long moment, she finally wagged her tail. "Sure, why not. It would be an honor to be friends with the famed Belle of Baton Rouge!"

As Belle, Fletcher, Georgie, and Whitey sniffed one another and laughed, Max, Rocky, and Gizmo sat in the center of the road, quietly taking it all in. Max couldn't help but wag his tail at the sight of them. Each of these Baton Rouge dogs had been alone in his or her own way. But now, it seemed, they were going to become a family.

Georgie peeled himself away from his friends and trotted to stand before Max, Rocky, and Gizmo.

"I guess this is good-bye," the big dog said, his head drooping. "I'm going to miss you guys."

"Oh, Georgie!" Gizmo cried. She darted forward, leaped back onto her hind legs, and hugged his front legs. "I'm going to miss you, too."

Rocky waddled forward and mimicked Gizmo's hug on Georgie's other front leg. "You seemed like a fraidy-cat when we first met you, big guy," he said. "But you turned out to be superbrave. Those gators were right to be scared of you."

Georgie's tail was a blur. "Aw. Thanks."

Tongue hanging down in a doggy smile, Max walked up to Georgie and gave him a quick lick on his nose.

"You keep an eye on Belle and the others, you hear?" Max said. "Something tells me they're going to need it."

Georgie's eyes went wide. "You think I could be their leader?"

"Maybe not the leader," Max said. "When dogs fight to be in charge, it never seems to end well." He tilted his head. "How about you just be their very good friend, and they can be your very good friends back?"

"You got it, Max," Georgie said. "Thanks for saving me from that swamp."

"Thank you for being the fearsome Mudlurker!"

All the dogs laughed at that. Reluctantly, Rocky and Gizmo let Georgie go, and the Saint Bernard wandered back to join his new group of friends.

The sun was arcing down toward the western horizon as Max, Rocky, and Gizmo walked side by side in the center of the road, leaving Belle's mansion behind and heading away from Baton Rouge.

"So where to now, big guy?" Rocky asked as they passed a sign in front of a farm that showed a cartoon puppy next to the words HAPPY PAWS.

"We keep heading west, I figure," Max said.

"Definitely," Rocky said. "But how will we know we're going the right way?"

Up ahead, only slightly visible in the late afternoon sunlight, Max saw an amber beacon blinking atop an orange-and-white barricade.

"Oh, look!" Gizmo said, catching sight of the beacon, too. "Dr. Lynn must have come this way."

Rocky nodded. "So we keep following the signs. Easy enough."

"Until we run into more gators," Max said.

"Or devious snakes," Gizmo added.

Rocky scrunched his nose. "Or dogs who don't know the value of proper hygiene."

And though all those monsters and serpents and canines had made their lives miserable, the three dogs laughed. It was all they could do.

The road ahead seemed to go on forever, but just like the river they'd followed for so long, Max knew it would end eventually.

Along the way, he planned to keep spreading hope to each animal they met. Just like Belle, everyone deserved to know that Dr. Lynn was going to save them all. The humans were going to return. The pets would be reunited with their families.

No matter what Max faced between then and now, he knew if he kept that dream alive, he'd finally reach the end of this journey.

And when that end came, he'd be embraced again by Charlie and Emma, once and for all.

ACKNOWLEDGMENTS

The Long Road comes to you action-packed and thrilling thanks to the insightful notes from my great editors, Julie Scheina and Pam Garfinkel, who saw both the forest and the trees and knew exactly which branches and trunks to cut down. They and everyone else at Little, Brown Books for Young Readers have been incredibly dedicated to making this series the best it can be, and I am amazed every day by all the work they've done to make these books a reality.

Endless thanks must go to the team at the Inkhouse as well. Michael Stearns and Ted Malawer helped conceive a page-turner of a plot, then once again let me run wild to bring it to life. And Ruth Katcher was there every step of the way to help tame my unruly pages and turn them into a sleek manuscript. Having her experienced eye give my words a second look throughout the writing process was a lifesaver.

As always, I am so impressed by how Allen Douglas has brought Max, Rocky, and Gizmo to life in his illustrations. I think this might be my favorite cover art so far!

And finally, thank you to all the kids, parents, teachers, and librarians who have come to see me in person or have written me letters about how much you've enjoyed these books. Your enthusiasm and tales of your own dogs have provided more inspiration than I could have imagined!